UNDER MY SKIN

JAMES DAWSON

HOT
KEY
BOOKS

First published in Great Britain in 2015 by Hot Key Books
Northburgh House, 10 Northburgh Street, London EC1V 0AT

Text copyright © James Dawson 2015

A CIP catalogue record for this book is available from the British Library.

ISBN: 978-1-4714-0296-8

1

This book is typeset in 10.5 Berling LT Std using Atomik ePublisher

Printed and bound by Clays Ltd, St Ives Plc

www.hotkeybooks.com

Hot Key Books is part of the Bonnier Publishing Group
www.bonnierpublishing.com

ALSO BY JAMES DAWSON

Say Her Name
Cruel Summer
Hollow Pike

This Book is Gay
Being a Boy

To all the 'strong female characters' but most of all my mum, Angela.

I thought how unpleasant it is to be locked out;
and I thought how it is worse, perhaps, to be locked in.

Virginia Woolf, *A Room of One's Own*

FINALE

I can't say I wasn't warned. This is what all those stories told us about. This is the dark at the heart of the forest; this is the Big Bad Wolf; this is both serpent and apple. There were warnings everywhere – in the Bible, on TV, in nursery rhymes. I always thought they were metaphors or allegories to get me to go to bed, to make me eat my vegetables. I ignored them. I think we all do.

And now it's too late. I was weak and now I am dead.

Oh, it's for the best. I hurt people every way people can be hurt. And I'd do it again.

This is not just badness.

This is not just wrong.

This is *evil*.

Chapter One

I'm not good enough.

The spotlight shone in Sally's face, blinding her. All she could see was dazzling, brilliant whiteness. It was entirely possible that she'd died of fright and was now glimpsing the glory of Heaven. She dug her fingernails into her palms. Saliva filled her mouth, lubricating it, ready to . . .

I'm going to vomit and everyone is going to see. People will talk about it for weeks. I'll be Sally Sick, Sick Sally, or maybe even Vomgirl. Or Chunks.

She swallowed hard, averting disaster. Not for the first time, Sally questioned her sanity. They say madness runs in the family, and there was a reason why the Feathers didn't see Uncle John so much these days. The only explanation Sally could think of as to why she was standing there was that she'd lost her mind.

Why did I agree to this?

'Who's next?'

Sally jumped as Mr Roberts yelled.

I can't do it. She heard him rustle through his sheets of paper.

'Erm . . . Sally Feather? Is that Sally?'

3

'Yes!' she squeaked. She felt dwarfed by the big, empty stage, reminded of the stunted wooden people in her old doll's house. 'I'm Sally.' Her voice echoed through the hall dull and lumpy-sounding. She hated her talking voice.

'Brilliant. Are you ready, Sally?'

She squinted through the spotlight and recognised the stocky, beardy silhouette of Mr Roberts. It wouldn't be so bad if it was only him. In the auditorium behind him was a neat row of identical glossy heads lined up like *Girl's World* hairstyling dolls. Dozens of eyes all fixed on Sally. Their judgement was palpable. *What's SHE doing here?*

I really must have gone mad.

'I'm ready,' she muttered into the microphone and a wail of feedback tore around the room like a banshee. Sally heard the other girls giggle. 'Sorry.'

'That's OK, dear. In your own time.' Roberts was a flamboyant black guy with the most neatly pruned chinstrap beard Sally had ever seen. He had a fiery temper, but she had mostly liked his music lessons in Year Nine.

She knew she should just leave. Quit now and she could just turn away and exit in a dignified and poised manner – well, as much as her clumsy gait would allow. That was her only shot at coming out of this unscathed. But she couldn't. This was the last show Sally could be a part of, and she'd *promised* her mum that she would at least audition. It would, after all, look good on her Cambridge application.

There was a part of her – a really small, neglected nubbin in her head – that quite wanted to be in a play. She'd get to sing, she'd get to dress up. She'd adored nativity plays in

4

primary school, back when people were kinder, but this felt very different. *For God's sake Sally, it's only a school play – get it together – it might even be fun.* Her stomach heaved again, reminding her this was *not* fun.

There was an impatient sigh from Miss Deevers, waiting at the piano. She looked like an older version of Sally in some ways – the same fine features and mousy, unruly hair – although Miss Deevers's was secured with a cheap plastic crocodile clip. Sally's, as ever, hung in its long plait, the end of which she now rubbed between her thumb and forefinger like a comfort blanket.

Deep breaths weren't having quite the magical healing effect her mum had promised they would. Nevertheless, Sally gave Miss Deevers the nod. The opening bars of 'Somewhere That's Green' started. The piano badly needed tuning; it sounded like bones clanking together.

You can do this, Sally told herself. *You know the words. You know you can sing.* But she also knew, deep down inside, in a toxic pit in her gut, that it was about so much more than having a pretty voice. What is it those awful TV talent shows say? *We're looking for the total package – for the 'X factor'.* Sally just wasn't one of those mannequins. To Sally, the beautiful, effortless sound that came out of her mouth when she sang must have accidentally landed in her body on its way to someone else.

Sally was so lost in doubt that she missed her cue. Nerves had sewed her lips shut. Miss Deevers let the notes die off. More giggling from the crowd. Sally didn't need to be able to see to know it was Melody Vine, Eleanor Ford and Keira Stevens. The unholy trinity.

5

'Sally? Are you OK?' Mr Roberts sat up straighter.

You've blown it. There was no way she was getting cast after this. And maybe that was OK. She could truthfully tell her mum she'd auditioned. 'Sorry.' She felt herself fluster. 'Can . . . can I start again?'

A subtle glance at his watch. 'Yeah, sure.'

Sally nodded to Miss Deevers. This time she closed her eyes.

I am no longer Sally Feather. I am Audrey from Little Shop of Horrors.

She conjured a picture in her head – beautiful and sexy, but naive and lost. She dug inside to capture the longing she felt for Seymour and the need to get away from Skid Row. The last one didn't take much imagining – Sally couldn't wait to get out of Saxton Vale High School.

This time the words came out. Her voice didn't fail her. Sally heard herself and felt better at once. God knew how she did it, but her singing voice – quite the opposite of her normal voice – flowed like liquid gold, intuitively finding the right notes. *If the rest of me was like my voice*, she mused, *there wouldn't be an issue*. She'd learned she could sing years ago at church and the choir mistress had quickly put her in the choir, but that was different; there she was hidden in a crowd with no eyes on her.

Before she knew it, she'd reached the end of the song. *I did it*. She opened her eyes and ceased being Audrey. Her shoulders hunched inward, shrivelling up. There was silence in the hall. Sally had become used to the empty seconds that followed her singing. It was the time required for the audience to recompose themselves following the mental turmoil brought on by the

6

conundrum: 'How did that gorgeous noise come out of that plain little thing?'

'Very good, erm . . . Sally. Excellent.' Mr Roberts snapped out of it quicker than most. 'Really, really lovely. Why aren't you in choir?'

'I . . . I am.' Sally's cheeks burned.

'Oh, OK. Even better.' She still couldn't see him properly for the spotlight, but she could see that he was smiling. But he was also stalling. This time, the delay was because he was now trying to do a drastic *Next Top Model* makeover in his head to see if he could turn her into an Audrey onstage.

He can't. I'm not right.

Sad, but true. As all the girls had to sing 'Somewhere That's Green' as their audition piece, Sally hadn't had a choice in the matter. She would happily settle for a place in the chorus. She would get to sing, and her mum could come to one show before she left school for good.

As tempting as the wigs and costumes were, there was no way she'd ever be able to handle a role like Audrey. Standing there in the spotlight, her skinny hands were shaking and her mouth felt so dry it could crack. Singing and performing are not the same thing. Getting all the solos wasn't worth the terror involved.

'Thank you very much, Sally. Again, that was just lovely,' Mr Roberts said. 'Keep your eye on the casting sheet.'

Sally nodded and headbutted the microphone, eliciting yet more hyena giggling from the third row. *So embarrassing.* Sally shuffled off the side of the stage like a sick thing looking for a place to die.

* * *

7

'Hey, Sally!' She was already halfway down the corridor when she heard her name. The exit was in sight – so close to freedom and yet so far. It was at times like these that Sally wished she could freeze time to make faster getaways.

Sally really, really didn't want to talk to Melody Vine. She *couldn't* talk to Melody Vine.

She turned to face them. Melody, Eleanor and Keira. Sometimes known as Melanora. They were so easy to hate because they were three perfect mirrors reflecting her own imperfections. It brought little relief to bitch and call them shallow or stupid; Sally was self-aware enough to know that her resentment was, at least in part, jealousy.

Six slender legs carried three Bikram yoga bodies holding three immaculately coiffed heads. Keira was known for her magnificent trademark afro and mischievous smile. With her display boobs and long blonde hair, Eleanor could probably run the school if she weren't so vacant. But of them all, Melody was the most radiant with her faux-wholesome Disney Channel loveliness: her button nose and anime eyes; her butterscotch tan and parted-pout lips. She smiled at Sally, and Sally couldn't help but adore her for a split second, hypnotised by the gleam of her teeth. *How easy life would be*, Sally thought, *if I looked like them*. The mesmerism lasted for a second until Sally reminded herself that Melody was Satan's school representative on Earth.

'Sally, wait up,' Melody said.

Sally's tongue turned to clay and she suddenly felt way too hot. 'Hi,' she managed, as they fell into step alongside her. Eleanor and Keira tapped away on their phones, barely bothering to make eye contact with her. They were much too busy with their followers and infinite friends.

'I just wanted to say . . .' Melody paused to sweep a glossy chestnut wave over her shoulder. There had once been a fairly convincing rumour that Melody Vine's hair had its own insurance policy. '. . . you were amazing in there.'

This always happened after Sally sang. People felt they were paying her a compliment by saying, 'Good for you – you have one redeeming feature after all!'

'Thanks. You too.' Sally couldn't look her directly in the eye. Although they were roughly the same height, Melody seemed so much bigger.

'Do you think you'll go for Audrey?' Melody's breeziness was a ploy. This was a clear warning as far as Sally was concerned.

'No,' she replied, looking at her toes. She tried to laugh it off, but instead giggled like a psycho. 'I'd be too scared.' Sally wanted to cry. *'I'd be too scared?' Could you be more of a loser?*

Sally glanced up to see relief flash across Melody's face. She wondered, momentarily, if Melody was threatened. By *her*.

'You're *probably* right.' Melody nodded. 'Being the romantic lead is about so much more than just the voice. You really need to be a triple threat. That's what my agent always says.'

Sally suspected she was only a single threat – if that. Singing, fine, the dancing and acting . . . not so much. Students at Saxton Vale High School heard about Melody's agent a lot, although as far as anyone knew the only thing she'd done to date was an advert for *The Sofa Emporium*. She'd played the coveted role of Smiling Girl with iPod on Sofa.

Sally reached the double doors at the end of the corridor and pushed down on the exit bar. A blast of cool, late afternoon air hit her. Between the last little winter nip in the air and being around Melody, Sally was suddenly wide awake, as alert as a deer in hunting season. As the auditions had run on for a couple of hours after school, the peachy sun was already melting behind the towering conifers lining the school grounds.

Sally kept her head down as they walked down the flagstone path, but Melody continued to blather on. 'You know, when my sister did *Little Shop of Horrors* a few years back, she was Mr Mushnik. You'd be perfect for that.'

Sally was speechless. A little, fat, male character? That was next-level bitchy, even for Melody.

'I'm not saying that to be a bitch,' Melody gasped, as if she'd *ever* be a bitch. 'It's actually a great part and you get a solo.'

Out of the corner of her eye, Sally saw Eleanor and Keira share a sly look.

'Cool costume too. She had to wear a moustache.'

Eleanor and Keira could barely conceal their giggles. Melody wasn't stupid. With her wide eyes and friendly tone, you'd never be able to accuse her of nastiness, but she knew that, and relied on it. No one at Saxton Vale had ever been able to bring her down; she was Teflon – nothing stuck.

By this time they'd reached the road. A couple of buses were stationary in the bay, but the school was now a ghost town. Melody and her friends seemed to be heading in the same direction as her and Sally hugged her books to her chest a little tighter, as if they were armour. Surely they wouldn't stick with her the whole way home? Sally started to think of pretend reasons why she might have to duck back into the school.

'Anyway, Sally,' Melody said by way of conclusion, 'good luck when they announce the cast list. I'm sure you'll do . . .'

She stopped rambling, her sentence hanging. Sally dragged her eyes off the pavement to see what had halted her mid-speech. Concern creased Melody's pretty features – something had spooked her. Sally looked over the road at whatever she was gawping at.

'Ew. How gross is that?' muttered Eleanor, her nose turned up.

There was a man, a tramp by the look of him. He staggered down the opposite side of the street and, as he zigzagged into the pool of a pink streetlamp, Sally got a better view. He was in a real state. It was hard to tell how old he was; he was so covered in grime and his beard was so unkempt he could be anything from thirty to sixty.

He had no arms. The left had been amputated almost at the shoulder, while the right ended at the elbow. As he ambled along, empty sleeves swung around him like an untied straitjacket. Sally felt a tug on her heartstrings – she always felt so guilty and impotent when she saw homeless people. She often gave them whatever coins were in her pocket, but always felt bad for not being able to do more.

He came closer and Sally heard him babbling, ranting and wailing. It sounded like gibberish, and, as much as she felt sorry for him, it was also unsettling. It was bad enough being with these girls but something worse, something dark and heavy, twisted in Sally's stomach. She wished she were anywhere but here.

He saw them.

'Oh God, he's coming this way,' Melody said. 'Keep walking.'

11

For the first time Sally was glad she was with them. There's safety in numbers. The little group set off at a pace away from the school, their backs turned to the homeless guy.

'Is he following us?' Keira whispered.

Sally resolved to keep calm. Homeless people are harmless.

'Hey!' He shouted over the road at them. 'Help me!'

'Just keep going,' Melody ordered. Sally obeyed without question.

'Pretty girls!' he sobbed. 'You can help me, pretty girls. Wait . . . wait for me. I don't wanna hurt you.'

Melody took charge. She whirled around to face him. Sally followed suit, hovering at Melody's shoulder like her other sidekicks did. The man had wobbled into the road, heading right for them. 'Just leave us alone, paedo!' Melody demanded. 'We haven't got any money, OK?'

His face contorted as if he was in great pain. Head back, he howled at the faint moon – a true lunatic. 'Please.' He bounced up and down at the knees, the way that tantruming toddlers do. 'Please get it out of me.'

'Melody?' Eleanor said. 'Maybe we should call the police.'

'Don't get your phone out!' Melody scolded.

What's he gonna do? Snatch it? He hasn't got any hands. Sally kept the thought to herself.

The tramp looked straight at Sally, and she flinched. Up close, he didn't seem so benign any more. Even from the middle of the road, she could see his eyes were arctic blue, and burned in the centre of his filthy face. They pierced her. 'You. You'll help me. You're a good girl.' He smiled to reveal yellow, spongy teeth.

Sally said nothing, cowering behind Melody.

12

He continued ranting. 'It never stops . . . never. It's . . . it's *inside* me. Get it out. GET IT OUT!' He charged for them, running the rest of the way across the street. The others shrieked, but Sally couldn't take her eyes away from his. Those eyes . . . they were like black ice and she was frozen to the spot.

Sally heard the horn, but didn't understand what was happening until it was too late. Brakes screamed and tyres screeched. The car slammed into the tramp's legs and he crashed over the bonnet, cracking the windscreen before tumbling onto the road. He landed with a damp thud.

Melody collided with Sally as she staggered onto the school lawn in her haste to get out of the way. Sally heard shouting and wailing, and honestly, it might have been her. In the midst of all the chaos she couldn't make sense of anything.

The car came to a standstill and the man lay still alongside it, not moving – not moving *at all*. His head was black and wet with blood, a puddle fanning out across the tarmac.

Sally realised she was gripping Melody Vine's hand.

Chapter Two

Sally prodded a thick, fatty chunk of beef underneath what was left of her mashed potatoes. Her plate swam in gravy, beads of orange oil gleaming like algae on the surface of a brown lake.

'Sally, please do not play with your food.'

Her eyes flicked up to regard her mother through her hair. 'I'm not hungry.'

'Sally.' Her father frowned, his face like a tombstone. 'Don't answer your mother back.'

As they did every night, her mother and father sat opposite each other at one end of an unnecessarily long, feast-length dining table while Sally sat at the head between them. Her mum reached over the table and squeezed her husband's hand. 'It's OK, dear. What she saw must have been absolutely dreadful.' Talking about her as if she wasn't there was also something they enjoyed.

Her father dabbed his moustache with a linen napkin. 'That's no excuse to be surly. Sit up straight, please. Your posture's terrible. You'll get a hump if you're not careful.'

Sally gave up on dinner, resting her fork in the swampy remains. 'I saw a man die, Dad.'

After the accident, the four girls had been made to wait to be interviewed by a stout, red-faced policeman before they'd been allowed to go, during which time they'd been forced to see paramedics scrape what was left of the poor man off the asphalt and into a black plastic body bag.

Her father seemed genuinely confused by her distress. 'No great loss by the sounds of it. One less junkie for the rest of us to take care of.'

'Dad!' Sally protested.

'It'll be a different story once you're paying taxes, believe me.' He quaffed his twenty-five-pound-a-bottle wine and most likely didn't see any irony in it.

Her mother changed the subject, sipping at her own wine with thin lips. She was so bird-like, Sally couldn't help but imagine the sparrows drinking from the bird bath in the garden. 'Unpleasantness aside, how did the audition go?'

That all now seemed so utterly trivial compared to what had followed. 'I dunno. OK, I guess.'

'Sally, answer your mother properly, please. We don't grunt.'

A deep breath. 'It was fine. I think I sounded acceptable. We'll find out tomorrow if we got parts or not.'

Mrs Feather smiled. 'I do hope so. It'd be so nice for you to get out of the house and actually do something for once. You need to join in more. I was in all the school plays when I was your age. I was once Lady Macbeth. And it'll look ever so good on your application forms.'

Even the words 'join in' gave Sally cold cramps in her stomach. She'd heard the pitch before. *I do go out*, she thought sulkily. Sally looked to her mother. 'May I go over to Stan's, please?'

'But you've hardly touched your supper, dear.'

Sally felt the same way about her parents as she did about algebraic equations: baffled and frustrated in equal measure. 'Please. I'm not hungry – and I need to talk about what happened with Jennie and Stan.'

'Have you done your homework?'

'Yes. You can check it if you like.' She'd done it while waiting for her turn at the audition.

Her mum relented. 'Well, if you think it'll help.'

'It will.'

'All right then, dear, but I'd like you home by ten. And leave your homework on the sideboard for Dad to check.'

'Sure thing.' Sally pushed herself away from the table, leaving her plate for her mum to clear away – why deprive her of her main joy in life? Cooking, cleaning, serving her dad. Their home was a time capsule. They could so easily be living in the 1950s: doilies, net curtains, chintz fabric and oppressive dark wood antique furniture, although that was nothing compared to the prehistoric roles her mum and dad played.

Her dad was a bona fide bank manager, although he never missed an opportunity to remind Sally that he'd started at the bottom and worked his way up the ladder through blood, sweat and tears, so her mother had never had to, or chose not to, work. 'Being a wife and mother *is* a full-time job, dear,' she would often say. Her parents were a good ten years older than most of her friends' parents – when she was little, people had often mistaken them for her grandparents.

After putting her homework out for inspection on the sideboard next to her mother's creepy collection of faceless porcelain angels, Sally jammed some Converse on her feet and made a prompt exit. The second she let the front door slam shut behind her, she was back in the real world. Her home smelled a lot like the historical museum in town and she rinsed the furniture polish haze from her lungs with a deep breath of night air.

Somewhere close by, her owl, and it was *her* owl because he was a nightly visitor, hooted in the trees behind the house as she scurried across the lawn. She was 'lucky' enough to live in Mulberry Hill, the 'nice' part of town that overlooked the rest of Saxton Vale. Their hometown was truly a caste system: in the valley were the dingy terraced houses, rundown flats over betting shops and don't-get-out-of-your-car areas; halfway up the hill were the nicer semi-detached homes and shiny new 'executive apartments' for commuters; while the richest residents lived up here at the very top of the tree. To Sally, Mulberry Hill was nothing more than a viper's nest filled with snakes like Melody Vine and her equally poisonous parents.

When they were about six, Stan and Sally had removed a plank in the fence separating their houses, to save themselves the trouble of having to go all the way down the drive just to come back up the other side. Sally was still skinny enough to fit through the gap even if Stan's shoulders would get wedged in these days. Although they were the same architecturally, Stan's house was the polar opposite of hers. The garden was perpetually overgrown and cluttered with his little sister's toys.

A warm, familiar voice called out of an upstairs window. It was Jennie Gong, her other best friend. It's OK to have two best friends. 'Sal! Get your ass up here! New *Satanville* in t-minus two minutes! And you better have sweets!'

'I come bearing Haribo!' Sally replied.

Stan's head appeared next to Jennie's in the window. 'Come on up, Feather, the door's open!'

Sally hurried onto the porch and let herself in. The door was always unlocked. Unlike her sterile abode, Stan's was always noisy and chaotic, the way a home should be. Edie, wearing Stan's hand-me-down Buzz Lightyear costume, ran up to greet her in the hall. 'Sally!' She wrapped herself around Sally's legs.

'Hey there, you. I'm gonna need my legs back!'

'They're mine now!' the little girl growled.

'Edie, let her go!' It was Mrs Randall, Stan's mum. She was heavily pregnant again, although just as full of cheer as ever. She approached and gave Sally a hug. 'Go on up, sweetheart, you don't wanna miss the start of your show.'

'Thanks, Mrs Randall.'

'How many times?' She smiled. '*Please* call me Lou.'

'Sorry!' Sally blushed – she had to be reminded every time. Edie unhooked herself and Sally dashed up the stairs. Stan's bedroom door was covered in stickers of bands they liked and a massive poster of the *Satanville* cast standing in a graveyard. She barged her way in and found Stan sitting cross-legged on his bed, Mr Squid sat in his lap, while Jennie was on the Pokémon beanbag next to the bed.

'Hey!' Stan shifted to make room for her. He put the well-loved stuffed squid with buttons-for-eyes on his pillow. 'You OK?'

Jennie sprang up like Tigger and threw her arms round her. Sally breathed in her familiar, sugary perfume. She smelled like Love Hearts. When Sally closed her eyes and thought of her friend, she always saw strawberry-milkshake pink. 'Relax, Jen, I brought the gummy bears! You don't have to wrestle them from me.'

'That wasn't for the gummy bears, dummy.' She tucked a magenta stripe of hair behind her ear. 'That was for the trauma. Stan told me what happened.'

'Are you all right?' Stan looked up at her, his wide, blue eyes peering out from under his floppy fringe.

She threw him the gummy bears. 'Yeah, I'm fine. It was awful, obviously, but I guess it's inevitable. Sooner or later, we'll all accidentally hold Melody Vine's hand.'

Her friends chuckled.

'God, I hope you sterilised your hand afterwards.' Jennie flopped back into the beanbag. 'But seriously?' *But seriously* was their code to stop joking around.

'But seriously? It was messed up. I wish I could sterilise my *brain* – there's no way I'll sleep tonight.' She joined Stan on the bed, fingering her bracelets. The three of them had matching ones – a tribute to Zeke from *Satanville* who wore the same ones – three straps of red, brown and black leather twined together.

'Man, you are so lucky to have seen a real dead person,' said Stan, morbid as ever.

'Oh yeah, I feel blessed.'

'But seriously. Who was he?' Stan asked.

Sally shrugged. 'No idea. The police couldn't find any ID on him. John Doe, I guess.' That's what they always said on American shows.

'Oh, that's so sad. Sadface.' Jennie made a sad face.

19

'Double sadface.' Sally paused, a little ashamed of what she was about to say. 'But it was really scary too. There was something . . . wrong about him . . . I've never seen anyone freak out like that.'

Stan gave her a gentle punch on the arm. It was weird; even though they'd known each other *for ever* and were best friends, they never hugged, held hands or touched unless absolutely necessary. They had very definite rules about personal space. 'It must have been awful – but . . . what about the audition? Enquiring minds need to know.'

'Oh, I'm so dense! I totally forgot that's why you were even there.' Jennie flipped her hair over her head.

Sally suddenly felt a fresh wave of nausea. Another thing to worry about. 'Yeah, it was OK. I sang.'

'And?' Stan prompted.

'And what?'

'Did you get cast?'

'Oh, I dunno. We'll find out tomorrow. But I don't think —'

'Well, if you don't, Roberts must be Helen Keller. You're the best singer in the whole school,' Stan said and Sally felt her cheeks flush.

'God, Stan, gush much?' Sally couldn't look at them, allergic to praise. 'Jeez, put *Satanville* on!'

'Now you're talking!' Jennie grinned. 'Nothing like dead people to take your mind off dead people.'

Stan left the bed and crossed to his computer where he'd downloaded the latest episode. Illegally downloading American TV is *wrong*, but there was no way they'd avoid spoilers until it was shown over here. It was a totally necessary evil. 'You ready?'

'Yep,' Jennie said.

'Wait.' Sally popped a red sweet in her mouth. Red ones were the best. 'I can't remember what happened last week.'

'You do,' said Stan. 'It ended where Taryn had to choose —'

'OMG! Yes! We'll finally find out if she chooses Zeke or Dante for Lucifer's Ball! Go, go, go!' Stan pressed play and joined her on the bed after killing the lights.

They say true friends are those who hate the same people as you, and that was definitely the case, but *Satanville* was the glue that bound them together. Taryn Van Pelt's long-running love for her guardian angel and lust for her half-demon assassin had been a weekly fixture of their lives for over three years now. They'd only been fourteen when it had started.

'She better choose Dante or Tumblr will explode.' Stan took a handful of gummy bears. This was true. Taryn and Dante – 'Daryn' – were Sally's OTP, her One True Pairing.

'Shh!' Jennie snapped. No discussion was permitted until the end of the episode. This was as good as it got for Sally. She plucked Mr Squid off the pillow and played with his tentacles absentmindedly while the opening credits rolled. If school was just her, Jennie, Stan and the teachers, it'd be pretty good fun. Sadly it wasn't, so it sucked.

They watched the episode in total silence, save for the occasional rustle of the gummy bears. Not a classic episode, but *always* awesome.

'Oh my God!' Jennie declared when it had finished. 'I can't believe she took Angela. What is she playing at?'

'Yeah,' Sally added. 'But remember Taryn doesn't know how Angela feels because she wiped her memory.'

21

'You don't think Taryn will go gay?'

'I dunno,' said Stan. 'It *is* season four. Maybe they're running out of ideas.'

'That would be amazing!' Sally grinned. 'I'm totally shipping Taryn and Angela.'

'Tarangela!' Stan laughed.

'Amazing!' Jennie giggled. 'I'm tweeting that right now!' She reached for her phone. 'Hashtag Tarangela!'

Sally went to retweet it, not that she had many followers outside of that bedroom – although they were all pretty popular in *Satanville* forums. 'You guys *know* that Taryn's gonna fall for Lucifer right?'

'You reckon?' Stan frowned.

'It's so obvious —'

Jennie suddenly leaped off the beanbag. 'Oh my God – I have to go!'

'Why?'

'I said I'd meet Kyle after band practice. How is it so late already?' She dashed around Stan's bedroom, searching for her coat and bag.

Stan and Sally shared a subtle glance. 'Why do you have to meet him?' Stan asked. 'Text him and tell him you'll see him at school in the morning.'

'No! He hates it when I cancel stuff.' Jennie struggled into her purple denim 'Taryn' jacket. 'He's already having a really bad day . . .' Another eye roll. If Jennie saw them, she didn't let on. 'I'll see you guys at the corner, yeah? Kisses!'

'Sure,' said Sally. 'See you in the morning.'

Jennie couldn't get out of the room fast enough – Sally

imagined a cartoon dust cloud in her wake. 'Do you think it's time for the intervention?' Stan asked once they'd heard the front door slam.

Sally shook her head. 'We can't.'

'He's a knoblin. And by that I mean a goblin made out of knobs.'

Sally laughed. 'Knoblin? Amazing. Consider that stolen. *But seriously* she might pick him over us. We can't risk it.'

Stan wrinkled his broad nose. 'She wouldn't . . . would she?'

Sally shrugged again. There was nothing left to say. It wasn't worth losing a friend over. Jennie had been going out with Kyle for about six months now. He wasn't good for her. It wasn't so much *him* as the *her* she was when she was around him: clingier than cling film.

Stan sighed. 'Man, I hate that guy more than pineapple on pizza.'

Sally laughed. 'Wow! That bad?'

'Yup. He soggifies the pizza base of life.' Stan smiled. He lay across his bed, propping up his head with a hand. 'You wanna do sleepover?'

Sally shook her head. 'I gotta get home.'

'No! Stay! We can make gifs from tonight's episode. Don't go! And you said you'd help me with my French homework.' That meant do his homework for him.

'I promised my mum. You can copy my homework before register.' This was awkward. Her promise to her mother wasn't the only reason she didn't want to stay at Stan's. Truth was, even though they'd had millions of sleepovers, people were starting to talk at school, and it wasn't like that *at all*. So Sally had vowed to phase out their sleepovers, hopefully so gradually that Stan wouldn't even notice. Having a BIG TALK about it would only turn it into a BIG DEAL, something she was keen to avoid.

'OK, but log on to chat when you get in, yeah?'

'Sure. You'll be able to see me from your window . . . I don't think you're gonna miss me.'

'Are you kidding? Every time you leave a part of my heart snaps off and withers like an autumn leaf.' He grinned.

'You're such a doofus.' Sally laughed as she pulled her coat back on. 'I'll see you at the corner.'

Stan held Mr Squid to his chest. He waved a tentacle goodbye. 'Hey, Sally.'

'What?'

'Are you really OK? After what happened with the homeless guy?'

'I'll be fine, I promise.' She stood in the doorway, ready to go.

'If you need me, just holler across the lawn.'

She smiled. Knowing he was thirty metres from her bedroom window was, and always had been, comforting. 'Thank you,' she said. 'Sleep tight.'

'Sweet dreams, Feather.'

Chapter Three

Sally Feather was *not* a morning person. She stayed in bed until the very last minute, desperately trying to think of something to look forward to, a ritual she performed every morning. Some days you need a reason to get out of bed. This morning she had three things: they'd post the *Little Shop* cast list today; Jennie's birthday was coming up; there would be more *Satanville* in six days. When *Satanville* was on hiatus, sometimes getting out of bed was pretty tough.

When she could no longer take her mother screaming up the stairs, Sally dragged herself out from underneath the duvet and made her bed, pre-empting wrath. Her room was surely the most immaculate room any seventeen-year-old ever had. She sloped over to her wardrobe and selected some jeans, a T-shirt and a baggy checked shirt to throw over the top of it. She hated clothes that were too clingy, she couldn't stand the thought of people seeing her body – she was way too skinny. There had been a period in Year Eight when a few of the girls, led by Melody, had started bringing cakes and chocolate bars to school for her to 'cure her anorexia'. To her shame, she'd eaten some of them publically to prove she wasn't.

Before bed the previous night she'd had a bath and her thick hair had dried overnight into wavy ropes all the way down her back. Sitting in front of her mirror, she plaited it into a messy braid and swung it over her back. She added a touch of Vaseline to her lips, but that was it as far as her face was concerned. Where Melanora found the time to do a face full of makeup before school was a mystery to her.

'Sally!' her mum called for the hundredth time.

'What?'

'You'll be late!'

Sally followed the smell of fresh coffee into the kitchen, knowing there'd be breakfast waiting for her. Her mum knew her well enough to know there wouldn't be enough time for a full breakfast, but there was some toast with homemade lemon curd ready for her to grab and go. In the mornings, she quite liked that her mum was a domestic goddess.

Sally already had the toast in her mouth when her mum stopped her. She wiped an imaginary mark off Sally's cheek with a wet thumb. 'Sally, please don't forget to go to the sorting office to pick up your father's new golf shoes.'

'What?'

She wiped her hands on her apron. 'Sally, we talked about this. I need you to collect them after school.'

'Why can't you go?'

'Because I have church flower group today on the other side of town. Please don't argue.'

Sally sighed. There was so little in her mother's life that small jobs and errands took on epic proportions. A trip to the post office or a haircut was a full day's endeavour. 'OK.

Do you have the little card thing?'

'Here.' Her mum handed her the delivery note. 'Be careful, though. There's all sorts of weirdos down by the depot and after what happened yesterday . . .'

Sally hadn't thought of that. To get to the depot, she'd have to go to the worst part of town. Her skin crawled as she remembered the amputee and his wild, unblinking eyes, but she shook it off. 'It'll be fine, Mum.'

'Good. Go right after school and come straight home before it gets dark.'

Sally nodded. *Heaven forbid a seventeen-year-old go to a post office unaccompanied.* 'I have a free period this afternoon so I'll be able to leave school early.'

'All right then, dear.' Her mother kissed her forehead and Sally swept out, toast between her teeth.

Jennie texted Sally to say she was running late so she and Stan walked to school alone, discussing the previous night's *Satanville* in great depth, and whether the cast in real life was as close as they seemed. According to the internet, Mia Meyer who played Taryn was a massive diva on set. Sally didn't want to believe her heroine was a real-life bitch, and no one ever accuses male actors of being divas.

When they arrived at SVHS, they headed straight for the library block. The library was a separate building and the only part of the school that hadn't been demolished as part of a recent upgrade scheme. The rest of SVHS now looked and smelled like a futuristic leisure centre – all glass and needlessly curving walls. The old library was locked at this time of day, but there were a couple of picnic tables outside and this was where their clique congregated before registration.

The hierarchy was very simple. A-Listers like Melody, Eleanor and Keira, along with their uniformly hot boyfriends, sat on the cafeteria steps. Hot jocks were allowed to join them, but ugly jocks (such as the plain-Janes on the lacrosse team) hung out by the tennis courts. Band and choir members mostly loitered in the courtyard by the fountain, stoners behind the toilets. That just left their little area for waifs and strays – they weren't some inspirational band of misfit outsiders, however, they were just disparate individuals who tolerated each other because there's safety in numbers.

Sally was aware that, although SVHS was a daily nightmare, she didn't get nearly as much grief as some of her periphery friends. She was lucky in that a lot of the A-Listers didn't know she existed. Poor Grace Doulton with her acne, or overweight Dora Petrowski, or effeminate Joshua Parnell – they really got it bad.

Sally and Stan sat with a few of their lesson friends on the benches. Stan had devised the term 'lesson friend' as someone who you sit with for social protection purposes, but make no plans to see outside of school. As Sally didn't have Jennie or Stan in all of her classes, these B-List friends were important to her.

'What's your day like?' Stan asked.

'Pretty sucky. Double maths first.'

'But I'll see you third period, right?'

'Yeah. You can carry on your story.' In the margins of her French notepad, Stan was writing some *Satanville* fanfic. It was

28

actually pretty good – another little thing to look forward to, another breadcrumb to lead her through the day.

Stan was about to reply when they saw Jennie and Kyle hurrying across the lawn towards the library. Sometimes Kyle hung out with them, sometimes he loitered by the fountain. He carried his guitar on his back, dyed jet black hair blowing over his face. Sally swallowed back a bitter taste as he approached. He really did think he was the reincarnated spirit of Kurt Cobain and it made her sick.

He and Jennie were clearly having some sort of spat. He wasn't so much holding her hand as dragging her across the grass. Out of earshot, Kyle whispered something in Jennie's ear before releasing her from his grasp. After a pause they walked the rest of the way side by side. Jennie nodded at whatever it was he was saying before smiling broadly and almost skipping the rest of the way to the table, as if he'd commanded her to cheer up. 'Hey, guys!'

Sparkle, Jennie, sparkle.

Stan frowned. 'You OK?'

'Yeah, I'm fine!' Jenny said with a rictus grin.

Sally decided not to let it drop. 'What was that about?'

'Nothing. Everything's fine.' Kyle answered on her behalf. 'Right, babe?'

'Right.' Jennie fiddled with the hem of her nautical baby-doll dress. 'I made us late. Kyle was supposed to drop some sheet music off but —'

'It's no biggy.' Kyle wrapped an arm around her shoulder. 'I'll do it at break.' He looked directly at Stan. 'You know what girls are like. She was getting all stressed out and I was, like, dude, chill.'

'Right,' Stan said, apparently uncomfortable at being dragged into it.

'We made the bell, so it's all fine.' Jennie smiled but her shoulders were rigid. Sally longed to know exactly what words he'd whispered in her ear. Standard Jennie and Kyle: they were tactile and smiley but a weird vibe seemed to follow them around.

Jennie looked right at her. 'Hey, Sal, did you see the cast list yet?'

'What? No. Is it up already?'

'According to Becca it is. She ran off to see if her name was on the list a minute ago.'

Sally sprang off the bench, her palms suddenly sweaty. 'Oh, OK. I guess I should go check, then.'

'Want us to come with you?' Stan asked, swinging his rucksack onto his shoulder.

'No.' Sally nudged at some gravel with her Converse-clad toe. 'I won't be on the list. I might as well get it over with. I kinda hope I'm not on it. I only auditioned to keep Mum off my back.'

'You sure?'

'Yeah. I'll see you at registration.' Sally took off across the lawn and under the archway that led into the courtyard by the fountain. The cast list would be pinned to the arts noticeboard, which was why the musical kids all hung out by the fountain – it was their hub of information regarding rehearsal times and practice rooms.

There was already a crowd at the noticeboard, kids climbing over each other to get a clear view of the list. A couple of girls came away from the huddle obviously disappointed. 'We're not even in the chorus? How does that make sense?' said one distraught girl that Sally remembered from the auditions. She'd been tone deaf, so it wasn't a massive surprise.

From the centre of the scrum, she heard a high-pitched voice cry, 'Who on earth's Sally Feather? Which one was she?'

'You know, that one with the . . . plait thing,' someone else replied.

The crowd parted to let Melody, Eleanor and Keira out of the centre. Melody threw her a glance so hate-filled that it almost knocked Sally off her feet.

There's no way . . .

Sally slipped in through a gap and fought her way to the board. The list was printed on a piece of acid green paper, no doubt selected to be the same shade as the man-eating plant from the show.

Sally's heart raced as fast as it had at the audition. The main part was Seymour and that had gone to Joshua Parnell. She was delighted for him – effeminate he may be, but the guy could sing circles around anyone else at SVHS. In the not-too-distant future, when he was on Broadway, Sally suspected he'd get the last laugh.

The next part was Audrey. She could scarcely look. The role had gone to . . . Melody Vine. Oh. Well, that was an anti-climax. What was the filthy look for, then? Sally continued to scan the list past Mr Mushnik, the voice of Audrey II – the plant – and Orin, the evil dentist. Then she saw her name. She'd been cast as Chiffon. Chiffon, Crystal and Ronette were the Motown girl group who narrated the whole play. Thinking logically, although she wouldn't get a big solo spotlight, she would get to sing more than any other individual character.

Her hand flew to her chest, her skin suddenly hot and prickly. She'd actually got a part. A really good part – her mum would be thrilled. The elation lasted about a second before a cartoon anvil of panic smashed onto her head. How on earth was she going to get up on stage, most likely in a tight, sequinned dress, and perform song after song? She felt sick. Maybe she could pull out and not tell her mum. *Yes . . . tell a white lie, get out of it.*

And then it got that little bit worse. While Ronette was being played by Keira, she saw that Eleanor had only been cast in the chorus. Initially Sally figured that was what Melody's death glare had been about, but then she saw the very bottom of the list. Seymour had an understudy and so did Audrey.

AUDREY (UNDERSTUDY) . . . . SALLY FEATHER

Oh, well that explained it. Sally's head spun like she'd been punched by an iron fist. This was all a lot to take in. She pushed her way out of the huddle only to find herself face to face with Melody and she did not look pleased – her face was flushed and her lips were pursed like she'd gorged on lemons. 'Don't get excited, Sally.' She sounded as sour as she looked. 'I've never missed a performance in my entire career.'

The congregation turned to witness their conversation. Who doesn't love a catfight? Sally's brain felt like a blob of chewing gum and she struggled to form words. 'I . . . I don't want to be Audrey.'

Melody didn't look like she was expecting that response. 'Well . . . good. Because you won't be.' She turned and stormed off with a flick of her mane. Sally caught a whiff of whatever fragrance she'd sprayed all over herself that morning; it was vanilla-tinged and sickly.

Sally waited until Melody was out of sight before breathing again. As much as her mum wanted her to be in the production, Sally wasn't sure a) it was worth it for two months of rehearsal time with Melody, and b) whether she had the guts to do it. First rehearsal was tomorrow after school. She had until then to pull out.

By the time she'd spent five minutes psyching herself up in front of the mirror in the girls' toilets, she only had a second to check in with Mrs Flynn, her form tutor, before she had to race to first period. She arrived at maths even more sweaty and dishevelled than usual. Eyes fixed on the floor, she tried to slip into her seat as inconspicuously as possible, but the rest of the class was already seated and Mr Pollock ready to teach.

Sally took a space next to Dee, a lesson friend known for her frizzy strawberry blonde hair and face full of freckles. She greeted Sally with a smile. 'Congrats on the play,' she whispered.

'Thanks. H-how did you know?'

'I'll give you one guess.'

Melody. Word travels fast. Luckily, as far as Sally could ascertain, Melody couldn't count beyond ten, so Sally was safe in her A-Level maths classes. Sally had always loved maths; solving the problems and looking for the patterns. You could rely on numbers too. However you played with them they always behaved in a predictable way. Numbers were numbers.

And then something truly weird and entirely magnificent happened. From the next table over, a handsome – like off-the-TV handsome – guy turned to face her. 'Hey,' he said.

'Don't worry about Mels. Just give her some time to cool off. And congrats.' He was Todd Brady and he was Melody's boyfriend.

Sally's first reaction was, *Who is he talking to?* Her brain cogs turned too late, leaving a vast, cavernous silence after he'd finished speaking. 'Oh. Erm. Yeah. Thanks.'

Todd grinned and turned back to face Mr Pollock. Sally's brain was whirling. On the one hand Todd represented everything she should despise. He was from a rich family in Mulberry Hill, he was genetically blessed in every possible way, he was co-captain of the football team *and* he dated the worst person on earth. TV shows do not look kindly on his type of character.

Todd was an OK guy, but his friends were buffoon jocks of the worst order – mean, racist, homophobic bullies who dominated the school, and, as everyone knows, standing back and watching evil happen is its own kind of evil.

However, as a heterosexual girl with eyes, Sally couldn't help but wonder what he was like under his shirt. His football shirt gave just enough of a hint as to how sculpted his chest was, and his arms were huge. Alone in bed at night, she often dreamed about what it would be like to lie wrapped up in those arms, his skin on hers. He was an exact mixture of Zeke and Dante – the former's blue eyes and the latter's thick chestnut hair.

God, she loathed herself. She had never told *anyone*, not even Jennie, how she felt about Todd. He had only ever spoken to her once before: two years ago he had said, 'Sorry, mate,' after he'd bumped into her on the top corridor. She remembered every detail of it. It had been *so* hot.

This was one for the deathbed. If this information ever leaked, two things would happen. Number one: she'd be a laughing stock for about thirty seconds before number two: Melody ripped her still-beating heart from her chest and ate it publically in the centre of the courtyard.

'Miss Feather?' It was Mr Pollock. He looked at her expectantly. She'd been so consumed with the idea of resting her head on Todd Brady's pecs she'd missed his question.

'Sorry . . . I . . . ?'

He smirked. 'I merely require you to confirm your attendance . . .'

From the back of the classroom, some douche guys snorted laughter.

'Here, Sir,' Sally muttered. It was going to be a *long* double maths.

On her free period, Sally was about to spill into a nap, her head resting on her folded arms on a library table, when she suddenly remembered her errand. 'Oh God,' she exclaimed. 'I have to go into town.'

'What?' Stan looked up from his French homework. 'Why?'

'I have to go collect my dad's new golf shoes.'

Stan grinned. 'Sounds thrilling! Oh, please say I can come!'

'Sure.'

'Wait.' His smile fell. 'I can't. I'm meeting Kareem here after school to do our physics assignment.'

'It's OK, I don't plan on making it a huge visit.' She scooped her books into her rucksack. 'Shall I come over tonight?'

'Yeah, yeah,' he said eagerly. Stan was so puppy-like it was hard to imagine him as a seventeen-year-old man, even with his height and square shoulders. She guessed even really big St Bernard puppies are still puppies. To her he'd always be the plump little boy next door who flicked bogeys at her.

'OK, I'll come round after dinner.' As she sloped out of the library, she threw a look back over her shoulder, only to catch her friend watching her. 'What? Have I got something on me?'

'No. No, it's nothing.' He seemed to be blushing. Sally shook it off as she left the building. There was no way that Stan could think of her like *that*. They'd known each other for ever – granted he *had* once shown her his penis, but they'd been four and he'd asked to see hers in return. Sally couldn't believe for a second that a guy who had seen her with measles, a guy she had personally infested with head lice, a guy who had seen her in *Spongebob* pyjamas could possibly find her attractive.

Who am I kidding? She couldn't imagine *any* guy finding her attractive. She suddenly didn't like this line of thinking and blocked the thoughts out, focusing on the pleasing orange warmth of the afternoon sun on her face. Freedom felt good.

Sally pointedly avoided the cordoned-off scene of the road accident yesterday, taking the long way around the back of the school. She walked away from the playing fields, on which Year Nine girls were scowling their way through a hockey lesson, and towards Old Town. Beyond the school perimeter there was a petrol station, a faux American diner – *Howdy's* – and a few shops that survived on trade from students. The diner was a staple for the afterschool crowd – Oreo milkshakes and chicken wings were a must – although Sally, Stan and Jennie had never really felt popular enough to monopolise a whole booth there.

Anything American fascinated Sally, it always had. There was just something shinier about American stuff – the TV shows and films make life seem so much glossier, that sunny, soft-focus haze over everything. High school looked so glamorous, with cheerleaders and valedictorians ferried to proms and pep rallies in yellow buses. One day she'd move there, she was determined. She'd live on 'biscuits and gravy' and chilli dogs and Mountain Dew.

She reached the corner with the hardware store, took a right and headed towards the depot. This wasn't the best part of town, but it was still broad daylight, so she felt safe enough. The shops in Old Town were mostly off-licences, bookies and cash-for-gold shops – not the boutiques and restaurants of Mulberry Hill or the New Quarter. Before she knew it, she was absentmindedly humming 'Skid Row' from *Little Shop*.

An electric saw growled from the garage on the junction, sparks flying out of the open double doors. Sally darted over the street, past the scrap metal yard, the smell of molten rubber catching in the back of her throat. From inside the garage, a gruff, bearded mechanic glared out at her. His eyes peered through thick smoke, seemingly questioning what a lone girl was doing walking around this neighbourhood.

Sally kept her head down. The grimy brick walls were strewn in graffiti and weeds sprouted up through cracks in the pavement. She came to the rec ground, signalling that she was only a few roads away from the depot. The park was perhaps in an even sadder state than the street. The swing set only held one intact swing and the roundabout was covered in spray-paint squiggles.

Sally sensed she wasn't alone. Sure enough, a trio of street drinkers sat on one of the benches in the park. Holding her head up high, Sally walked with purpose, remembering some assertiveness seminar she'd sat through last year about how victims of crime often carry themselves like victims.

'You all right, darlin'?' a toothless man catcalled. 'Spare change?'

Sally pretended not to hear him. She couldn't do this again; it was like the previous night all over again. She quickened her pace.

'Oi! Where you goin'?' The man rose from his bench. His cheeks and nose were bright red with drink, his white beard stained nicotine yellow.

Her eyes were so fixed on the pavement that she didn't see the dog until it was too late. A sleek black shape reared up against a chain-link fence, its claws rattling the metal. Sally screamed and staggered into the road. She threw her hands over her face before she realised the Doberman was held securely behind the fence that ran around a gas canister warehouse. It was just a guard dog. Breathing again, Sally backed away. The animal barked and barked, drool spraying from its curled lips, baring white needle-sharp teeth. The black eyes were wild, rolling back in its head as if it were rabid.

There was something familiar about the deranged expression; something in the eyes. The same madness as the man with no arms. Sally's legs suddenly felt hollow and unsteady. She dearly wished Stan had come with her.

'Oi!' It was the drunk. He was staggering towards her. She whirled around, looking for a safe place. At least the people in the shops would be sober, if not exactly friendly. Breaking into a run, she looked for a safe haven. 'Where are you goin? I ain't gonna hurt ya!'

Find help. The nearest shop was boarded up, a downbeat notice thanking loyal customers taped to the door. So was the next. With horror, she realised everything on the street was closed or derelict. An old jeweller's, a burned out Kebab Palace – even the pub had metal grills over the windows. There was nothing. Sally's trainers pounded the pavement, but, chancing a look over her shoulder, she saw that the man still pursued her.

Something caught her eye: down a narrow side street there was a flashing neon light. A sign of life. Instinctively, Sally ducked into the alleyway. Sure enough, a flashing, hot-pink sign pointed down to a basement shop. It read, *HOUSE OF SKIN*. While the neon light flashed, a painted sign below read, *Tattoo & Piercing Parlour*.

The tramp turned the corner into the alleyway, which Sally now saw was a dead end, with bin bags piled up against a brick wall she had no hope of getting over. At the foot of the steps, she heard the electric whirr of what could only be a tattooist's needle. Sally careered down the worn stone steps and almost fell into the tattoo parlour.

As the door swung open, a bell chimed above her head. Sally slammed the door behind her and released the latch, locking herself inside. She hoped the shop owner would understand. Peering though a glass panel in the door, Sally saw the homeless guy hovering uncertainly at the top of the stairs before backing away. For now, she was safe.

The air inside the parlour was treacly with smoky incense, which failed to mask a whiff of antiseptic. Sally took in her surroundings. The shop wasn't as seedy as she might have expected. Rich crimson drapes hung down the walls, parted and tied with gold rope to allow curving bronze wall lights to snake into the dim room. There were towering palms in every corner of what seemed to be a reception area or waiting room; there was a plush, emerald green chaise longue next to a coffee table and receptionist's desk, although it wasn't presently manned.

'Hello?' Sally said, stepping properly into the waiting room. 'Is anyone there?'

Beyond the desk, a further blood red curtain hung over an archway to a back room. The buzz of the needle was louder now that she was inside and it set her teeth on edge, reminding her of a dentist's drill. She took a nervous step towards the studio, a little wary of who she might meet in this part of town, but unwilling to go back outside just yet.

The wall nearest her was lined with framed pictures containing dozens of images for clients to choose from – a colourful catalogue of mermaids, pirates, anchors, swallows and skulls. There was a bookcase filled with tattoo books but also candles, statues of the Madonna and leering *Dia de los Muertos* skulls. Sally ran a finger along the nearest shelf.

'Can I help you?'

Sally yelped and twirled around, tripping over her feet in the process and knocking a Virgin Mary to the floor. A woman stood *behind* her. How? How was that even possible when the door was locked? Sally guessed she must have been lurking in the alcove next to the barred window.

40

'I-I-I'm sorry,' Sally stuttered. At first, Sally thought the woman was wearing face paint, but then she realised her whole face was *tattooed*. She looked just like one of the Day of the Dead skulls – a spiderweb covered her entire face; thin black lines made it seem as if her lips were stitched shut, and gaping dark circles surrounded her eyes, making the sockets look hollow. She was deathly pale, with midnight blue-black ringlets tumbling around her shoulders. In her hair she wore a single red rose, the same sanguine shade as the curtains.

'What are you doing here?' She had a faint accent, possibly Portuguese or Spanish, maybe Eastern European, Sally wasn't sure.

'I . . . I was being chased,' Sally blurted out. 'I had nowhere else to go and I saw your sign was on.' She stooped down to pick up the fallen statue.

It was hard to tell because of the tattoos, but the woman seemed to soften. From the middle of the haunting black holes in her face, green eyes sparkled. 'You poor thing. You must have been so scared.'

'Yeah.' Sally nodded, embarrassed about making such a fuss. 'Can I stay in here for a minute? I won't be any trouble.'

'Well, of course. Stay as long as you want. Young girls like you shouldn't be wandering around this part of town alone. It's dangerous. Do you want me to call the police?'

Sally considered this for a moment. 'No, it's OK. I . . . I think he'll go away now he knows I'm with you. It was, erm, just a homeless guy.'

A hand covered in fingerless lace gloves reached for Sally's arm. 'Come, child, be seated. Can I bring you some tea?' The lady wore a rib-crushing black velvet corset from which silk skirts erupted like a scarlet fountain at her waist.

'No. I mean, no, thank you. I'm sure it'll be safe in a second.' Sally perched on the chaise longue, hands nervously in her lap.

'Such a polite little girl. What's your name?'

Don't talk to strangers, but what about saviours? 'I'm Sally.'

'And you can call me Rosita.'

'Thanks for letting me . . . hide.'

A smile danced on Rosita's bruise-coloured lips. 'Not at all. Welcome to the House of Skin.'

Sally wasn't sure what to say. 'It's . . . it's very nice.'

Rosita smiled broadly. She was picking up on her unease, Sally could tell. She doubted they had very many clients like her: shy schoolgirls with plaits. 'Why, thank you. Boris, the artist, is one of the most respected tattooists in all of Europe . . . all the world. Men and women come from all around the globe to be inked by him.'

'Really? To Saxton Vale?' Once upon a time their town had been famous for its mills, but now it was famous for nothing except its commuter links. Nothing good ever came there.

As she moved, Rosita almost seemed to float on air, her skirts hardly shifting as she glided across the shop floor. 'For now Saxton Vale. Who knows where tomorrow? He and I are circus people at heart – wanderers.'

Sally decided it might be best if she sat on her hands to stop them fidgeting. 'OK.'

Rosita paced the far wall, the one that held the array of tattoos. 'Do you have any piercings?'

'Oh, no,' Sally said, aware her over-the-top reaction was a touch Amish. 'My mum and dad wouldn't even let me get my ears pierced; they think it's common.'

'That's a shame.' Rosita smiled. 'I think that would look pretty. I suppose a tattoo is out of the question, then?'

Sally laughed, feeling more relaxed. She'd probably brave leaving the parlour in a minute if Rosita didn't mind checking the coast was clear – like, who was going to mess with tattoo-face lady? 'Are you kidding? They'd *kill* me!'

'Oh, how would they ever know?' Rosita said with a conspiratorial wink. With the tattoo elongating her lips, each smile almost seemed to split her face in two, like the Cheshire Cat from *Alice In Wonderland*. 'There comes a time in her life when every girl must defy her mother and father. It's all a part of becoming a woman.' She ran a gloved hand over the contour of her chest, her fingers tracing her ample bust. Sally looked away, embarrassed. 'Don't be shy,' Rosita said. 'Come and have a look.' She gestured at the wall of designs.

'Oh, I'm OK.'

'It's fun! Humour me! If you *were* going to have a tattoo, which would it be?'

Hmmm. Well, if she absolutely had *to* . . . 'Do you watch *Satanville*?' Sally asked. Rosita shook her head. 'It's this TV show and the demon assassins all have a tattoo on their wrist to show what order they belong to. That'd be cool. I'd get Dante's order, the Order of —'

Rosita cut her off. 'Come. Show me what it looks like.'

Sally bounced off the sofa. She scoured the images on the wall. The Order of the First had an ornate numeral I in a wreath of ivy. Sally could see nothing like it, although there were both numerals and floral designs.

In her whole life, Sally had probably spent a sum total of about twelve seconds thinking about tattoos, but she saw now that some of them were quite beautiful. Orchids, lilies and roses so lifelike she was compelled to reach out and touch the petals. Swallows, doves and peacocks with such intelligence in their onyx eyes, they almost seemed to follow her as she moved along the wall. Rosita watched her keenly.

There was a whole frame containing hearts. Some broken, some on fire, some with daggers through their core. All had blank scrolls underneath, waiting to be dedicated to a loved one. Sally smiled. How love-addled would you have to be to get someone's name branded on your skin?

Finally she came to a slightly grander frame, sturdy and gold, a little larger than the rest. The contents were less busy. This frame contained four beautiful 1950s pin-up girls and they were all breathtaking. 'Oh, they're so cool,' Sally murmured, almost to herself.

'Aren't they?' Rosita replied. 'Each of those girls is very special to me.'

'They're based on real people?'

'Of course! People Boris and I met on our travels.'

'Who are they?'

Sally looked at the first girl, an exquisite geisha. She held a paper parasol to match her kimono. 'That's Kazumi. We met her in Osaka. She's our winter girl, pure as fallen snow.'

The incense fumes made Sally's eyes heavy; a wave of sleepiness hit her. She could so easily imagine snowflakes swirling around Kazumi, her waist-length hair billowing in the wind. The next pin-up was a perky, busty blonde, her Easter eggs almost tumbling out of her basket as she tried to keep her bonnet on. Her red lips formed a shocked O. 'That's Marilyn.'

'Monroe?' The similarity was striking.

'Of course not,' Rosita said with a smirk. Her eyes twinkled. 'How old do you think I am?'

The third girl was a stunning redhead, her skirt blowing up as russet autumn leaves twirled around her bare legs. For a second, the leaves almost seemed to move on the paper.

'Adelaide in Autumn,' Rosita explained.

'She's love—' Sally started and then stopped because she saw the next drawing. *Drawing* didn't really do her justice, because her violet eyes *burned* from the poster. Unlike the other three girls, the final figure had no props or gimmicks to show she represented summer. She was quite hot enough by herself.

The final girl had raven black-and-blue hair curled at the nape of her neck. She cast a come-and-get-me look over her left shoulder, inviting the viewer to follow her off the straight and narrow. Her ruby lips curled into a smile full of men's secrets. She walked with her hands on her denim-clad hips, jean shorts cut high to emphasise the curve of her bottom. Sally could tell that her checked shirt, although she had her back to onlookers, was unfastened and secured in a knot under her breasts. 'Who's she?'

'That's Molly Sue.' Rosita smiled. 'And she's trouble.'

Chapter Four

So captivated was she by Molly Sue's eyes that Sally entirely phased out whatever Rosita said next, as if she were underwater. 'Sally?'

'Sorry . . . what?'

Rosita smiled. 'I asked if you liked her.'

'Erm . . . yes. Very much so. She's beautiful.' Sally still couldn't break the tattoo's gaze.

'Well, then,' Rosita interlaced her fingers under her chin with glee, 'why don't you get her?'

That snapped Sally out of her funk. She backed away from the frame, shaking her head. 'Oh, I couldn't. There's no way.'

'Why?'

'Because if my mum and dad didn't kill me, they'd ground me forever. Seriously. There was this one time I giggled because someone farted in church and they cancelled my birthday party.'

Rosita laughed before turning her back on her. She swept her hair to one side like a curtain. On her left shoulder blade there was an octopus tattoo, its tentacles making elegant curves and curlicues all over her back. 'See this little guy? I had him done when I was fourteen years old. My first.'

'It's . . . very nice.'

Rosita faced her once more and guided her back to the sofa to be seated. 'My father was . . . an angry man.' She paused, considering her words. 'He was . . . how would you say? A bully. I would take his beatings so that he might leave my little sisters alone. Once I got my octopus, he became my secret strength. Something only I knew about. He made me *powerful* because, if nothing else, it was I who was in control of my own body.'

The octopus suddenly seemed so much more than just a tattoo. It stood for something. Sally turned back to Molly Sue and wondered what the pin-up girl could mean to her. 'I guess I'm not really a tattoo person.'

'Don't be so sure. How old are you?'

'Seventeen.'

'Then you are a woman. You have your own secret strength, Sally. I can feel it.'

'I . . . I really don't.' Warmth rushed to her cheeks.

'Oh, it's there, we just need to bring it to the surface, perhaps. Molly Sue can make you powerful. We could put her somewhere out of sight. No one but you would ever know, until you felt it was time to unveil her – share her with someone special. A young man, perhaps?'

For some reason, Sally imagined Todd Brady's eyes light up when he saw there was something wild and exotic etched on her thoroughly vanilla skin. 'I don't have a boyfriend,' she muttered, and although it was meant to sound empowered, it came out so, so lonesome.

'Not yet.' Rosita's eyes sparkled. 'But you've thought about it, I can tell. What it would be like.'

Sally said nothing, letting her red cheeks do the talking.

'Or maybe it's not a boy,' Rosita went on. As she moved, she ran a finger around the gold frame containing the girls. 'Maybe it is a girl? Or . . . maybe it's status your heart desires . . . friends and popularity, money and clothes? We all have our little wants.'

Sally shook her head, but thought of Melody Vine and *that* hair. 'I already have friends.' *Just not many.*

'I am sorry, I have embarrassed you. I forget what it's like to be you.'

'To be me?'

Rosita smiled. 'To be a teenage girl. Lots and lots of rules. So many things you shouldn't be doing. So many things you're not supposed to say. So many things you're not supposed to even think.'

Sally gave a slight nod. She wasn't sure she'd ever met a grown-up who'd spoken to her like Rosita was: like an equal. Because she was so shy at school, teachers always treated her like she was a simpleton, while her parents treated her like one of her mother's decorative porcelain figurines on the sideboard.

Rosita, somehow, seemed to understand her despite having known her for less than ten minutes.

Walking back to the display wall, Sally allowed herself to look once more into Molly Sue's eyes. She was everything Sally wanted to be – not just cupcake-pretty, but cool, aloof, bold . . . *strong*. Sally would be satisfied with just one of those traits. If she was more like Molly Sue, she'd tell Melody Vine to curl up and die. *She'd* be Audrey. She'd tell her mum and dad she wasn't going back to church to pretend to pray to a God she didn't believe in. She'd tell Todd Brady that she thought about his lips each night as she fell asleep . . .

She staggered back as though the floor was swaying under her feet. It was all too much. Her head felt wobbly, like the time she'd sneakily downed two glasses of champagne at her cousin Alba's wedding.

'Are you OK?' Rosita asked.

'Yeah. I'm fine . . . I just . . .' Sally raised a hand to her temple.

'You want her. I can tell.' Rosita, materialising at her side, reached out and stroked the glass. 'Perhaps on the small of your back.'

'I can't.' Sally was surprised at how much she *did* want her. She remembered crying outside the pet shop the day they'd had puppies in the window. She hadn't even known she'd wanted one until she saw them and, when her mother dragged her away citing allergies, it had felt like her heart was being stretched – like an invisible piece of elastic from the little dog. She'd never wanted anything so much. This was the same.

'Of course you can. Our little secret. She'll be all yours too. Boris never does the same tattoo twice.'

Jealousy snapped, crackled and popped at Sally's core. The thought of anyone else taking Molly Sue was almost more than she could stand. A tattoo as stunning as Molly Sue should only belong to someone who felt as strongly as she did.

Her heart deflated like a punctured balloon. 'Even if I wanted to . . . I don't have any money. I'm broke. My mum won't even let me take a babysitting job.'

'Well, isn't this just your lucky day? Most of our clients are, let's say, a little older than you. Boris takes a special pride in tattooing beautiful young skin. It's extra special. No charge.'

'No charge?'

'On the house, as they say. It would be a treat for Boris. Pure, unmarked skin like yours will make his day. His week.'

'Oh, I couldn't possibly.'

Rosita clamped her hands on her hips but smiled warmly. 'Why ever not? What reasons do you have left?'

Sally opened her mouth but no sounds came out. She had no reasons left. She imagined the looks on *their* faces – *them* being the rest of the world. What would they say if they knew? Shy little mouse Sally Feather has a *tattoo*? She imagined the horror and disbelief her mum, dad, Melody, Stan, Jennie would wear on their faces.

She thought about how *naughty* she would feel having a secret – not some lame crush on a football player – a real secret. 'OK,' she said.

'Really?' Rosita clapped her hands together. 'Oh, Boris will be thrilled! Are you sure?'

Sally appreciated Rosita offering her a way out, but the seed had taken root in her mind. 'Yes.' She looked at Molly Sue one last time and felt like the girl was welcoming her into some sorority. 'She's just too gorgeous to refuse.'

A smile danced on Rosita's lips. 'Spoken like Molly Sue herself! Come, child. Follow me.' Rosita placed a hand on her shoulder and guided her towards the partitioned archway.

The back room was now silent, the needle had stopped its intermittent buzzing. 'Isn't there already someone in here?' Sally asked.

'No,' Rosita said simply. Sally was confused – why was the needle going if there was no one back here? Sally stalled as they passed over the threshold. The back room was a far cry from the opulent waiting area. Stark grey tiles covered the walls floor to ceiling, while the floor was wipe-clean linoleum. In the centre of the room was a reclining dentist's chair next to a steel trolley housing an array of inks, black latex gloves, piercing guns and, finally, the tattoo needle – a wasp-like metal gun.

A green-tinged angled lamp cast strange, jagged shadows up the walls. The room was dark, claustrophobic and windowless.

A hulk of a man waited in the shadows, his broad shoulders filling an entire corner. As he stepped into the light, Sally saw that he wore a surgical mask over his mouth and a black rubber apron over his unusually smart clothes: a crisp, stiff-collared white shirt, a black tie and matching sleeve garters. In the dim pool of the lamp, his eyes sparkled as he saw her for the first time. Behind the mask, he growled appreciatively, hungrily.

Perhaps I should just be going . . .

Sally backed away instinctively, colliding with Rosita. 'Oh, I should have said.' Rosita pushed her further into the studio. 'Boris speaks no English.' She said something to the artist in his native tongue. Sally had no idea what she said, or even what language it was. She'd done French and Spanish at school, and it sounded nothing like either of those. It was a strange, guttural sound. Maybe Slavic? Rosita did most of the talking, with Boris growling and grunting by way of reply. Rosita stroked Sally's lower back, presumably directing Boris as to where Molly Sue was going.

Sally's heart galloped. This was *wild*, but it felt like she'd been led here for a reason. It felt *right*. Today was the day she grew

51

up – like the season two episode of *Satanville* where Taryn's grandmother died and passed the Amulet of Forbidden Truths to her. She tried to draw strength from that . . . if Taryn could leave childhood behind, so could she.

As Rosita spoke, Boris never once took his eyes off her. Sally felt the weight of his stare and shrank back. His eyes, almost feline, were the most unusual amber shade, somewhere between brown and gold.

Rosita turned back to her. 'Come, child, sit.' She pulled up a simple metal chair and gestured for her to be seated. 'Sit sideways on and lean against the big chair. Oh, and you'll need to take off your shirt.'

Sally had expected nothing less. With nervous fingers, she unbuttoned her plaid shirt and laid it on the dentist's chair, which was fully reclined, before pulling her T-shirt over her head. Her mother bought all of her clothes and her bra was the plainest, most nun-like one they sold at *Lucy's Locker* in the shopping centre. It was almost military issue and Sally was deeply embarrassed, folding her arms across her chest.

'Sit,' Rosita prompted again, before adding, 'you have a beautiful body, Sally . . . and the most exquisite skin.'

Was her unease that obvious? 'Um . . . thanks.' Sally sat side-saddle on the chair, pulling her long braid around the front of her shoulder. She couldn't believe Rosita thought her body beautiful – it was angular and bony, not comely like Rosita's curves.

'Lean forward,' Rosita instructed and Sally folded her arms on the armrest and lay her head on them.

'Will it hurt?' She already knew the answer.

'Yes. But it's unlike any pain you'll have known. Do not worry, though, the soft part of the back isn't the worst place to have done.'

Boris snapped on a pair of the black latex gloves.

'OK.' If her dad ever found out she'd be *dead*. Her mouth was desert dry. What was the worst he could do? Throw her onto the streets? She was leaving for university next year anyway and then she could be as tattooed as she liked. In fact, she cherished the idea of starting afresh in a new town with a new identity she'd curate for herself. She'd be the cool girl with the awesome tattoo. *Just do it*.

Wordlessly, Boris sat on a wheelie stool and pulled himself close behind her. She smelled alcohol disinfectant about a second before she felt the icy cold stuff being smeared over her skin on a cotton-wool ball. He grunted at Rosita.

'Are you ready?' she translated.

Sally nodded, feeling far from sure. Once that needle touched her skin she was past the point of no return. Whatever happened, there was no way she was leaving this room with a half-finished squiggle. That would only prove to the rest of the world that she was weak. She wasn't weak, she was quiet. There's a difference.

With gloved fingers, Boris turned a dial on what looked like a voltage box. The meter jumped and the needle started up, buzzing like an angry bee. And then it stung. She wasn't ready for it. The pain shot up and down her spine like a bolt of lightning. Boris held her still with a bear paw. He kept going. Why it came as a surprise that it felt like there were needles burrowing into her skin was beyond her, but that was exactly what it felt like. He *dragged* the thing across her flesh.

53

She bit her lip to stop herself screaming. She screwed her eyes shut, blinking back tears.

Only then it changed. It was as if the pain drilled down into her bones. It was no longer a sharp, stabbing agony, but more of an ache. It was warm and it was manageable. Sally breathed again. She imagined a pink tide, the warmth spreading in waves from the base of her spine, washing across her torso and down her legs.

It hurt, but it hurt in the way a massage hurts. It was excruciating and blissful at the same time. A cocktail of pleasure and pain.

The wave reached her fingertips and toes, all of her skin buzzing in time with the needle – finding a resonance. The warmth reached her lips and then her eyes, like she was filling up with bathwater, and Sally completely zoned out.

When she came to, the buzzing had stopped. She sat upright with a jerk, wondering if the whole thing had a been a blue-cheese dream and she was still dozing in the library with Stan. But no, she was still in the tattoo studio. Her back felt warm and tingly.

'All done.' It was Rosita. 'Would you like to see?'

Boris washed his hands over a stainless steel sink in the corner.

'Yeah . . . you're finished?' She'd closed her eyes for like a minute – how could it possibly be done already?

'Yes. She looks beautiful.'

'Oh.' Sally stood, tempted to reach around and feel. 'Did I pass out or something?'

'I don't think so. You sat very well, though – no wriggling. Boris was impressed.' From the corner, he growled by way of agreement.

'I . . . I thought it'd take longer.' She reached for her back, but Rosita pulled her hand away.

'Don't scratch it, no matter how itchy it gets.' Rosita guided her to a full-length, freestanding mirror. 'Can you see over your shoulder?'

Sally closed her eyes and took a deep breath. *What have you done? You stupid, stupid little idiot*. There was always laser removal, she figured. She opened her left eye a fraction, terrified she'd see a hideous bloody mess running onto her jeans.

It was fine.

It was more than fine. Sure, the skin was a little red and raised, but there was no blood and Boris had apparently smeared her back in some sort of shiny ointment so it didn't even feel too sore. 'Oh, wow.'

'Isn't she beautiful?' Rosita beamed.

She really, *really* was. The Molly Sue on her back was an exact replica of the one she'd seen in the gallery, only this one looked even more real, if that were possible. The pin-up girl looked delighted to be on her flesh and Sally was delighted to have her. 'That's . . . that's amazing.'

'Do you like her?'

All of Sally's nagging doubts dropped away in a second. Molly Sue made her whole body look different, her slinky walk following the curve of Sally's own spine. Sally looked older, her waist and hips curvier and more womanly somehow – although she was quite sure it was all psychological. 'I don't like her. I *love* her.'

Chapter Five

Hazy, lazy sun was still shining through thin cloud when Sally reached the top of the basement stairs outside the House of Skin. It was warm too, sunset still a while away. Sally squinted against the light, confused. She was sure she'd heard that tattoos take hours and hours – Molly Sue was quite large too, covering the expanse of flesh from under her shoulder blade to the small of her back.

Sally started in the direction of home, before remembering why she'd come to this god-awful part of town in the first place – her father's golf shoes. Still a little wary of the drunk, she looked around anxiously, ready to pelt back down the stairs if necessary. He was nowhere to be seen – he must have got bored and given up ages ago. Sally let out a calming breath and set off towards the parcel depot.

Like the anaesthetic wearing off after a trip to the dentist, the full horror of what she'd done didn't hit her until she walked through her front door.

What have you done to yourself? You've scarred yourself FOR LIFE.

By that time the sun was setting and a chill breeze shivered the trees of her cul-de-sac, although she couldn't be sure if it was the wind or her nerves making her back teeth clatter.

'Where have you been?' Her mother skittered from the kitchen into the hall, brandishing a whisk. 'You said you'd be back before dark.'

Sally almost vomited then and there on the welcome mat. *She's going to know. She's going to know as soon as she looks at me.*

Sally had always been a terrible liar; she was going to be in so much trouble. In her parents' eyes, girls had been locked in iron masks for less. Her skin was suddenly unbearably hot, the tattoo at the epicentre of the heatwave.

Her mum just looked at her. 'Well?'

'Sorry – I forgot to get Daddy's parcel. I had to go back.'

Her mum brushed a lock of hair out of her face. 'Oh, you're such a scatterbrain, Sally.' She took the box out of her hands and headed back to the kitchen. The conversation was apparently over. 'I can't trust you with the most basic errands. Go and wash your hands for supper, please. It's your favourite. Corn beef hash.'

Number one: Sally hadn't liked corn beef hash since she was about five – it's a meat tumour. Number two: she'd got away with it. She looked around the frilly house – the lounge to her right and dining room to her left. Everything was as it should be: the grandfather clock ticked away, the immaculately polished photographs lining the staircase, the vases overflowing with fresh hydrangeas. If she angled her ear towards the lounge, she could hear Tweetie, her mother's canary, picking through the seed in her cage. Everything was the same, but she was different.

And no one else knew but her.

She recalled Rosita's words about secret strength. Supressing a smile, Sally dashed upstairs towards the bathroom.

Getting through dinner was a struggle. She was sure her dad would spot something was wrong, but he seemed far more concerned about uncovering the identity of the co-worker who'd dinged his car outside the bank.

As Sally tried to stomach supper, her initial dread turned to something like hysteria. She had to supress the urge to giggle manically. The words, 'I GOT A TATTOO,' sat right at the very tip of her tongue. The more she thought of potential punishments her father might dole out (being dragged through the town centre behind a horse-drawn cart, being made to wear an *I'm a heathen* sandwich board while ringing a bell outside church), the more she wanted to laugh.

It was so clear now. They might well be her parents but these were not her people. Despite her and their best attempts to make a cookie-cut daughter, Sally did not belong in this house – a fact pencilled in since birth. Getting a tattoo signed it in ink. It didn't bother her so much, though. In fact, admitting it was quite freeing.

After maintaining invisibility over dinner, Sally ducked through the fence to Stan's house. She was sore and exhausted, but she figured if she didn't go over like she'd promised, he'd know something was up and she wasn't sure she'd hold up under interrogation.

Stan was in the kitchen when she arrived, waiting for microwave popcorn to finish. He was wearing his pyjamas even though it was only a little after seven. 'Hey,' he said after she'd run the gauntlet of their cluttered hallway. 'Can you get the Coke out of the fridge? Kareem lent me *Hacksaw 5* on DVD. We can watch that if you want.'

'Is that the one with the evil clown?' Sally went to the fridge.

'It sure is!' He gingerly pinched the steaming bag out of the microwave and tipped it into a bowl, sucking his burned fingers. Job done, Stan turned round and looked at her for the first time. 'Are you OK?'

'Yeah. I'm fine.'

'You look different.'

Sally's heart plummeted into her feet. She steeled herself and avoided the truth. 'I'm wearing exactly what I had on at school.'

Stan scrutinised her. 'Yeah, but . . . I don't know . . . you just look different.'

'Nope. Same as ever.' She wasn't even sure why she lied. It popped out of her mouth before she could reason that he and Jennie would probably think it was quite cool. But they might tell people at school and *they* might tell a parent and then *her* parents would know within the hour. The town worked like that.

They'd only just reached Stan's room when they heard the front door close and Jennie chatting to Mrs Randall in the hall. She made her way up the stairs at half her normal speed. As soon as she stepped into the bedroom, Sally could tell that she'd been crying. 'Hey, what's up, Mitten?'

'Nothing.' Jennie took her jacket off but wouldn't look her

in the eye. This was not the pastel-grunge-bubblegum Jennie they were used to.

'Jen . . . something is clearly wrong.'

Stan pushed the popcorn to one side. 'Is it Kyle?' His nostrils flared along with his temper.

'We had a fight and now he won't return my texts. I don't know where he is. I'm really worried about him.'

Stan muttered something under his breath, but Sally guided Jennie to the bed so she didn't hear him. 'I'm sure he's fine. What was the fight about?'

Jennie blinked back fresh tears. She fiddled with her *Satanville* bracelets as she spoke. 'It's so stupid. Kyle read some stuff I'd written on the Order of the First forum and he saw that I'd been chatting to some guy in America.'

Sally frowned at Stan. 'Well, so what?'

'He said that I was flirting. I wasn't, though! We were just chatting – but he's still really cross, because you know how months ago he found out I'd been talking to my ex on Facebook.' Jennie checked her phone again only to throw it onto the mattress in dismay.

Stan, at his laptop, flicked onto the forum Jennie was talking about. 'Jennie, this is not cool. He can't stalk you online like that! You didn't even say anything remotely flirty.'

'I know!'

Sally tried to keep her tone even and non-judgemental. 'And he shouldn't be going through your stuff like that. Do you hack into his Facebook too?'

'No! Well, maybe a couple of times . . . if he leaves himself logged in.'

Sally sighed. 'Jen! That is so messed up!'

'I know, but I didn't do anything. I don't know why he's ignoring me.'

'Because he's a knoblin,' Stan mumbled.

'What?' Jennie looked to him.

'Because he's annoying,' Stan said, joining them on the bed. 'Jennie, he's making you über-miserable.'

Jennie scowled at him. 'No, he isn't!' she said vehemently. 'I love him.' In that moment, she sounded *young* and Sally fought an urge to shake her friend by the shoulders.

But Sally held her tongue, the way she always did. 'Jennie, you and Kyle fall out all the time. You always work it out in the end. It'll be fine.'

Stan started to argue. 'This is bullsh—'

'Stan, you're not helping.' Sally's voice was steady but firm. 'But he shouldn't be checking your Facebook. It's a violation of privacy and it's not cool.'

Her cool tone seemed to lure Jennie off the ceiling. 'I know. I know. Thanks, Sal.' Jennie flung her skinny arms around Sally and squeezed her tight. Too tight. The tattoo burned and Sally's eyes bulged in pain.

'Ow!'

Jennie let go. 'What?'

'Nothing.' She lied again, but too quickly. She felt like a little kid standing inside the pantry, icing all around her mouth.

'What's going on?' Stan asked, scrutinising her.

'Nothing,' she repeated, before adding, 'That time of the month.'

Stan dropped it at once, the way she suspected any guy would. 'Oh. Right . . .'

She could have so easily told them, but she didn't want to share. Molly Sue was *hers*.

Later that night, Sally couldn't sleep. A mugginess had crept in, the first taste of spring with any luck. It was more than that though: the tattoo. It was sore, it was itchy and Sally couldn't lie on her back. All evening she ping-ponged back and forth from feeling like the most rock-and-roll girl in all of Saxton Vale to *I have made a terrible, terrible mistake*. She shifted, trying to get comfortable. In the end she kicked back her duvet and just lay on top of the bed with the window open a crack.

The slide into sleep was so gradual she didn't even realise she was asleep until she awoke with a start.

There was someone in her room.

She heard a voice. Or voices. She couldn't tell which. Low, muttering voices.

Who is it? Where are they?

Her first instinct was to freeze, lie as still as she could and play dead; she held her breath.

Nothing.

Eyes open, but facing into her pillow, she could only see the corner of her rug. There could be someone standing at the foot of her bed. Worst-case scenarios arrived in her head. *Has someone broken in? Burglars? Are Mum and Dad dead in the next room? Am I next?*

Sally waited, still not exhaling. The room was silent. Her second thought was to get the hell out, to get her dad. She sat upright in bed, ready to grab anything that could be used as a makeshift weapon.

Her room was empty.

Sally *swore* there'd been voices.

You were dreaming, go back to sleep, she told herself.

She listened more closely.

There it was again. A low whispering so quiet that Sally could hardly distinguish the words. Someone giggled. This time, she definitely wasn't imagining anything.

'Ssssssss . . .'

She couldn't make out words, it was little more than a hiss.

'Aaaaaahhhh . . .'

It didn't sound like her mum or dad, though. Not daring to hang her legs off the bed where they'd be exposed, she oh-so-slowly lowered her head off the edge of the bed. Her hair trailing onto the carpet as she hung upside-down, she peeked underneath. There was nothing, not even dust bunnies.

'Sssssssaaaaaahhh . . .' There it was again . . . in the distance, but somehow close by.

Confident she was alone, Sally swung her legs off the bed and walked to her window. She pulled the lacy curtain to one side and looked out across their immaculately mown back lawn. The cherub water feature babbled into the pond and the wind chime in the Randall's garden clattered like cowbells, but she couldn't see anyone talking.

She heaved up the sash window and stuck her head out into the night. The voice continued.

'Eeeeeeeee . . .'

At least that's what it sounded like. The voice was far away, maybe around the front of the house. It was hardly human at all. There was something almost snake-like about it. Sally listened for a minute longer and her neighbourhood fell silent again. Her owl was elsewhere tonight.

Maybe a big snake ate it.

Looking to her left, she saw Stan's bedroom window on the side of their house. He too had his bedroom window open a crack, the ash black curtains billowing through the gap. Green light flickered from within – he must have fallen asleep in front of the TV or something. Suddenly it made sense. The voices must be from whatever he was watching. Probably *Satanville*.

Satisfied, she ducked back through the window and slid it down. The heat of her healing back reminded her that yesterday most definitely hadn't been a dream.

Oh God, you're stuck with it now, she told herself. *This is going to look awesome when you're forty.*

Now wide awake, she crossed to her en-suite and flicked on the light above the mirror. As well as she could, she craned her neck around to see the reflection of her back.

Sally's eyes were fuzzy from sleep. She blinked hard. For a second there, it had looked like Molly Sue had her eyes closed, but she now saw it was just a trick of the light. The tattoo's eyes were wide open. Sally shook her head and sloped back to bed.

On the very brink of sleep, so close she wouldn't remember when she awoke, Sally idly wondered if the airy hiss was sounding out the letters of her name.

Chapter Six

By the time Sally reached the benches outside the library the following morning, two things were clear. One was that spring had truly arrived. It was already pleasantly warm by eight thirty. Sally couldn't bear to think what the temperature would be like by midday. The thought of her T-shirt riding up and revealing Molly Sue scared Sally so much that she'd opted to wear a tent of a shirt over it – one she normally wore only to sleep. She was going to boil to death. The tattoo was already itchy and she'd only just applied the ointment to it.

The second obvious thing was that Jennie and Kyle had made up and wanted the whole world to see. Jennie sat on his lap at the picnic table, stroking his hair. He ran his fingers up and down her bare arm like he was playing a harp. The mere thought of his hands on flesh made Sally's own skin crawl but the really sad part was that Jennie looked delighted. For now, she was *winning*. Based on what she'd seen at school, Sally sometimes wondered if that's all relationships were – one big competition to gain the upper hand.

'Oh my God!' Jennie beamed as she approached. 'Sal, I'm hot just looking at you! Lose a layer!'

'I'm fine,' Sally lied. 'It's not that warm.'

Beside her, Stan had bust out shorts for the first time that year and a vintage Green Day T-shirt. 'You do look pretty hot,' he said before turning a distinctive radish shade in the cheeks. Kyle laughed like Nelson from *The Simpsons*. 'Not like *that*,' Stan quickly amended.

'Slick, dude.' Kyle said. 'Slick.'

Stan gave him a look of barely concealed hatred. Stan wasn't subtle at the best of times and Sally saw Jennie tense ever so slightly.

'Hey.' It was Annabel Sumpter, one of their B-friends. She was OK, but like *really* intensely Christian, which Sally found off-putting. She'd once made a big speech about 'Muslim Hell' which hadn't sat well with Sally at all. 'Given that this could be the entire British summer in one day, we might go for a picnic up at the lake right after sixth period, if you fancy it? Ollie says he'll drive. He's got the people carrier.'

'Ooh, that sounds like fun!' Jennie clapped.

'I can't,' said Sally, although she knew her parents didn't like her going up to the lake, anyway (the 'wild parties', the 'drinking', the 'wrong crowd'). 'It's the first *Little Shop* rehearsal.'

'Oh, bummer.' Stan looked genuinely disappointed.

'You should go anyway,' Sally told him.

'Well,' Stan said, 'Jen and I said we might come and offer our services to the production team . . .'

'Yeah. Kyle's in the show band, anyway, so it could be fun,' Jennie added.

'You guys are the best.' Sally feigned excitement. She was

already nervous about rehearsal – and now she'd have a keen-eyed audience.

The rest of the day was as average a school day as you could imagine. The highlights, if they could be considered such, were the ice lollies they found to serve in the canteen, a glimpse of Mr Rudd, the gorgeous PE teacher, in his gym shorts, and Stan continuing his *Satanville* fanfic in French – even if his shipping of Taryn and Angela was getting a little X-rated.

The day passed without troubling Sally too much mentally, even if her back was on fire. School never felt especially nourishing – more like brain chewing gum. The work was just too easy for her, but she certainly wasn't going to draw attention to herself by announcing her brilliance from the rooftops. What was the point? She couldn't do any better than the A-grades she was already getting. The last thing she needed was the likes of Melody calling her 'swot' and 'nerd' and 'teacher's pet'. Keeping her head down and playing the game had worked out well enough so far and she intended to keep it that way.

Of course, now she had to stick her head way above the parapet.

Sally's palms were damp as she climbed the endless stairs to the top corridor, which led to the main hall, the venue for the first rehearsal. There was a giggly buzz as the cast assembled for the first time. Naturally, Melody was at the epicentre of the attention with Eleanor and Keira like bookends beside her. Sally noted that Melody had adopted her leading man, Joshua, as one of the gang. *Two-faced bitch*, thought Sally. She'd heard Melody calling him 'gay boy' and 'faggot' on numerous occasions. With utter horror, she wondered if she might get the same treatment until Melody threw her enough side-eye to cause her to stumble right into Stan's arms.

'You drunk, Feather?' he chuckled.

'Melody Vine death stare,' she whispered. 'DON'T look!'

'Oh, wow. She finally developed telekinesis. Bummer.'

Sally turned to Stan, gripping both his arms. 'Stan, can we just go? I don't know if I can do this.'

'Of course you can. You'll be dope.'

She laughed despite herself. 'Dope?'

'Yeah. What? I'm street. Just, y'know, sing.'

'Like it's that easy.'

Stan shrugged. 'Why isn't it? You're the best singer in our year.'

'Yeah, right.'

'Don't forget I can hear you across the back garden. I leave my window open because you're better than whatever's on the radio.'

Sally considered him with a tilt of her head. 'You listen to me sing?'

He shifted uncomfortably, suddenly very interested in his feet. 'Yeah, sometimes. You're pretty loud, you know. But good. That's how I know you can do this. Just look for your inner lion or something.'

Or something. Sally remembered the powerful creature at the base of her back and tapped into the strength in Molly Sue's eyes. *What did Rosita say? Her own secret strength. She could* do *this. And she would.*

Mr Roberts entered the hall, balancing a stack of photocopied scripts and song-sheets in one arm and a coffee in his spare hand. Immaculate as ever, today he wore a matching tangerine shirt and tie combo. He'd barely had a chance to set his coffee down atop the piano before Melody advanced on him, Eleanor and Keira still at her side.

'Mr Roberts,' Melody said sweetly. She brushed her hair over her shoulder as if she were offering her bare neck to a vampire.

Barking up the wrong tree there, thought Sally.

'We had an idea we wanted to talk to you about.'

Roberts sighed. 'Can it wait, Melody? We need to get started.'

'It'll only take a minute.' She smiled. 'We just thought it'd make much more sense if Eleanor was Chiffon instead of Sally. That way we could rehearse more because we always see each other outside of school.'

Sally looked to her feet. The conversation wasn't quiet and Melody knew Sally was in earshot. Luckily, the teacher didn't look thrilled at having his directorial choices questioned. 'No, Melody, absolutely not. I'm not changing the cast now.' He looked worriedly over at Sally but she pretended she hadn't heard.

Suddenly a new voice rang around the room. It boomed in Sally's ears. A strong, American voice with a distinctive southern twang. 'WHAT A GODDAMN BITCH!'

Sally hid a giggle behind her hand and turned around looking for the source, but only saw a last few stragglers arriving in the hall. Everyone else was going about their business. That was weird.

'Oh, darlin',' said the voice, as clear as day. 'Don't worry, there's only you that can hear me. It's me, Molly Sue.'

Chapter Seven

'Can you hear that?' Sally grabbed Stan, pulling him away from his conversation with some B-friends.

'What?'

'That girl?' Sally once more scanned the hall.

The American spoke again. She was so loud, she must be close by. 'Girl, when you're done whippin' your head around, we should probably talk alone.'

Stan frowned. 'Sally, I can't hear anything. Are you OK?'

Sally felt the colour purge out of her face. Her legs turned to spaghetti and she realised too late she was going to fall. She clung to Stan.

'Sally!'

That got Mr Robert's attention. 'Sally? What's wrong?'

'God, what a drama queen.' Melody rolled her eyes.

The American seemed to agree. 'Five Gs, baby. Good God, Girl, Get A Grip.'

'Sally?' Jennie, who'd been with Kyle, came to her side.

'I'm fine,' Sally blurted out. 'I . . . I just need the bathroom.'

'Oh, that's nice,' Melody sniggered.

'Didn't her mama learn her no manners?' the voice said.

The voice only I can hear, thought Sally.

'You want me to come with you?' Jennie asked, clearly concerned.

'No! No. I'm fine. I promise.' Sally just had to get out of the room. If her head was going to explode – and it felt like it might – she didn't want anyone to see. Trying as hard as she could to walk in a straight line, no small feat with the ground spinning, Sally made it to the exit and into the corridor. Steadying herself against the wall, she felt her way to the disabled toilet, knowing no one would disturb her in there.

She locked the door behind herself and collapsed onto the toilet, gripping the handrail. Bleach and illicit cigarette smoke assaulted her nostrils.

This isn't happening. This SERIOUSLY isn't happening.

'It surely is, darlin',' the voice replied. 'Get used to it.'

Sally jammed her hands over her ears. 'Go away!' she hissed, worried someone would hear her.

'Now where amma gonna go?'

This can't be real. I'm cracking up. Oh God, I've gone mad like Uncle John.

'Sugar pie, we need to get past this. I know it's a shock and all, but the quicker y'all adjust, the better it'll be for ya. It's gon' be fine and dandy, just you wait.'

Sally stood and faced the mirror. Scared to look but unable to not, Sally lifted the baggy shirt and vest underneath. Turning around, she saw Molly Sue, still peering over her shoulder.

And then Molly Sue turned.

The tattoo moved, fully animated, turning to face her.

'No!' Sally cried aloud.

Molly Sue's ruby lips moved. 'I'm gon' square with ya. I know this must be a trip. But ya wanna try being a tattoo sometime! How'd ya think I feel?'

Sally dropped her shirt and stumbled backwards, colliding with the sanitary bin. 'What . . . ? I don't understand . . . am I going mad?'

'No, ma'am. I am one hundred per cent the real deal. I sure am sorry I didn't say somethin' last night. It takes a few shakes to sink in, y'know? I wasn't gon' say anything 'til we were alone, but that Melody Vine sure is a piece o' work, ain't she?'

Sally clutched her head, squeezing her skull as hard as she could. She tasted tears running into her mouth. 'Please, stop . . .'

'Now lookee here. It's gonna be fine, sugar.' The voice changed – cooler and more authoritative. 'All you need to do is get yo' pretty little ass back into that hall before someone comes a-lookin' for ya. Think ya can do that?'

'No!' Sally slid down the wall. The floor was tacky and strewn with stray white squares of toilet paper.

'Aw, c'mon! This ain't such a bad thing. Look! I'll shut ma trap til ya get home. How 'bout that? You won't even know I'm here. And you don't have ta worry about talkin' to me – I can hear ya thoughts loud 'n' clear. Whatcha say, darlin'? Think ya can keep it together for a bitty rehearsal?' Molly Sue purred in her ear, her voice like Texan silk.

Sally nodded, although tears still ran down her face.

There's a talking tattoo on my back. NO. *I'm cracking up.*

Hearing voices: never a good sign.

'C'mon,' Molly Sue said. 'You got this. Get up. Get up an' knock 'em dead.'

Sally hauled herself to her feet. The reflection in the mirror wasn't pretty – she looked like a wreck: her eyes, nose and lips soggy.

'Atta girl. Splash some water up on your face.'

Sally did as she was told and looked fractionally better.

'There. Now let's go hear this angel voice I been hearing all about.'

Chapter Eight

By the time Sally got home, she was starting to think the whole thing had been in her head. That was fine with her – a hallucination was probably better than a talking tattoo. Maybe it was a 'psychotic episode'. That's a thing – sometimes her Uncle John had them and you could get pills for it. She'd gone back into rehearsal only to be taken out by one of the other music teachers to start learning the songs. Her tattoo stayed true to her promise and shut up, although the other singers in the group kept their distance, wary of the girl who'd obviously been crying.

Straight after they'd finished, Stan and Jennie had headed up to the lake with Kyle, so Sally made her excuses and left them to it.

She let the front door slam behind her and headed for the stairs. Her mother swooshed out of the kitchen in a cloud of steam. Sally could hear pan lids tapping away as potatoes bubbled. 'Sally, how many times have I asked you not to slam the . . . ? Where are you going?'

'I feel ill.' Sally didn't even look at her.

'But I made your favourite. Shepherd's pie.'

She still didn't turn back. 'Save some for me.' Sally headed straight for her room. Not taking any chances, she drew the curtains and switched on her laptop. As soon as it was fired up she Googled *multiple personalities*. She'd seen enough TV to know that that's what this was.

The first result thrown up was for *Dissociative Identity Disorder (DID)*. Sally clicked on the link. 'A mental disorder characterised by the presence of at least two enduring identities . . .' she muttered to herself. As best as she could given how much medical jargon there was in the description, Sally read through the article and learned DID was extremely rare indeed, although the first onset of so-called 'alters' was most likely to occur in girls around her age.

Her fingers tapped nervously on the edge of the desk. Perhaps this was it. As she continued to read, her heart sank. There were so few confirmed cases and they nearly all went hand in hand with other mental illnesses or following a great trauma.

'You don't buy that horse dung, do ya?' The southern twang struck again.

Sally recoiled, expecting there to be someone standing behind her. Gathering her wits, she leaned forward and started the radio streaming on her computer.

'I told ya – no one else but you is gonna hear me and ya don't even have to speak out loud back if ya don't wanna.'

Once again, the voice seemed to be coming from right next to her ear. 'You aren't real . . . this is . . . a sickness,' Sally said, gritting her teeth.

'You read it, sugar! Most people saying they got voices in their head are makin' it up so they don't get sent to the chair!'

She had a point; on Wikipedia, doctors were advised to check for 'malingering'.

Pushing away from her desk and entering the bathroom, Sally pulled off her shirt and vest to get a better look at Molly Sue. She'd moved around to the front so Sally no longer had to contort herself to see the tattoo, and had formed a new position – sitting insouciantly on her hip, long legs crossed, one hand behind her head.

'It *is* you,' Sally breathed.

'Is a pig's ass pork?' Molly Sue grinned. When she spoke, her cherry lips moved like Betty Boop's.

'What are you?' Sally asked. Her voice shook, but if this was really, truly real, she had questions now. Lots and lots of them.

'I told you – ya don't have to speak out loud, I can hear you anyway.' Molly Sue relaxed her pose, letting her arm fall. She sashayed over Sally's torso in fluid, sensual moves. She almost danced. But Sally could *feel* her moving, like an itch deep under her skin. Molly Sue wasn't just ink. Although Sally had nothing to compare her to, she could feel something solid moving inside her, shifting, squirming and twisting within. The tattoo was alive.

Sally covered her mouth with her hand, afraid she might vomit. 'I want to. I want to speak out loud. It feels more . . . more normal.'

'Suit yourself.'

'I'll ask again: *what are you?*'

'Now don't be gettin' uppity, darlin'! Y'already know who I am. I'm Molly Sue Savannah Claybourne the Third. Oh, shoot, I made that last part up, but I always did want a last name.' Sally glared at the tattoo, scarcely believing what she was seeing. 'You better believe it, sugar, cos this whiny racket in yo' head sure ain't getting any more fun.'

Sally closed her eyes. Like it or not it was *real*: Sally's hip, her skin, her belly button . . . it was all flesh and bone and, somehow, incredibly, so was the tattoo. The voice was crystal clear and the phone calls were coming from inside the house. It really was like Molly Sue was in the room with her, and in a way, she was. She was right there, waiting for Sally's next move. No amount of gormless blinking was going to erase Molly Sue.

No. This wasn't Dissociative Identity Disorder. Sally knew when it was time to move on, and denying what was happening in front of her eyes wasn't going to get her anywhere, she understood that. But how she *wished* it was something there was a pill for.

Then the wishy-washy confusion solidified into a red-hot anger. She'd been so *stupid*! Free tattoo . . . what had she been thinking? *There's nothing for free in this life* was one of her father's favourite mantras. It was too late now, though.

Sally tried again. 'I know *who* you are. I want to know what you are.'

'I heard the question, I just didn't like the question. Kinda nosy question. I'm all woman, darlin'.'

'You're a *tattoo*.'

'No kiddin'.' Molly Sue sighed and sat on her left hip, resting her face in her hands. 'I used to be a gen-u-wine woman, long time 'go. Some people move on when they're done, others . . . stick around is all.'

Sally clutched the rim of her sink. 'You're a ghost?'

77

Molly Sue laughed. Even now, she was so beautiful, her smile radiant. 'Well, I ain't never walked through no walls, if that's what you mean.'

'But this is impossible!' Sally couldn't help herself, even though there were early episodes of *Satanville* where Taryn had said that a lot and they'd all wanted to slap her, saying, '*Get with it, Taryn! He's an angel – deal with it!*'

'Don't ya think I don't know that? I just had more time to get used to my situation is all.' Molly Sue smiled, uncrossing and crossing her legs. 'But the good news is we got a whole bunch of time for you and me to get acquainted now! We gon' be together for a long old while.'

Sally fought back a sob with all the strength she had left. 'So you're like a haunted tattoo or something?'

A perfect eyebrow shot up. 'Oh, now that just sounds so tacky!'

'Sorry. What else am I meant to call you?'

'I'm a wanderer, sugar,' she said, a wistful, faraway look on her cartoon face. 'I'm a lost soul, rollin' stone kinda gal. I'm just a-lookin' for a friendly port in a storm, always was, always will be.' Molly Sue winked. 'Look, darlin', I know this musta come as a shock . . .' Sally balked at that. 'But I'm the best friend a girl can have. I'll keep quiet unless ya want me to, I swear on my dear old mama's grave.'

'I wish I hadn't ever . . .' Sally blinked back a tear.

'Well, if wishes were fishes, we'd all cast a net.'

'Stop! Just go away!'

'What? You sure as hell wanted me yesterday. What changed?'

Sally laughed bitterly. 'Are you kidding? I just wanted a tattoo!'

78

'I'm the same girl you fell in love with yesterday. Look!' Molly Sue swam back into her original position on Sally's back. 'See? Ya won't even know I'm here. Quiet as a mouse!'

'What if I *never* want you to speak?'

Molly Sue walked back around to her stomach, strutting, hands on hips. 'I won't lie, my feelin's would be pretty darn hurt, but if that's what you want . . .'

'That's what I want.'

Molly Sue lay down on her stomach, resting her head in her hands and kicking her kitten heels up. 'You sure, darlin'? You seemed pretty lonely to me. 'S why I chose you.'

'What? I chose *you*.'

'Oh, please! I felt your sadness from miles away, sweetheart!'

'What?'

'Well, you're a lost girl too. Takes one to know one an' I never seen anyone so lost my whole life. All that fire inside o' you with nowhere to go – you done well not to scream, darlin'.'

Sally's mouth fell open. It was true. In a few words Molly Sue had captured how Sally felt she'd been sitting on a bulging suitcase of frustration her whole life, willing it to stay shut. These were the darkest, cobweb-strewn thoughts at the very, very back of the cupboard. *How does she* . . . ?

'I know it all, sugar! I seen inside o' ya and it's pretty blue up in here. You ain't OK.'

Sally looked her in the eye. 'I'm fine.'

'Who you tryin' to kid? I felt all that pain and a-sufferin' as soon as you walked in the store. I know about your mama and daddy. I know about them teachers that don't know you exist. I seen the way them pretty girls talk about ya. I know all about that mighty fine Todd Brady too. And you . . . the loneliest girl there ever was. I thought you could use a friend.'

'I've got friends!'

'Some friends. They don't know the real you and you don't show 'em.' Sally went to argue but Molly Sue carried on. 'Stan keeps you around to do his homework, and little Jennie . . . well, all she can think about is that scrawny asshole.'

'That's not true.'

'Honey, those aren't *my* thoughts, they're *yours*. But if that's how you wanna play it, go on . . . go next door and watch your stories on TV. I ain't gonna stop ya.'

Sally was gripping the basin so tightly her knuckles were bleached bone. If the tattoo could hear her thoughts she'd never have privacy ever again. Ever. Every thought, every single wicked thought would be Molly's to hear. Sally grinded her teeth. 'Just . . . just please . . . shut up. I . . . I can't handle this.'

'If that's whatcha want . . .'

'That *is* what I want.'

'Suit yourself, darlin'. But you know where I am . . .' Sally caught a faint smile on Molly Sue's lips before she floated around her torso and disappeared onto her back. The writhing under her skin ceased and Sally took that to mean that, for now, Molly Sue was still . . . for now.

Chapter Nine

The next morning, Sally awoke to dappled magnolia light pouring through her curtains, while birds twittered in the garden. For a gorgeous second, everything was 'Morning Has Broken' before the skin on her back started to sting and itch. Everything that happened yesterday could so easily have been a dream, although Sally somehow knew that wasn't the case.

Experimentally, Sally thought, *Are you there?*

'Yes ma'am,' Molly Sue replied at once.

Go away.

'You just asked if I was here! Jeez!'

And now I want you to go away again.

'Oh, this sure is fun.' But Molly Sue fell quiet again.

Sally pushed her duvet back, imagining how she felt was what it must be like to wake up with a hangover. At least it was a Friday and at least Molly Sue had let her sleep through the night – well, what little restful sleep she'd been able to get, for her dreams had been full of Molly Sue, of Rosita and of Boris. She'd dreamed of saying no to having the tattoo done, only to stir and remember the awful reality of things.

After she'd showered – very gingerly washing her back – Sally fired up her laptop, the loading time agonisingly long – why is it, she wondered, that when you're desperate to get on the internet your computer decides it needs to install updates?

Very much hoping that Molly Sue was looking elsewhere, Sally Googled *laser tattoo removal*. She found a clinic in the city and looked at their website. It was all pretty confusing, but she saw before and after pictures – they could erase anything apparently.

She sensed she had to do this quickly, like tip-toeing around a sleeping lion. Sally made a mental note of where the clinic was before clicking onto their price list. She still had about a hundred quid left over from her last birthday and she hoped that would be enough. Her heart sank as the page loaded. She saw that, for a tattoo the size of Molly Sue, a single session would be one hundred and fifty pounds – and they recommended between four and eight sessions. *What? That could be over a thousand pounds!*

'Don't even think about it,' Molly Sue drawled.

'I'm not talking to you. Go. Away.'

Sally was so tired that she felt like she was out of sync with her classes and friends – one of those YouTube clips where the dialogue doesn't match the mouths. She looked awful, even worse than usual, and Stan and Jennie pestered her all day with concern. In the end, she did something she'd never done before – she cut class. Period five and six on a Friday was double chemistry and there was no way she'd be able to sit through ninety minutes of molar equations. And it's not like Dr Farmer would even notice she was gone.

Molly Sue, true to her word, stayed silent the whole day, and Sally didn't rouse her.

As soon as she'd registered for the afternoon, Sally slipped out of school the back way, knowing that anyone who saw her would assume she had a reason to be out of school – she wasn't the truancy type. She took the same route into Old Town, past the diner, garage and rec ground. Today the disinterested Doberman licked a paw, half in and half out of his kennel.

But it was there Sally found herself lost. *Where am I? This isn't right.* She passed three side streets, keeping an eye out for the flashing neon *House of Skin* sign, but by the time she reached the derelict video-rental shop, she realised she'd gone too far. She doubled back on herself, paying better attention. From what she could remember, it had been down the first alleyway past where the dog had jumped up at her.

She knew there was nothing Rosita or Boris could do for her, but she hoped to glean more information about Molly Sue – if she was a real, live woman perhaps they had known her. Rosita did say they were based on people they'd met.

OK, I'm clutching at straws.

Fairly confident she'd got the right side street, Sally walked down the alley. She stopped. The end of the street looked the same: rubbish spilling from the mountain of bin bags at the dead end, but the *House of Skin* sign had gone. This *was* the right alley though, Sally was sure of it – she recognised the peeling paint on the railings leading down to the basement shop.

She approached the stairs. There was no evidence the sign had ever existed, no outline in the grime, no holes for the bracket. At the bottom of the stairwell was the door, but instead of the ruby red wood veneer was a rusted metal security gate.

What the hell is going on? Sally felt a sting of tears behind her nose. She had *not* imagined this place and she was *not* hearing things. The frustration felt almost physical, like a hand around her throat. She clomped down the stairs, utterly resigned. The door was open a fraction, perhaps from squatters, and so she pulled it open, sweeping away a tide of plastic bags, fliers and beer cans that had built up on the floor.

Her hand flew over her mouth and nose. It was nothing. Just a rank, urine-scented cellar with stained mattresses on the floor. For now, at least, it was deserted. Sally threw her hands up, blinking back tears. *Oh look*, she thought, *there's something underneath rock bottom*. She shook it off. Crying wasn't going to help her.

A haunted tattoo parlour? Why not? No more ridiculous than a smart-mouthed tattoo. She remembered what Molly Sue had said – how Sally had been 'chosen'. Maybe the House of Skin was some sort of urban Hogwart's Room of Requirement that had only appeared when she needed it. *But I don't need her . . . I don't need any of this.*

The smell was threatening to make her gag, so Sally turned and left the cellar, taking the worn stairs two at a time. She considered asking Molly Sue how any of this was possible, but she already knew the answer. None of this was possible, and three years of solid *Satanville* fandom had done nothing to prepare her for what would happen when fantasy bled into the edges of her tedious little world.

Or is this what happens? Sally thought. *Does too much TV rot your brain like Coke does teeth?* Had her brain finally given up on the real world? It was certainly tempting, to swap spotty schoolboys for muscular guardian angels; to let go of reality for good because reality's not worth clinging to.

A stiff breeze rolled rusty lager cans and plastic bags down the alley. Sally hugged herself almost like she was ready for the straitjacket. There was nowhere left to go and no one she could talk to. Wherever she went she couldn't get away from *her.* There was this *thing* on her back and she was stuck with it.

And that was when divine intervention struck. Literally. At the end of the alleyway, Sally could see the spire of St Francis De Sales church.

Well, that's what you do when you're possessed, she thought. *You see the exorcist.*

Sally wondered why she hadn't thought of this before – all those hours watching fallen angels and she hadn't thought to speak to a priest. As she understood it, going to her mother's Methodist chapel wasn't going to cut the mustard. For demons you go hard or go home – you go Catholic. More importantly, no one would know her here.

The church was graffiti and litter-free, as if even the dregs of the town knew to leave it alone. Sally ran up the grand white stairs, only pausing to look at the serene Virgin Mary statue, which seemed to regard her with her sad eyes. Mary seemed disappointed in her.

Worrying momentarily that the church might be locked – *do churches shut?* – Sally tapped on the door before trying the handle. With a pained screech, it swung open and Sally grimaced. *Could you be more conspicuous?* Stepping inside, she was greeted by the overwhelming smell of church – this one even more pungent than her mother's – that musty, incense-laced, Bible-pages fustiness.

The door creaked shut behind her, echoing through the chapel. She hadn't burst into flames on entering, so that was a good sign. Sally couldn't see anyone else around, the pews were empty and there was no one at the altar or organ. There was a sign saying, *Open for private prayer and contemplation.*

'I might need something a little stronger,' Sally muttered. She wondered if the priest was in confession – isn't that what they did at Catholic churches? She wasn't even sure what her confession was. 'Hello?' she said quietly. There was no response.

Stroking the pews as she passed them, she wandered down the aisle towards the confession boxes but found the first one empty, although there was another on the other side and the curtains were drawn across it. Sally cut along one of the pews and bent down to see if she could see feet underneath the curtain.

'Can I help you?' a soft voice said.

Startled, Sally spun around, almost stumbling into the booth. In the aisle stood a nun. Sally wasn't a fan of nuns. In one episode of *Satanville* a hoard of floating ghost nuns with no faces had tried to recruit Taryn into their faceless hoard.

'Are you lost, child?' the nun said. She had the most gentle Irish accent Sally had ever heard, as soothing as the babbling streams that ran down from the lake.

'No . . . no . . . I . . . I was, well, looking for the priest.' Sally held her hands together to stop them fidgeting.

The nun came closer. As she approached, Sally saw she was young – surprisingly young. The sister wore a simple, austere kilt and cardigan rather than flowing robes while her wimple framed a pretty, delicate face from which huge doe eyes peered. They were the most unusual shade, such a deep blue they were almost violet. 'Oh, I'm sorry, my child, he's at St Joseph's Primary on Friday afternoons. Is there anything I can help you with?'

Sally's heart sank. 'No. It's OK.'

Perhaps the nun picked up on her tone, or perhaps it was just so unusual for someone her age to be here, but the nun glided up to her and took her hand. 'Young women like you don't come looking for Father Gonzales when things are OK.' She said things like *tings*. 'Why don't you talk to me? My name's Sister Bernadette. You don't have to tell me yours if you don't want.'

Sally fought back tears. The nun reminded her of Miss Dorset, the classroom assistant from when she'd been in Year One. Their teacher had been a tough old boot, but Miss Dorset – who even looked a bit like Sister Bernadette – would always pick them up when they fell or give them a hug when they missed their mums. She could use a hug now. 'No, it's OK. I'm Sally.'

'And what seems to be the trouble, Sally?'

'I'm not Catholic.'

'Oh, that doesn't matter now, does it?

'I'm not even sure I believe in God.'

The nun didn't bat an eyelid. 'And yet you came to a church. Now. Tell me: is it a boy?'

Oh. She thinks I'm knocked up. 'Oh, God – sorry. No, it's not that kind of trouble!'

Bernadette let her hand fall and led her to an alcove filled with shelves of votive candles of all shapes and sizes – some long and white, others stout and blood red. 'I thought not.' Taking a long match, Bernadette lit the nearest candle.

Sally had no idea where to begin. 'I . . . I . . . this is going to sound nuts, but do you believe in *demons*?'

Sally whispered the final word, but the question didn't throw the nun in the slightest. 'With all my heart.' Sister Bernadette looked her dead in the eye.

'Really?'

'Of course. They come in all different shapes and sizes and we all have them. Once they take hold, they sink their claws in ever so deep. Like wee limpets, they are. Jealousy, anger, hate, fear, lust . . . and they make us do such shameful things.' Sally looked into the pools of her eyes and saw that the sister, perhaps surprisingly, was no stranger to these demons, but they weren't what Sally was talking about.

'No. I mean *real* demons . . . like Satan.'

'So do I, child. He lives in the hearts of men.' A brief smile. 'And women. There's darkness in all of us, Sally. Just some people give it a name.'

Yet Sally couldn't bring herself to pull up her T-shirt and scream, '*I have a tattoo demon on my back!*'

Sister Bernadette continued. 'Now don't go around telling people I told you this, but there are no black and whites in this life, Sally. Only greys. Of course there are those who do harm – to themselves, which is sad, and to others, which is wickedness – but I don't think there are fundamentally good and bad people. Just people, tussling with their demons – some succeeding more than others. The ones you really want to watch out for,' she said with foreboding, 'are the ones who claim to be perfect.'

Sally didn't need a sermon. 'But how do you get rid of them? The demons?'

Sister Bernadette said nothing for a moment, her hand hopping from candle to candle the way a bee travels between flowers. 'I don't rightly think you ever lose them, you just learn to keep them somewhere where they can't cause harm. We build cages inside,' Bernadette said wearily. Sally wondered what her demons looked like and how long she'd been holding them at bay.

'How do you do that?'

'You pray for strength, child. You pray for the strength every day.' Her pale hand trembled over the candles. She closed her eyes and exhaled. 'I was so lost once upon a time, Sally. I hurt people, people dear to me, so now I help others, I do what little I can. I found solace in our saviour, but everyone has their own path to find.'

Sally feared she could pray all she wanted but it wasn't going to remove the tattoo from her back. 'But what if that isn't enough? Don't you do, like . . . exorcisms?'

Sister Bernadette smiled to herself and blew out her match. 'You've been watching too much television.' Sally couldn't argue with that. 'There are rare cases where a priest might carry out an exorcism, but the priests have to be specially trained and then act only in exceptional circumstances. Myself, I'm not so convinced.'

'You don't think people get possessed or you don't think exorcisms work?'

'I don't think the devil makes it so easy. If only it were so simple that a priest might say the right words and all the evil in the world would go away.' Bernadette's smile fell. 'Sally, you don't think you might have a *friend* in need of an exorcism, do you?'

She so wanted to say yes, but her mouth wouldn't form the word. She shook her head. 'I should go. I'm sorry I wasted your time.'

Although the nun looked disappointed, her face remained so kind. 'Not at all. I'm always here, Sally.'

More tears pushed behind her nose. 'Thank you.' Sally bowed her head and hurried out of the church. The sunshine was a hundred times brighter than she was expecting and she put up a hand to shield her eyes.

'If you really think that's gonna work,' said a familiar Texan voice, 'you been watching *way* too many bad movies.'

'Oh, who asked you?' Sally said aloud.

Chapter Ten

I should have gone straight to Stan.

On reflection, he should have been Sally's first port of call – who knew more about demons than *Satanville*'s biggest fan? By the time she got back to Mulberry Hill, Stan was already home and had changed into a pair of cut-off tracksuit bottoms and an oversized New York Knicks jersey. 'Where were you this afternoon, abandoner?' he asked as they trotted up to his room. 'I can't believe you left me with Jennie and the Knoblin King.'

'Sorry,' Sally said. 'I came home. Women's problems again.'

Stan sat on his beanbag and unpaused the game he was playing. He appeared to be toting a very large gun/penile extension through a derelict art-deco hotel that was suffering a zombie infestation. 'OK, I know that's a lie because you had your women's problems, like, two weeks ago.'

Sally felt her cheeks redden. 'We spend way too much time together.'

He paused the game again to pay full attention. 'I didn't want to push it the other night, but what's actually wrong? Is someone giving you a hard time? I'll duff them up for you.' Sally avoided his gaze and wondered if she could change the subject. Stan had a mountain of uneaten toast and Nutella next to his computer. He'd even toasted the end crusts. *Who does that?*

'No. Well . . .' Sally thought on her feet. 'I'm just massively freaking out about *Little Shop*. I don't want to do it, but I can't pull out either. If you really must know, I have a nervous tummy,' she fibbed.

Stan grimaced. 'Ew. Nutella?' He grinned.

'You're disgusting.'

'Says Miss Poopy-Pants.' He shoved a whole slice of toast in his mouth. 'What are we doing tonight? Can we *not* go to the lake? I say sleepover! We could watch this week's *STV* again or we could see what's on Netflix? Mum and Gary said we could have the lounge.'

Sally wondered how to tackle the Molly Sue issue subtly. 'What's that episode of *Satanville* in season one where Zeke had the parasite demon thing?'

Stan's eyes lit up. 'Ooh, *The Hitchhiker*. That episode blew so hard.'

Nodding, Sally sat on the bed and plopped Mr Squid in her lap. It *really* hadn't been a classic episode, not one that she rewatched. 'What was that demon called?'

Stan ran a hand through his mop of hair. 'Erm . . . Parasite Demon? I don't think it had a name, to be honest.'

'Can we watch that one?'

'Really?' he said with mild disgust. 'Why?'

'No reason.'

'If we're going to watch season one, we should watch the one where Taryn turned into a cat.'

Ooh, that was a good one. 'You know what? We should probably just watch season one from the start.'

And that was what they did. Nine hours, two stuffed-crust meat feasts, one tub of Phish Food and two litres of Diet Coke later they had finished the boxset and it was a little after one a.m. With *Satanville* as her catnip, Sally was wide awake and had agreed to sleepover despite her previous vow. It was a Friday, after all.

But she was no nearer to understanding Molly Sue. The Parasite Demon took the form of a grotesque baby ghoul thing that latched onto Zeke's back, while the only other comparable demon was a succubus who took the form of a beautiful woman, although her MO was to drain the life-force from hot guys by having sex with them. So far, as Molly Sue hadn't tried to do *that*, Sally figured she wasn't a succubus. There was also a homunculus demon – a tiny version of a guest star that lived in a fold in his stomach, but that didn't feel right either – although she guessed Molly Sue was a homunculus in some ways.

'I gotta say,' Molly Sue said as Sally changed into some of Stan's pyjamas while he brushed his teeth in the bathroom down the hall. 'I'm pretty darn hurt you think I'm a demon.'

Shut up.

'Aw, c'mon, girl, can't we just get along? We gotta show the ladies some love.'

OK, we'll start with some questions. Sister Bernadette and *Satanville* hadn't provided any answers so there was only Molly Sue left to interrogate. *Where did the House of Skin go? Where are Boris and Rosita?*

'Somewhere safe.'

What's that supposed to mean?

'They look after me, an' I look after them. They been very good to me down the years.'

That doesn't answer my question and Stan will be back any second.

'Don't worry, I'm gonna give you your privacy. You get yours, girl!'

Ew! No! It's not like that!

Molly Sue laughed a low, throaty laugh. 'Maybe not for you.'

Or him. He's like my brother!

Right on cue, Stan ambled back into the bedroom, a blob of toothpaste on his chin. 'You OK?'

'Fine!' Sally said brightly, pushing Molly Sue out of her head.

As ever, Stan let Sally take his bed and he went sidecar in a sleeping bag on the floor. They chatted about *Satanville* and school for a while as Sally grew sleepier, before Stan promptly changed the subject. 'Are you going to go to the Year Twelve dance?'

That woke her up. It was months away. 'What? No. As if.'

'I'm thinking about it.'

'Oh God, why? This play is bad enough – I think I've reached my "joining in" quota for the year.'

Stan rolled to his side and propped himself up on an elbow. 'Yeah, I know they kinda suck, but we only have three socials left until we leave school for ever.'

'I'm striving for a hundred per cent non-attendance rate.'

'But it's like prom! Taryn went to prom!' He paused. 'Why

do you think Americans always say "go to prom" instead of "go to *the* prom"? Surely that's bad English?'

'I have no idea. But I don't want to go.'

'Jennie's going with Kyle.'

'All the more reason to stay home.'

'Come on! We could go together . . . just as friends. It'll be fun.'

'Told ya so . . .' Molly Sue said in a sing-song voice.

Sally ignored her. 'Sorry, Stan. I honestly think I'd rather die.'

Stan pouted. 'OK, whatever, but don't come crying to me when you're thirty and sad you didn't go to prom.'

'Goodnight, Stan!'

'Sweet dreams, Feather.' He rolled away from her and rested his head.

'Sweet dreams . . .' cooed Molly Sue.

Oh, pipe down.

The following day Sally was presented with a rock / hard place duo of options for her Saturday. The first was accompanying her parents to the garden centre to look for new border shrubs (staying at home wasn't an option, apparently – her dad felt it wasn't healthy to spend such a pleasant weekend stuck indoors). The second, slightly less hideous, option was heading up to the lake with Stan, Jennie and some of Kyle's music friends. There was talk of getting rowing boats out to one of the islands in the middle of the lake. Stan promised they could get their own rowing boat, so she agreed.

Once again, Sally layered up like she was getting ready to visit a mosque – every inch of skin covered in case anyone got a glimpse of Molly Sue. Today she wore a long vest top and a lacy cardigan, which would at least allow some ventilation. They didn't really team well, but it'd have to do.

It was about a twenty-minute drive from Mulberry Hill to the lake in Kyle's mum's car. As they drove even further up the valley, Kyle all the time lecturing Jennie on why she was wrong for liking pop – *it's not real music because they don't play instruments* – Sally relaxed for the first time since she'd had Molly Sue. The tattoo had stayed quiet all through the night and all morning, and Sally started to think that cohabitation *might* be an option. Two days had passed and nothing disastrous had happened, after all.

Through the trees, Sally caught glimpses of the lake, glimmering like mercury in the sunshine. The lake was so beautiful. Even though she'd lived near it her whole life, she knew to never take it for granted. Sometimes, if you were lucky, you got a little cove to yourself; no kids paddling, no screaming babies, no raucous guys from school swinging off the rope into the water – it was dictionary-definition tranquillity. Every so often she and Jennie caught the bus up the hill, found a boulder to sit on, and simply read together in companionable silence.

His bandmates already at the lake, Kyle pulled into the car park next to the boat kiosk, and they stocked up on water, crisps and sweets before hiring a pair of rowing boats. Sally was left to row while Stan devoured a sausage sandwich he'd bought.

'You're doing a great job there, Feather,' he said as the boat veered in the wrong direction. A blob of ketchup squelched out of his sandwich and landed in his crotch. He cursed loudly.

'I'm hopeless,' Sally laughed, 'and you're hopeless!'

'You're better than Kyle!' Jennie shouted from their boat. Kyle did seem to be rowing them in circles.

'I'd like to see you try!' Kyle snapped, his ego obviously dented.

Stan rolled his eyes. 'Oh, here we go . . .'

'Stan, don't start,' Sally warned under her breath.

'You want me to take over?' Stan asked, shoving the last of his sandwich in his mouth.

'I can cope. You can do the return journey.' Sally had found her rhythm, but a lifetime of avoiding PE (she'd discovered at quite a young age that some teachers really will believe you have your period every week) hadn't prepared her arms or back for the exertion, and halfway across she let Stan take over.

Cormorant Island, as Stan had christened it, was the biggest clump of trees in the centre of the lake. On one side, the edges were sheer and eroded, with tree roots dangling into the water, but around the circumference were several beaches. In reality they were little more than muddy slopes into the lake, but they were the nearest thing to beaches in Saxton Vale.

After much, much hilarity trying to steer, both boats arrived on one such beach. 'That was really hard!' Kyle said, lightening up.

'I can't lift my arms!' Sally agreed. Then she heard someone laughing. At first she thought it was Molly Sue, but then she realised it was coming from the other side of the island. 'Can you hear that?'

'Yeah. There must be someone else out here.'

'Man, I hoped we'd have it to ourselves,' Jennie pouted.

'On a day like this? No way,' said Kyle, pulling a crate of beer from the bottom of their boat. 'And can you smell that? They have pot! Let's go see who it is!' He darted into the trees with the beers.

'Kyle! Come back!' Jennie moaned. 'For God's sake. Why doesn't he ever listen to me?' She followed him into the forest.

Sally and Stan pulled the boats as far up the beach as they could to make sure they wouldn't drift away before they followed the giggles and shouts.

Cormorant Island was basically a mound, so they had to head uphill until the terrain levelled out in the middle before dipping on the other side. As they got closer to the largest beach, the one with the rope swing, Sally recognised Keira's voice. *Oh God, that means only one thing . . .* They reached the cove to find Melody Vine sat on Todd's lap.

It was quite the party – three boats had ferried three coolers and two disposable barbecues over. They had some portable speakers and tinny hip hop played. Sally tensed immediately. 'Oh God,' she said to Stan. 'Can we go?'

'Yeah, let's get Jennie and head to one of the other islands or something.'

'Stan the man!' yelled a piggish-looking guy. This was Jess White, former nobody who'd worked his way up the social ladder by selling whatever weed and MDMA powder his older, even shadier brother passed on to him. He and Stan had been pretty good friends until a year or so back when Jess started his transformation into a bottom feeder.

'Hey, Jess. You OK?'

'Yeah, man, it's all good. Grab a beer dude. Get your drink on! Get your smoke on!' Like all try-hards, he never got it quite right.

There were eight of them in total – Melody and Todd, Eleanor and Keira (obviously), Jess and some other ass-hat guys from the football team. If this island were to be unexpectedly nuked after they'd departed, Sally would be fine with that. 'Oh, hi Sally,' Melody said. 'How are you?'

It was ridiculous how such a mundane question could throw her so far when it came from Melody. 'I'm fine,' she mumbled like an idiot.

'I *love* your cardigan,' Melody said, suggesting precisely the opposite. Keira smirked from her beach towel, pretending she wasn't listening. 'Join us! We've got plenty of food. We can talk about the musical.'

Jennie had already sat alongside Kyle as he sparked up a joint with Jess. If he was smoking so would she. That was how it went. Like it or not, it looked like they were staying.

'I don't think we'll stay,' Stan said to Melody, and Sally could have hugged him.

'Don't be gay!' Melody snapped, adding homophobia to her repertoire. 'You just got here. Stop being a loser and get a drink. We don't bite.' Some of the football guys sniggered, but one of them handed Stan a beer, which he reluctantly took.

'Where's your bikini?' Eleanor asked Sally, wearing little more than dental floss herself. 'Aren't you boiling?'

Sally flushed. 'I . . . I'm not swimming today.'

'Did you forget to wax or something?' Melody smirked. 'Or do you go *au naturelle*?'

'Mels, don't be shady,' Todd told her, and Sally's stupid heart fluttered. Melody didn't look thrilled at being chastised but let it drop.

As she took a seat out of the direct sun, Molly Sue spoke. 'Donchya be listening to that bitch, OK? She ain't worth the salt in her bread.'

Not now, please, Sally implored her.

'You know what happens to girls like Melody Vine?' Molly went on regardless.

No.

'Well, let me tell you, darlin'. She's a small town Barbie, and y'know what happens to them? They get forgotten at the bottom of the toy box. She'll either wind up stuck here for the resta her life, find a Ken and pop out a bunch o' rugrats or she'll head into the city like those girls who go to Hollywood to be the next big waitress. She's a big, fat nothin', darlin'. Ya don't gotta worry about her. I seen lots of hers come and go.'

She's got an agent.

Molly Sue laughed heartily. 'Girl, that's *all* she got. She thinks the world owes her somethin' cos she's got a pretty smile. Her elevator don't go all the way to the top, if you catch my drift. You're ten times better than her, sweetheart. Cross mine and hope to die.'

Sally felt a little better. But Melody had more than just a pretty smile. She had *him*. Todd stood up and pulled his T-shirt over his head. It was a beautiful car crash and Sally couldn't look away. It was only May but he was already California-tanned, airbrushed perfection. How was his body so good? Had no one told him about chocolate? His chest was hard and defined, as were his flawless abs. She thought six packs were only for TV, but apparently not.

He picked up a bottle of sun cream and started to rub it onto his muscular arms. His eyes flashed in her direction and she whipped her gaze away, praying he hadn't caught her staring. She couldn't help it though, she had to look again.

When she looked at him, she ached.

'Oh, girl, you got it bad!' Molly Sue chuckled.

It's not like that.

'Aw c'mon! You and me ain't got no secrets! The boy's a cutie! Don't be ashamed . . . I gotta say, darlin', you've had some pretty nasty thoughts about that one . . .'

Stop it!

'I'm not judgin'! It's not like you can help it, sugar! It's how we're wired. We're red-blooded women, don't be sorry 'bout it! I could teach ya a thing or two!'

Melody massaged sun cream onto Todd's shoulders and Sally shifted uncomfortably. Jealousy stabbed through her ribs. *Oh, to be that cream.*

Molly Sue giggled at the thought. 'Ya want him real bad?'

Yes, Sally admitted for the first time.

'Then get after him, darlin'. 'Tween you and me, pageant queens like her never like gettin' their hair mussed up – all talk, no action.'

I couldn't. He doesn't know I exist.

'Sure he does!'

He goes for girls like Melody.

'What? Mean-as-a-snake girls?'

Looks like it.

101

'That ain't the face of a happy camper. Look at him!'

Todd did look a little uncomfortable. If Melody was trying to arouse him, it didn't look like it was working. Melody treated Todd the same way she treated Eleanor and Keira – they were all accessories and nothing more. Like her Louis purse and Gucci shades, they told onlookers about her status and little else. Sally had seen the way Melody barked orders at him across the cafeteria stairs: 'Todd, text your mum to tell her you'll be late!' and 'Todd, you can't that night, we're seeing a film'. Maybe he wasn't enjoying it; maybe he was fruit ripe for picking.

Oh, as if. Dream on, Sally.

'Cards on the table. You want him?' Sally could imagine Molly Sue's no-nonsense expression without having to see her.

If Sally did have him, she wouldn't know what to do with him but . . . *yeah. Yeah, I do.*

'Well, you've come to the right gal. We got this.'

What?

'I wouldn't normally go 'round shopping in some other girl's store, but this bitch got it comin'. And anyway, that boy likes ya. I can tell.'

Yeah, right.

'You don't see what I see, darlin'. You got something Melody Vine never had – mystery and enigma. That's currency! Just trust me. If you want Todd Brady you can have him.'

She was so entranced by the dimples at the bottom of Todd's spine, she didn't even see Jennie approach. 'Sally? You OK?'

She snapped out of it. 'Yeah, I'm fine.'

'You looked a million miles away.'

102

'Just thinking.'

Molly Sue spoke again, more quietly. 'Girl, I gotta plan to get you the man. You on board?'

Todd held his hands behind his head, opening his chest wide. She'd never expected to find armpits sexy, but OH GOD. *Yeah*, she told Molly Sue. *OK*.

Chapter Eleven

The mirror on Sally's dressing table was lined with photos – her, Jen and Stan pulling faces with fake moustaches; one of her in an inflatable paddling pool when she was two; Dante; a grainy photo of her mother when she'd been beautiful. The carefree girl in that picture, her head tipped back in laughter, wasn't the mother Sally knew – she'd never seen her so joyful.

Sally looked doubtfully at Molly Sue in the mirror. Her new friend had migrated to her chest and Sally wore only her bra so they could talk face to face. 'But this is stupid,' Sally said aloud, knowing her mum and dad were at church. She'd got out of it by saying she wasn't feeling well. 'A haircut isn't going to make Todd like me.'

'It's a start,' Molly Sue replied. 'How long ya had this rope hangin' off the back of your head?'

'I don't know . . . since I was little.'

'Precisely, sugar! You want Todd to see you as a little girl?'

Ew, creepy. 'No! Of course not!'

'So trust me. You'll look like a whole new woman. *Woman* being the oper-a-tive word.'

'I won't, but whatever. Anyway, it's just a haircut. I'll

still be a massive loser. He wouldn't touch me with a barge pole.' *What did that phrase even mean?* Sally wondered. She'd heard her mum use it but had no idea what a barge pole actually was.

Molly Sue scoffed, fluffing her own sleek hair. 'Never underestimate the power of the 'do, darlin'.'

Sally held back her plait and tried to picture what she'd look like with less hair. She gave up in disgust at herself. 'So I turn myself into a Melody clone for a guy? That's healthy.' She sucked in her cheeks and pouted her lips like a duck, the way girls did on the front of magazines.

The pin-up rolled her eyes. 'OK, sweetheart, lesson one: men think they're stronger than us every which way. We gotta use every gun in the gallery. Now I'm not some ten-dollar hooker sayin' you gotta sleep yo way to the top, but I *am* condonin' blindin' guys with a little glitter. If they're dumb enough to think you're nothin' *but* hair and heels, that's their funeral. We know different. It ain't about how you *look*, it's 'bout showing the world you're ready for battle. It's standin' up and gettin' counted, which ain't never gonna happen in those disguises you wear. Ya gotta stop hidin', girl.' The tattoo winked. 'And who said anything about makin' you look like a supermodel? You're the brains, *I'm* the beauty in this set-up!'

Sally smiled despite herself. She couldn't believe how accustomed she'd become to Molly Sue. She'd slept all through the night and felt like a different person. Things didn't seem so otherworldly any more.

'You ready?' Molly Sue asked as Sally grabbed one of Stan's old baseball shirts that she'd acquired and yanked it on over her head.

'Pretty much.' Sally opened the lowest drawer in her dresser and took out the envelope containing her birthday money. She had a quick look and counted just over a hundred pounds.

'That's not enough,' Molly Sue stated.

'How is that not enough for a haircut?'

'Girl, I think we need more than a trim, don't you? And we need some threads to go with the hair.'

Sally sighed. 'My allowance is paid into my bank account, but that's supposed to be for university.'

'When was the last time you spent your allowance? You buy, like, what, three DVDs a year? I think ya can splash out a little.'

'I'm not supposed to use my card. My mum keeps it in a drawer in the study.'

'Go get it,' Molly Sue told her.

If she put the card back quietly later, they might not even know she'd used it. Her mother would have no idea what a decent haircut actually cost. Sally started towards the study. 'OK.'

'Good girl. Let's get this show on the road.'

Sally stood on the pavement outside the salon. Molly Sue had suggested Ford & Co in the New Town Arcade, knowing it was regarded as the best in town – and almost certainly where Melody et al had their manes managed. However, Sally couldn't bring her feet to cross the threshold. It was like the deck of the Starship Enterprise: glossy, sleek, modern and so, so white. The salon gleamed. The men and women inside all wore black head to toe, including the tattoos on their arms.

I wonder if their swallows and anchors give them back-chat, Sally thought ruefully. They all seemed to sport asymmetrical hairstyles that looked as if they'd been cut with lawnmowers. In other words, way, *way* too cool for Sally.

'Come on, girl, let's move it!'

'I can't. I'm too scared. I feel sick.' An old lady walking a pug glared at her as she passed. *She thinks I'm talking to myself!*

'You're not going to be sick.'

I am.

'You're not, darlin'. I got ya.'

I don't know what to do. I don't know what to ask for.

'You ain't never had a haircut before?'

Mum always trims it.

'Jesus, Mary and Joseph, this is worse than I thought. Look, I'm gonna take over for a bit, OK?'

Sally backed away from the salon, aware the receptionist was staring at her. *What?*

'Let me in the driving seat for the next couple of hours. I'll do all the talkin'.'

You must be kidding! You might tell them to shave my head or something. Sally had seen enough *Top Model* to know that one girl always lost the lot.

'Oh, will you relax? Why the hell would I go and do that? Girl, you seen me . . . do I look like I don't know what the inside of a salon looks like?'

I don't know . . . it's weird.

'It ain't weird. It's just while you get the cut done! Leave it up to me, girl! You stick to the books and math and I'll do the hair and beauty!'

Sally sighed. They were here now, might as well get it over with. *OK. How do I let you take over?*

'It's a piece o' cake. You'll feel me in your head, like ya do on your skin, and when you do, just let me in. It'll be like having a little daydream. You'll enjoy it.'

Sally couldn't pace like a weirdo outside the salon a second longer. Someone from school might see her. *Whatever. Please don't shave my head.* The thought of Molly Sue entered her mind. The cherry lips; the amethyst eyes twinkling; perfect white teeth. Sally embraced the idea.

'OK, ya ready?' Molly Sue asked. There was a coldness in Sally's head, almost a headache but not quite. More like the brain-freeze you get when you eat ice cream. Molly Sue was in her head and Sally simply closed her eyes.

It was like falling asleep.

She could be dreaming.

Time was different. One step didn't necessarily follow the other. She was dimly aware of the receptionist; *yes, one of our senior stylists has a cancellation if you're happy to wait..?* A black overall being swung over her shoulders; a glass of champagne, a handsome guy with a nose ring and flesh tunnel in his left ear. He took her plait in one hand, a pair of scissors in the other and in three swift snips, the rope came away.

Then she really blacked out.

Images and snippets came to her. Water running over her forehead. Another pair of hands worked on her face – her eyebrows were under attack from what looked like two bits of string. Someone else sawed away at her fingernails.

More darkness.

And then gleaming light. She was back in the salon one hundred per cent. The lights were so bright she was momentarily blind. She rubbed her eyes. 'So, what do you think?' The handsome hairdresser grinned down at her. He spoke with an Australian accent. 'Just a little different, huh?'

'Wakey wakey, darlin',' said Molly Sue. 'Get a load o' yourself!'

Oh. My. God. Sally was genuinely surprised to discover that the woman sitting opposite was, in fact, her reflection. She gasped. She was usually dubious of characters who 'gasped', but she had cause to. Her hand flew to her mouth. She looked *so* different.

'I'm blonde,' she muttered.

'You certainly are,' said the hairdresser, who she somehow knew to be called Steve.

It wasn't white straw like Eleanor's hair, hers was now *golden*, falling in gentle waves off her face to just below her shoulders. It changed everything about her face. Her eyebrows, instead of two chubby brown caterpillars were now graceful arches above her eyes which, rather than grey, now looked blue for the first time. 'Oh my God.'

'OK, Sally,' said Steve. 'You've got me sweating slightly . . .'

'Sorry . . . I . . . I *love* it.'

'And is it like her's? From *Satanville?* I did my best.'

Clever, clever, Molly Sue. It was *totally* the blonde version of Taryn's season four haircut. 'It really is. It's spot on.'

'Phew!' Steve continued to babble on about rebooking discounts or something, but Sally wasn't listening. She couldn't take her eyes off herself. She looked about ten years older. If she was so inclined, she reckoned she'd be able to get into Cellos in Old Town without ID, not that she ever would.

'Did I do good?' Molly Sue asked.

You did really good.

'Just call me Fairy Godmother. But we're not done yet. Now we gotta do the rags.'

It didn't occur to Sally that she might be in trouble until she was almost home, two glossy department store bags swinging at her ankles. She suddenly had the same nauseous feeling she'd had right after the tattoo – the *WHAT HAVE I DONE?* sensation. Her mum and dad were *always* telling her to brush her hair and her mum was *always* buying her hideously girly dresses that hung in her wardrobe with the labels intact. OK, they'd never said, 'Sally, you should bleach your head,' but perhaps they'd like the new look?

Fat chance. As soon as Sally stepped through the front door all she could do was brace herself for the tidal wave.

Her mother swept in from the kitchen, the meaty smell of the Sunday roast filling the air. Pork and apple sauce. 'Where have you been? You're meant to be ill —' She stopped. 'Heavens above! What have you done to your hair? Oh, Sally!'

Her dad padded in from the lounge, the *Mail on Sunday* in his hands. 'What's all the racket?' His face fell. 'Oh, for crying out loud!'

'It's OK,' Molly Sue muttered. 'Just follow my lead.'

Sally started. 'I got a haircut.'

'Well, I can see that!' Her father barked. 'And how much did that cost?'

'Tell him it's your birthday money,' Molly Sue whispered.

'Not much,' Sally lied. 'And I used my birthday money.'

110

Predictably that calmed her father down. Her mother edged closer as if she wanted to clarify that it wasn't a wig. 'Oh, Sally, it's a bit drastic . . . and you'll get terrible roots.'

Sally sighed. 'Mum, I really like it.'

Molly Sue chipped in. 'Tell her it's for the play . . .'

'And it's for the play. I thought I'd look more like Audrey.'

That seemed to appease her slightly. 'You look so grown up, though. I don't want you to be one of those tarty girls trying to get into Cellos on Friday nights.'

'Oh dear God —' Sally rolled her eyes.

'Do NOT take the Lord's name in vain.'

'Mum! As if I'd want to go to Cellos! But I *am* going to university next year. I . . . I am a grown-up now.'

She saw her mum's eyes glass over. Molly Sue whispered, 'Whoa, girl, bring out the big guns.'

Her dad relented. 'Well, it's your money to waste.' He returned to the lounge with his newspaper.

Sally so wished there was some common tongue she could speak with her mother other than the strange semaphore they were stuck with. 'Do . . . do you like it?'

Her mum sighed. 'It's a nice job, I suppose. You look very different.'

'That's the idea,' she whispered to herself, and Sally swore she heard resignation in her mother, like she too had now realised they were different species. The gap between them was becoming a chasm.

Chapter Twelve

Sally really didn't need a battle first thing on Monday morning. 'I can't wear *that*.'

'Sure you can!' Molly Sue urged. 'It'll work with the new boots.' The dress in question was one of the ones her mother had bought her last summer – a simple white cotton summer dress. It was so . . . *virginal*. 'That's the point, darlin'!' The tattoo, predictably, read her mind.

Molly Sue had said the goal wasn't to make her look like a hooker, but this was one extreme to the other. 'Just try it – humour me.'

This morning, the perfect salon waves had dropped out of her hair but the effect was effortlessly tousled, which she liked even if she didn't look quite so much like Taryn any more.

Huffing and puffing, Sally pulled the dress over her head. 'I look like a human sacrifice,' she said aloud to her reflection in the mirror.

Molly Sue, waiting on her upper arm, did a lioness-like yawn before saying, 'Let me tell ya something about boys. In the long-run, they don't want some man-eater in leopard-skin and red pumps – it scares 'em. They want a Sunday School girl to go a-strollin' through fields o' daisies with.'

I'm not changing who I am just for a boy.

'Oh, calm down, Scarlett O'Hara! If you walk around in that camouflage, never darin' to speak up, how is anyone gonna know you exist? You are somethin' worth seein', girl! You want this Todd trick or not?'

She really did want Todd. She couldn't wait to see his face when he saw her new look. If she was honest, although she was nervous about all the attention she'd no doubt get, she was also buzzing with the possibilities. All those people who thought she was a delicate little wallflower . . . *eat it, suckers.* For the first time in a long time she was excited to get to school.

'OK,' Molly Sue instructed. 'Now put the boots on.'

Sally deeply inhaled the brand-new-leather smell as she pulled the trooper-style boots over her knee socks. She loved them because Melody wouldn't wear them in a million – no, a *billion* – years. Also, and more importantly, Angela had had a pair in season three.

She regarded herself in the mirror. *Oh, wow.* OK, Molly Sue might just be a genius. The boots turned it from a little girl's party dress into something edgy, rock and roll even. And even if it did look good, which it did, she felt naked. Her shoulders and collarbone felt utterly exposed.

'Aw c'mon, girl. You're not in Yemen. You *can* show a little skin, y'know.'

I'll be cold.

'Nah, ya really won't because you'll have the jacket.'

113

The most expensive item she'd bought was a fitted leather biker jacket, which Molly Sue had assured her she'd wear for ever. She slipped it over her shoulders and she no longer felt bare. It was quite literally like donning a thicker skin. She was pretty sure people were going to take the piss, but she felt ready for it somehow. She *knew* she looked good, so what did it matter what anyone else thought? 'OK, I must be mad, but let's do it.'

Over breakfast her mother didn't pass comment on her outfit but the look on her face couldn't have been more strained. In her mum's world, a dress with boots probably made about as much sense as going to school in a wetsuit. All of the faffing around with clothes made her late. She texted Stan and Jennie to tell them to go ahead without her and so she walked to school alone.

'Ain't no bad thing,' Molly Sue had assured her. 'This way you get to make an entrance.'

At first the reaction was a little disappointing. Sally, although she knew it was a little self-obsessed, had expected at least a tiny reaction. As she walked towards the library, people *did* look in her direction, they stared a little bit but no one seemed especially impressed.

And then she learned why.

She passed a group of Year Eleven boys sitting on a low wall trying, in vain, to make their uniform blazers look cool by rolling the sleeves to the elbow. The cockiest of the group spoke deliberately loud enough for her to hear. 'Dude, check out the hot new sixth former! Want me to show you around, love?' he yelled.

What? They think I'm someone new.

'Well, aren't you just, darlin'?' Molly Sue chuckled.

Sally scurried past the Year Elevens, head down, but her skin felt like it was glowing. The invisibility cloak had finally slipped off. *And* he'd said she was hot. Was it that she looked different or that she felt different? Perhaps it was that, for the first time ever, she wanted people to notice her.

'Who cares, girl? Keep on keepin' on. Own it,' Molly Sue said as she continued through the courtyard.

The next domino fell. Annabel Sumpter clocked her as she walked past the orchestra crowd. Her face registered her twice – first as a stranger and then as Sally. 'Oh my . . . is that Sally Feather?'

Sally kept on walking. That seemed like the cooler thing to do. The picnic tables came into view. She saw Stan gesturing wildly, telling a story, and Jennie laughing. There were a few others lapping up his tale too, so they didn't see her approach. It was Kyle who saw her first. He sleazily scoped her out, his eyes scanning her body like she was a walking barcode, before realising who she was. He swore loudly and the others turned to see her.

She couldn't help it, she smiled. This was kinda fun. She threw her arms wide. 'What do you think?'

Stan's mouth fell open. If he'd been a cartoon his jaw would have hit the floor, tongue unfurling like a red carpet.

Jennie blinked hard, as if she might be hallucinating. 'Oh my God!' she said. 'Sally! What is happening on your head?'

'You like it?'

Jennie jumped up and ran over to get a better look. 'Are you kidding? You look incredible! When did this happen? I

115

am so mad at you for not telling me!' Jennie laughed, playfully punching her shoulder.

'I wanted to surprise you!'

'Consider me surprised! You're . . . you're blonde! And so hot. Look at the boots! I love the boots! I *need* those boots in my life! Stan, doesn't she look amazing?'

Stan stared at her. His face was more like her mother's had been than Jennie's; he looked more confused than impressed. 'Yeah,' he said, finally finding his voice. 'You look great. What . . . ? Why . . . ? What prompted the extreme makeover?'

That stung and she didn't know why it stung. 'It . . . it's not that extreme, is it?'

Stan squinted at her. 'You look totally different.'

'But good different?'

He blushed. 'Totally. Sorry. I keep saying *totally*.'

Jennie tutted. 'Don't listen to him! You look amazing! If I was a lesbian I totally would.'

Sally laughed but Stan's reaction irked her. Why did he look so . . . sad? Sally shrugged it off; this wasn't about Stan Randall. For the first time *ever* it was about her.

Sally had double maths first thing on a Monday – a perfect opportunity to see if Todd even noticed a difference. So far she didn't mind the spotlight being on her – even Mrs Flynn had passed comment with, 'Gosh you scrub up well.' Sally wasn't sure if that was a compliment on her current appearance or a slight on her previous one. Classmates that had never so much as given her the time of day stopped to tell her how fantastic she looked.

It confirmed something she'd suspected for a long time: most of the people in her school really were as shallow as they seemed.

'Hey, don't knock it, sugar,' Molly Sue had told her. 'There's a power in beauty, sweetheart – and it ain't just us girls that use it. You reckon that Todd fella o' yours don't get treated special on account o' how he looks?'

That's so superficial.

'It's like any power. 'S all about how you use it.'

As she settled into her seat next to Dee, who had already got her hairdresser's details and asked where she got the dress from, she waited for Todd to arrive. She had a horrible feeling it wouldn't make any difference – and that she'd been naive to think it would. What was he going to do? Drop Melody like a hot potato and whisk her off to Vegas? Unlikely.

Todd finally entered with a couple of his friends from the football team. As she did every time he walked into a room, Sally went to watch him, only to find that this time, Todd and his friends were staring at her.

'Don't look at him!' Mary Sue commanded. 'Play with your phone or somethin'. Look as bored as you can.'

Sally did as she was told, checking Tumblr on her phone. She could hear them, though. Todd's best friend, Lucas Greer – a total sexpest – said, 'Whoa! Was she always that smokin' hot?'

'Chill, man,' Todd snapped as he dragged his chair across the floor to sit.

'Oi, Sally!' Lucas said. 'Loving the new look. If you wanna come over to mine to watch that show you like sometime, I'm well up for that.' He mimed poking his right index finger into his curled left fist. Nice.

Sally blushed, no clue what to say. This was her very first sexual harassment.

'Just ignore him,' Todd said, swiftly punching his friend on the shoulder. 'You wanna know a secret? Lucas here is a massive virgin and if you said yes, he'd actually pee his pants.'

Sally laughed, although Lucas looked less than impressed. 'Thanks, man. Whatever happened to bros before hos?'

Todd leaned over his desk and Sally caught a whiff of his deodorant – clean and sporty and oh-so male. 'We heard rumours about your amazing makeover,' he smiled. 'And it's true – Sally, you look bananas.'

There was a cube wedged in her throat.

'Say somethin'!' Molly Sue shrieked.

'Thank you,' Sally muttered, suddenly very aware she had a lot less hair to hide behind. Her nervous hands dearly wanted to fly to the now phantom plait.

'Don't stop there, darlin'. You need to keep the conversation going.'

'I . . . erm . . . had it done at Ford & Co.'

'Tell him that ya fancied a change.'

'I just . . . fancied a change.'

Todd grinned. 'Well, you look awesome. Melody's trained me pretty well, so I am qualified to say the cut suits your face shape, and the colour brings out your eyes!'

The word 'Melody' was a gut-punch, but Molly Sue continued to whisper in her ear. 'It's gonna be tricky, but you need to make a little joke . . . tell him you didn't realise he was such an expert in women's hair.'

'I didn't realise you were such an expert. Or were gay.' Sally added her own little bit at the end with a grin.

Todd rocked back in his chair. 'Ha! You know my eldest brother's gay, right? He taught me everything I know!'

She did not know that. She realised there was quite a lot she didn't know about him. 'Really? That's so cool.'

'Yeah, he moved to London last year – he works for the BBC. You're an only child, right? You live next door to Randall in those big houses on Acacia Lane?'

Wow, how did he know that? 'He knows that because he likes ya, dummy,' Molly Sue chuckled. 'Ask him if he's been stalkin' ya. That's cute.'

'Yeah. Have you been stalking me?'

He laughed again and it was the best sound she'd ever heard. 'Oh, totally. That guy in the bushes outside your house. That's me.'

'I'll bring you out a sandwich next time.' She had no idea where that came from, but it seemed like a funny thing to do.

Todd grinned. 'Anything but tuna. Tuna is Satan's faeces.'

Sally didn't have to think of a comeback to that as Mr Pollock walked in, looking frazzled as ever. 'Settle down, please!' Sally rolled her eyes and swivelled in her chair to face the front.

'You did good, girl,' Molly Sue whispered. 'Real damn good.'

After the final bell had pealed, Sally dragged her feet towards rehearsal, exhausted from her day. It turned out that, although flattering, thanking people for compliments was *exhausting* and the balmy, lethargic weather wasn't helping. She was ready for bed, but had to get through ninety minutes of *Little Shop*. Worse still, today she actually had to perform – they were rehearsing the opening number, the title song. Acting, dancing and singing. It was 'triple threat' time.

'It's gonna be fine,' Molly Sue told her as she panted up the stairs towards the top corridor. 'Just do as I do.'

And what exactly is that?

'Put a little honey in ya hips when ya walk for starters.' Sally practised a strut along the top corridor when no one was looking. 'Atta, girl!'

Sally slipped into the bustling hall and it looked like she was a little late. 'Can we get started, please?' Mr Roberts clapped his hands together like a seal. 'Oh wow, Sally! Loving the new 'do!'

Sally dipped her head. 'Thank you.'

'You should always be blonde, but please get here on time in future.'

'Sorry.'

'No time for that – chop chop! Get into starting position. Go!'

The song 'Little Shop of Horrors' was a short piece – only about a minute to get through, but it dawned on Sally that she was essentially opening the show. *WWMSD? What Would Molly Sue Do? In fact, why couldn't Chiffon be Molly Sue?* That sort of worked now she thought about it. The music started and Sally decided to go for it. She knew the words, she knew how she was *supposed* to act (she'd YouTubed *The Supremes* at Mr Robert's request), all she had to do now was get the hyperactive butterflies in her stomach to settle the hell down.

The three of them waited in the wings for the guy playing the narrator to get his American accent right. Crystal was being played by Holly Harman, a lovely girl who should have also probably been Audrey based on her talent, but was at least a size sixteen so that was never going to happen. Keira, playing Ronette, gave Sally a warm smile that caught her off guard. 'Let's just be super fun and girly, OK?'

Sally was taken aback. 'Yeah, sure. I'll . . . follow you.'

'Cool,' Keira said to both Sally and Holly. 'We should be like sisters.' Keira seemed to have made her normally bouffant afro even huger as a tribute to Diana Ross.

A new voice interrupted. Melody. She was already wearing a tacky blonde wig and a sling over her arm for Audrey's first scene. 'Nice hair, Sally.'

Sally waited for the bitchy follow-up, but it didn't come. 'Oh. Thanks.'

'Looks really good.' The words were nice, but her eyes were deader than a shark's. Perhaps Melody's facial muscles just couldn't stretch to a smile.

Unlike Todd, Sally had no desire to make small talk with Melody and Molly Sue didn't prompt her to. 'Just ignore her,' she said.

'Don't listen to Mels. I never do,' Keira said, echoing Molly Sue's sentiment once Melody had crossed to the other side of the stage.

'What?'

'Oh, she's such a brat,' Keira said with her trademark smile. 'She had leukaemia when she was, like, three so her parents totally ruined her. She's a lost cause.' Hearing Melody's best friend talk about her behind her back was an eye-opener. Sally assumed everyone at SVHS worshipped her.

'I thought she was your best friend.'

'Oh, she is. If it wasn't for Mel's little dramas I wouldn't have a single thing to talk about!' Sally laughed with her. 'But contrary to popular belief I'm not her minion. After we leave here, I'll never see her again if I can help it. One year of this hellhole left and then I'm gone!'

Whaaaaaaaat? One third of Melanora hated school as much as Sally did? Mind officially blown. The day just got more and more interesting with every passing minute. Molly Sue was wrong – the makeover hadn't just changed her hair . . . everything was different.

Chapter Thirteen

For the next couple of weeks, Sally became Sally's obsession and Molly Sue was always on hand to help. Sally had to admit, it was kinda fun; working out how to make her old clothes look good; thinking of ways to style her new hair; experimenting with make-up. Molly Sue had truly taken her on as a project and one day of attention wasn't enough – it was addictive.

Sally had maths four times a week so that was four opportunities to talk to Todd. After a few lessons, she got the most positive sign yet. HE PASSED HER A NOTE. How many times had she yearned for someone to include her in a private joke, and when she was, it was Todd who reached out to her! This particular note read, *Check out Pollock's trousers. He has a piss stain.* Oh bless, the poor guy did have a little wet patch in his crotch. Sally turned around and rolled her eyes at Todd. 'He probably splashed when he washed his hands,' she whispered.

'I'm telling you . . . the guy needs an incontinence pad.'

She laughed aloud, drawing a death glare from the teacher. Sally didn't care.

'Keep it up, girl,' Molly Sue commented. 'You're way more fun than ol' Fingers-For-Dessert Vine. Just be patient.'

The only raincloud in the sky was Stan. He was being decidedly frosty with her. She'd been over a couple of times for brand new *Satanville* but he seemed sullen and unnecessarily harsh on the episodes ('Season four is the *worst*. I don't know why we're even bothering any more.'). It just didn't make sense.

Things reached boiling point at the New Quarter mall one Saturday. Even though the weather was getting hotter and hotter and most of the year was up at the lake, Sally, Stan and Jennie had gone shopping. They liked to hang out in the coffee shop and order tank-sized mugs of coffee the way the *Satanville* gang did. They huddled around Jennie's laptop, exploiting the free wifi.

'What shall we do now?' Sally asked, fingers sticky with cinnamon bun icing. 'You don't have to go home yet, do you?'

'Don't you want to hang with your new friends?' Stan asked pointedly. 'They'll be up at the lake no doubt.'

'Stan!' Jennie chided.

'What's that supposed to mean?' Sally asked crossly.

Stan shrugged. 'Now that you're Miss Popularity you can hang out with your new bestie, Keira.'

Sally saw red. The fact she chatted to Keira at rehearsals and that people now acknowledged her existence at school didn't make them her *new friends*. 'Well, maybe if you don't stop whining like a giant man-baby, I will!'

'Wow,' Molly Sue said quietly. 'Couldn'ta said it better myself.'

Stan flinched like she'd punched him in the face.

124

'I'm sorry, Stan,' Sally went on, 'but ever since I got that haircut you've been acting like I'm a alien clone shape-shifting bodysnatcher or something.'

'It's true.' Jennie came down on her side. 'You've had a face like a smacked bum all week.'

'Gee, thanks, guys. I so needed ganging up on.'

'We're not!' Sally said. 'OK, we are, but what's the problem, Mopey Moperson? Look, if I've done something to annoy you, just tell me so I can fix it.'

Stan squirmed, scraping the foam out of his coffee mug with a wooden stirrer. It looked like he regretted saying anything in the first place. 'I just hate that you're leaving us to go off and be one of the shiny people.'

Sally narrowed her eyes. 'Is that what you think I'm doing? Do you really think I'm that shallow? If you do . . . then that makes you just as shallow.'

'What?' Now it was Stan's turn to look cross.

'Oh, I don't know!' Sally threw her hands up, exasperated. 'But that's not what's happening. Stan, I just fancied a haircut.' Sally sighed. 'Is there something wrong with me wanting to look nice? Is there some secret rule? That you get two choices – ugly and deep, or pretty and shallow? That blows.'

Stan seemed to warm a fraction. 'OK, I'm sorry. I know I'm a sulker, I can't help it.' He looked at her with wide, honest eyes and it was difficult to be mad at him. 'You know, I don't know about you, but I pretty much hate school with all my heart. If it weren't for you guys, I don't know if I could, like, get through a single day. I just don't want stuff to change.'

'It has to,' Jennie said sadly. 'We're all leaving next year . . .'

'Don't even talk about that!' Sally sipped her coffee. She didn't really like coffee, it remained so bitter even after three sachets of sugar, but they never drank tea on *Satanville*. 'We'll always be best friends. Wherever we go next year . . . or whatever my hair looks like!' She wondered if maybe she had gone too far, too fast with her makeover. She really didn't want to change who she was just because of Todd – she knew enough to know that wasn't cool. 'Come on, let's go look at things we can't afford.'

Stan bought some comics from the SFF Emporium, where Sally wondered if a Dante action figure was a step too far, before Jennie decided she'd like to get some new clothes for her birthday party. Her parents were going to Korea to see her family in a few weeks but Jennie was allowed to remain for *Little Shop of Horrors* and had been granted a house party in their absence. For her OCD parents, this was a big deal.

Clothes shopping with Jennie was quite painful. It usually involved her seeing something in one shop (always the first), being indecisive and then trailing them around another six shops before deciding she did want the original item after all.

They set her a time limit of an hour and started in the first shop – one of those preppy places that was too dark, too loud and smelled like a gym changing room. Sally sat with Stan on the leather sofas outside the fitting room while Jennie tried a skirt and some tops on. 'Sorry I was such a douche,' Stan said. 'You know what I'm like once I get an idea in my head.'

Sally fiddled with her *Satanville* bracelets. 'No. It's OK. It's my fault too. I did the whole surprise reveal thing at school.

I should have told you and Jennie first – but I just wanted an honest reaction.'

Stan looked sheepish. 'And my reaction was douchey.'

'Perhaps a little.'

Stan tucked his feet under his legs to sit cross-legged. 'What I should have said is: Sally, you look freaking aaaaamaaaaazing.'

Sally's heart floated up her chest like it was full of helium. 'Really?' Her voice came out quiet and girlish, barely audible under the pounding house music.

'Really. Although, you know you were beautiful before the haircut, right?'

'Oh, cringe!' Sally grimaced.

'You need to learn to take a compliment, Blindy McNoeyes.'

Sally was about to enter a full-on embarrassment spasm at the way this conversation was heading, so abruptly changed the subject. 'No, what I need is to get out of this shop. Are you melting?'

'I am in danger of turning to a pool of goo, yeah.'

Sally rose from the sofa, her legs sticking to the leather. 'I'll go hurry her along. She won't buy any of it, anyway.' Sally ducked past the sour-faced shop assistant, whom she recognised from Year Thirteen, and entered the changing rooms. It was just as dark in here – presumably to fool you into thinking the clothes looked nice. The area divided up into booths with saloon doors and a large communal area in the middle. 'Jen?' Sally stooped down to find Jen's feet.

'I'm here,' Jennie replied. 'I'll just be a minute . . .'

'Me and Stan are boiling, can we wait outside?' Thinking nothing of it, Sally barged into Jennie's booth, the way they

127

always did. They'd shared changing rooms for ever, it was no biggy.

This time, Jennie seemed to mind, however. 'Wait, you don't need to —'

Too late, Sally was already through the doors. 'Why? Is the skirt hideous or . . .' Sally tailed off, seeing what the problem was. Jennie stood in her polka-dot bra, arms folded across her chest, but she couldn't hide the vicious bruises on her upper arms. They were vivid purple patches with yellowish outlines and they were the exact shape of handprints, as if someone had squeezed her arms way too tightly. 'How on earth did you . . . ?' Sally's words hung in the air again, because there was only one way she'd got those marks. Kyle.

Jennie tried to brush it off with a hollow laugh. 'Oh God, they're nothing. They don't even hurt.'

Sally felt Molly Sue stir in her, like a shark surfacing. 'That son of a bitch,' Molly snarled.

'Did Kyle do it?' Next to Molly Sue's, Sally's own voice sounded stupidly small.

'No! God, no! No, nothing like that. It must have happened while we were making out. You know what I'm like, I bruise like a peach!' Jennie was panicking, Sally could tell. She looked so, so guilty – which was so stupid, Sally could have cried. Tears pinched behind her nose.

'That bastard's lucky I can't get a shotgun in this pansy-ass country o' yours.' Molly Sue was pacing around her back; Sally could feel her getting hotter and hotter.

'Jennie.' Sally's voice wobbled but she closed the doors so they were protected by the booth. 'What happened? Please tell me . . . you can tell me anything. I won't tell anyone, I promise.'

'I already said! It's nothing!' Jennie snapped. 'Look, I'm standing here in a bra. Will you just let me get dressed, please? Thank you!' She pushed Sally out of the cubicle. Sally was speechless.

Dazed, she shuffled back to where Stan was waiting, leafing through one of his comics. 'Is she ready?'

'She'll be a minute.'

'Are you OK? You look awful.'

She couldn't tell Stan. She just couldn't. He'd blow up and try to be all manly, which would almost certainly result in Stan's ass getting squarely kicked in by an entire garage band. 'I . . . I just feel so hot. Can we wait outside?'

'Sure.' He led the way towards the exit.

'You're not gonna let that piece o' white trash get away with this, are ya?' Molly Sue raged.

No, Sally thought. *No, I'm not.*

Chapter Fourteen

That night, Sally had never felt so useless in her life. In the end, after much Googling of helplines and scouring blog posts about domestic violence, she curled up into a ball on her bed and cried. Just wept. She was powerless to help. What was she going to do? Call the police? That was exactly what she should do, but what was she meant to tell them? *I haven't witnessed anything and she'll probably deny it but I think my best friend's boyfriend is hurting her*. What's more, she'd promised Jennie she wouldn't tell anyone. She should have never agreed to that; she'd backed herself into a corner.

She sobbed anew. The thought of that . . . that . . . *arsehole* hurting Jennie. Jennie – one of life's little unicorns. Worse still, apparently Jennie considered having a boyfriend to be more important that her own well-being. How had she and Stan let that happen? Sally felt responsible, like she'd failed in her most basic of best friend duties. Quite simply, she didn't know what to do with herself.

So she cried.

'Let it all out, girl.' Molly Sue told her. The tattoo rested on the back of her shoulder blade, and Sally swore she could actually feel Molly Sue patting her back maternally. There was an *almost* comforting warmth under the skin.

What am I meant to do? Whatever I do it'll make things worse . . . what if he takes it out on Jennie? What if he really *hurts her?* She knew what Angela would do in *Satanville*: she'd pull on a pair of skin-tight leather trousers, some thigh boots and roundhouse kick the smirk off his slimy face. But she wasn't a bad-ass demon hunter, she was just . . . nothing.

'He's a coward, darlin'. What kinda man picks on an itty bitty thing like her? She wouldn't throw rice at a wedding. No sorta man at all, if y'ask me.'

What if he does it again?

'I don't doubt he will. Men like that get off on feelin' big an' powerful.'

I have to do something. *I can't ignore it. I can't.*

'Damn straight. Ya gotta talk to him, sugar. Let him know you're watchin' him. Threaten him a little.'

Sally knew with absolute certainty that wouldn't work. He'd wriggle out of it like a weasel somehow – *she walked into the door* or something just as lame. And Sally was scared of him. 'I can't,' she said. *You know I can't.*

'I can,' said Molly Sue. 'I ain't afraid o' that skinny son of a bitch. He'd have to stand up twice to cast a shadow.'

Sally rolled off the bed and went to her dresser so she could see her friend in the mirror. Molly Sue strutted over her shoulder and onto her chest. 'What do you mean?'

'Just like when I got ya hair did. Let me do it.'

'What? No. No, you can't.'

'Sure I can!'

131

Sally rolled her eyes. 'And just what are you going to do? With my body?'

'Calm down. I'm just gonna talk to him.'

'No way,' Sally shook her head no. 'Kyle thinks I'm an idiot. He won't listen to me.'

'He'll listen to me,' Molly Sue said with iron-clad certainty. 'I'm not gonna give him much of a say in the matter.'

Sally plucked a tissue out of the box on her dresser and dried her eyes. 'What would you tell him?'

Molly Sue let out a whistle through her teeth. 'Well, I'll just let him know that if he hurts sweet lil Jennie again, I'll make sure he gets it back ten times over. He musta seen you talkin' to Todd . . . we'll threaten him with the football team or somethin'.'

'This isn't going to work. And what if he takes it out on Jennie?'

'Girl! That's exactly what bullies like him want y'all to think! It's how they keep a hold on ya – buy your silence! Ya can't play along with men like that, you gotta show 'em who's got the real balls!'

Sally still wasn't convinced.

'Look, where's he gonna be this weekend? Just gimme five minutes with him and he won't be botherin' any more girls for a long time.'

Sally racked her brain, trying to remember what Jennie said they were doing. 'I think tomorrow night his band are playing at The Old Boat Shed up by the lake.'

'Can under eighteens get in?'

'Yeah.'

Molly Sue's violet eyes darkened. 'Then let's do it.'

* * *

132

The next night, Sally didn't select a pair of leather trousers because she didn't own any, but she did choose her most Angela-like outfit – skinny jeans, the army boots and the leather jacket. It was a rock gig after all, so she'd even gone overboard on the black eyeliner. It felt like war paint.

Not wanting her parents to see her so dolled up, Sally slipped out of the back door, calling into the lounge as she went. 'I'm going to Jennie's! I might be late . . .'

'What?' her mother called from the living room.

'There's a film on we both want to watch! Bye!' She slammed the door before her mum could stop her. She'd deal with any fallout in the morning. There was no way they'd let her go to a gig alone; the lie was necessary.

It was already dark by the time she reached the lake. She had no idea how this was going to work. Scanning the queue, Sally looked for Jennie – if she was here, how was she ever going to get Kyle on her own? She guessed that was Molly Sue's problem.

There was already a dirty bassline shaking the walls of the shed, which sat on the very edge of the lake. At this time of the evening, the lake was a black mirror – the trees and islands charcoal drawings reflected upside-down in the water. There was a steady stream of people from SVHS filing into The Old Boat Shed and even more laughing and drinking outside at the water's edge.

''K, ya ready?' Molly Sue asked as they joined the queue.

Ready as I'll ever be. Just don't do anything to make me look stupid.

'Darlin', have a little faith! When have I ever let ya down?'

OK, do it, then. Once more she imagined the tattoo sliding up into her head and there was a sharp, sudden chill in her skull. It was like the tipping-point plunge into sleep . . .

Sally woke with a start, face down in a pillow. *I can't breathe.* Surprised and scared, she swatted it away, sitting bolt upright. Her eyes were sleep fuzzy and unfocused. *Where am I?* She blinked hard and took in the familiar surroundings of her bedroom. Her owl hooted not far away. It felt late . . . or early even.

I was just at the club . . .

How long had Molly Sue taken over for? Why didn't she remember anything? She tried to force herself to remember getting home, or getting into bed, but there was only a black space, like the night had been coloured in with thick black Sharpies.

Sally pushed her hair off her face and saw that she was still partially dressed. The boots had been kicked off and the jacket had been slung over the back of her chair but she was still in her jeans and top. Both were covered in thick brown mud – it caked her bedsheets. 'What the . . . ?'

Climbing off the bed, Sally stumbled to her en-suite, tripping over a discarded boot. She flicked the bathroom light on and her hand flew to her mouth to stifle a scream.

Her cream T-shirt was red with blood.

Chapter Fifteen

'Molly Sue!' Sally hissed, the colour seeping from her face, leaving her skin sickly chalk white. 'What did you do?'

The tattoo didn't answer. Sally yanked the T-shirt up and saw Molly Sue was in her original position, statue still. 'Molly Sue!' She was wary of waking her parents, but a frustrated tear found its way out. 'Tell me what you did! Molly Sue!'

Still no reply.

Her hands were covered in tacky brown-red that she could only assume was blood. Nothing on her hurt; the blood wasn't hers. The ground lurched like a funhouse floor and she gripped the edge of the sink to steady herself. A wave of nausea, a feeling like carsickness, rose in her chest.

Sally closed her eyes. She *had* to remember. It *had* to be in there somewhere. There was nothing – only a thick, oily blackness where her evening ought to be. Another tear ran down her face, forging a channel in the dirt. She felt . . . wrong . . . violated. Molly Sue had stolen her body and done God only knew what.

Molly Sue! Tell me what you did! TELL ME!

The pin-up girl just looked coyly over her shoulder – *I've-got-a-secret-and-I'm-not-telling* all over her face. Sally sank to the bathroom floor, pressing herself into the narrow gap between the sink and the toilet. She pulled her knees to her chin and cried.

What have I done?

Sally awoke on the bath mat when her mother banged on her bedroom door. 'Sally! Are you awake?'

'Yes!' Sally shouted at once, not wanting her mum to see her like this. She sprang to her feet and looked in the mirror. It hadn't been a dream.

In the light of day everything was different. There's an old Russian saying she'd learned from an episode of *Satanville*: *the morning is wiser than the night*. It was so true. She'd done all her crying last night. This morning, if Molly Sue wasn't going to tell her, she needed to find out what had happened during the blackout.

But first things first. She peeled off the jeans and threw them into the shower with the T-shirt. She got in with them and turned the shower on. The filthy water ran black and maroon down the plughole, and she washed her clothes as best she could. The T-shirt would have to be burned, but the jeans could go in a regular wash without attracting too much suspicion. She'd put her bedding in too and just hope her mum didn't notice. As luck would have it, in the Feather household, Monday was laundry day and always had been.

After she was dry she found her phone in her leather jacket pocket. Without hesitation she called Kyle. It went straight to voicemail. 'No,' she mumbled. It felt like a brick dropping into her stomach. *Surely she didn't* . . . but maybe Molly Sue had. She *had* threatened it.

Panic bled in around the edges and Sally had to sit on her bed for a moment to stop shivering. *Did she kill him? Did I kill him?* She was no Kyle fan, but she didn't want him dead. Or did she? She reminded herself what he'd done to Jennie – those finger marks on her arm. *No, it wasn't you*, she told herself, *it was* her. *I was a fool to trust her.*

Sally thought about calling Jennie to ask if she'd heard anything from Kyle, but knew it'd look suspicious. She had to trust that Molly Sue hadn't left evidence – the police hadn't arrived on her doorstep yet. For now, Sally knew she mustn't draw attention to herself. She probably just punched him in the face or something. *So why is his phone dead?*

She couldn't manage any breakfast and walked to the corner almost in a trance. Stan and Jennie were waiting for her. 'Oh, she's on time for once!' Jennie called down the street. 'Oh, sweetie, what's up? You look awful!'

'Gee, thanks!' Sally attempted a carefree smile.

'Are you hungover?' Jennie grinned. 'I heard you got pretty wild at The Old Boat Shed last night.'

'What?' Stan's head whipped around as he walked a step ahead of them. 'What were you doing there?'

Sally processed the information. Did that mean Jennie hadn't been there? 'Yeah, I went and met some of the *Little Shop* cast,' she lied and Stan could barely hide his annoyance. 'How come you didn't go?' she said to Jennie.

'Duh!' Jennie sighed. 'Grandma was over for a family dinner. Major suckfest. I hate missing Kyle play. Was he good?'

'Yeah, great.'

'Where was my invite?' Stan said huffily.

'Don't start,' Sally snapped. She didn't have time for his wounded ego this morning. 'It was a cast thing. You are not in the cast. OK?'

Stan backed down. 'Sorry, Stresspants. *Are* you hungover?'

'No!' Sally said, although suspected this was *precisely* what a hangover felt like.

'Oh, really?' Jennie smiled slyly. 'When Kyle texted he said you were drinking shots.'

'Well, I wasn't,' she lied. She could kill Molly Sue. That would explain her dry mouth and churning stomach. 'Hey, are we meeting Kyle on the way in?'

'Don't think so. He hasn't texted to say to wait for him.'

Of course he hadn't – his phone was lost.

His phone's lost? How do I know that? It came back to her. A single image: a mobile dropping into the black lake with a clear plop. Nothing else – just that one image. *The lake? What was I doing on the lake?*

'Sally? Sure you're OK?' Stan asked, genuinely concerned.

'Yeah. Fine.'

'OK, let me know if you're gonna hurl. I'll hold your hair back.'

'You're such a gent.' Sally smiled, trying to hide her fear. It was another Monday morning where she couldn't wait to get to school.

Sally told Mrs Flynn that she had to talk to Mr Roberts about rehearsal so she ducked straight out of registration and went to the Newton Building where Kyle had form room with Dr Farmer. She loitered long after the bell for first period, waiting for everyone to file out, but Kyle was not amongst the masses. Her palms grew sweaty and she realised, almost too late, that she was going to vomit. She got to the girls' toilet with seconds to spare. *What did Molly Sue drink last night? What did she do?*

She felt better for being sick, like she'd expelled something toxic from her system. *I have to think clearly.* Sally was alone in the toilets so took her time, washing her face and rinsing her mouth out at the sink. She checked her jacket pocket for a tissue. She couldn't feel one, but her fingers found something square and hard in her inside pocket. Confused, Sally pulled it out. It was a Zippo lighter, the metal cold with a chipped American flag painted on one side. Sally flicked it open to see if it worked and found that it did. And remembered that Kyle had one just like it . . .

I should call the police. But if he was dead, it would be *her* DNA all over the body. Molly Sue didn't have little cartoon fingerprints. She could hardly tell the police that the tattoo on her back did it – she'd be put in a straitjacket and carted away.

Don't panic. Find out what happened first. Molly Sue? Are you there? There was still no answer. Fuming, she shoved the lighter back in her pocket. Again, if anyone saw it, they'd ask questions.

When the ground had stopped spinning quite so fast, she went to maths as normal, still wary of drawing too much attention to herself. Mr Pollock was already droning on when she tried to slip into the classroom like a shadow. 'Sally . . . glad you could join us. Hurry up and take your seat, please.'

'Sorry,' Sally muttered, head down. She tripped over someone's bag and managed to knock a pencil case off a desk with her satchel before finally arriving at her own desk. So much for not causing a scene. She was rummaging in her own bag for her textbook when she saw a scrap of white paper enter her periphery vision. It was Todd trying to subtly slide a note into her hand. She took it and sat up. Sure Mr Pollock wasn't looking, she unfolded the piece of paper.

Last night was AWESOME! Where'd you go? Xxx

Her eyes widened. *Oh God, what did I do?* All Sally could do was turn around and smile dumbly. Todd looked right back at her, the blue eyes peering out from under his heavy brow. It was like he was seeing past her and right at Molly Sue . . . who had done God knew what with him. His full lips curled up at the edges – a knowing half-smile. There was no way . . . surely she'd remember *that*. Sally turned away to hide the extent of her fuchsia blushing.

She needed to know what happened in those missing hours and she needed to know *now*.

By break it all became real.

'Have you seen Kyle?' Jennie was now visibly concerned. 'His phone has been off all morning.' She stood outside the library, hands on hips, looking hot and sticky from marching around the school on her search.

'Maybe's he's off sick,' Stan said through a mouthful of ham and crisp sandwich. 'If I was off sick, I'd still be asleep.'

Jennie humphed. 'I bet he got wasted after the gig and stayed in bed. Sal, did you see him after the gig?'

'Not really,' she replied, non-committal. *Maybe I should just turn myself in now.*

'God, it drives me mad! What's the point in having a phone if you're not going to use it!' Once more, Sally saw the phone vanish into the water. Jennie stomped off in search of Kyle. Sally knew she wasn't going to find him.

'Maybe he finally dropped dead?' Stan said.

At that Sally whirled to face him. 'What?' Had he seen something? Now that she thought about it, Molly Sue must have gone past his house on her way home.

Stan grinned, just kidding. 'You think? I wished pretty hard . . .'

'Well . . . don't!' Sally hoped her hammering heart wasn't audible. The rising panic was dizzying, and the thought of vomiting in front of half her class only made her more panicked.

'Steady on! Good lord, Sally Feather, you are not good after a late night.'

'Sorry . . . sorry. That's just a terrible thing to say.' Sally fought to keep her trembling hands steady.

'C'mon, Grumpy, let's get you a coffee!' Stan took her hand and dragged her towards the cafeteria. Sally could see Todd watching her every step of the way as they climbed the stairs. Just in case, Sally pulled her hand out of Stan's palm. She didn't want Todd to get the wrong idea.

Finally, in second period, it all got too much. She drummed hyperactive fingers against the table and she couldn't even feign interest in the fanfic Stan was writing in her notepad. The classroom felt airless, stifling.

Sally could think of five options available to her. Option one: do nothing and hope the whole thing blew over. Not likely. Option two: go to the police and tell the truth and

141

accept the consequences. That didn't seem fair when she hadn't done anything – hell she didn't even know what she'd be confessing to! A bubble of anger kept popping in her chest; Molly Sue had taken advantage of her. Was this a plan – to slowly take permanent control of her? To possess her body? No, that didn't feel right. If that were the case then she wouldn't have relinquished control so soon. Another thought occurred to her: maybe Molly Sue *couldn't* remain at the wheel for long – perhaps that was why she was so quiet now – she was spent after whatever she'd done last night.

Options three and four were to go to Kyle's house or the hospital. The final option was to go to the lake, to see if there was anything there that might jog her memory. The phone being swallowed into the water was the only pixel of the night she had.

'Stan, I have to get out of here,' she said suddenly.

'What? Are you OK?'

'I . . . I really don't feel well.' Not a lie.

'Want me to come with you?'

'No, no, it's fine.' She started to sweep her things into her satchel.

'Mademoiselle Feather,' said Madame Renoir, 'are you going somewhere?'

'Miss, I feel really ill . . .'

She mustn't have looked too brilliant either because the teacher nodded. '*D'accord. Vite!*'

Sally careered into the corridor, feeling like she was suffocating. She saw the fire escape at the end of the hall and lurched towards the open air. She started to run, her Converse slapping against the polished floor. Pushing against the bar, she tumbled into the yard and gulped in fresh air. The pigeons and crows gorging on leftover break-time snacks scattered, cawing their disapproval. Sally gathered her wits and hurried towards the main gates so fast she didn't see the figure coming around the corner of the science block until she ploughed into him.

It was Kyle, and he looked *angry*.

Chapter Sixteen

No. Sally backed up. He wasn't angry, he was shocked . . . scared even – a rabbit in her headlights. He backed away from her, eyes wide. Well, as wide as they could physically go with all the swelling – he had two black eyes and a nasty red gash on his cheek. He was so disfigured, he was only just recognisable as Kyle.

Did I . . . ? Did she . . . do that?

'OK, darlin' here's what you're gonna do.' It was Molly Sue and she was back, loud and clear. 'Before ya start freakin' out, I want ya to stand up real tall and ask him if he's done what ya told him to do.'

They faced-off at opposing sides of the playground like a pair of cowboys at high noon. Empty crisp packets rolled across the concrete in place of tumbleweeds. Sally did as she was told, trying to stop her voice from shaking. 'Did . . . you do what I told you to do?'

Kyle scanned the deserted path for help. Sally could see it even in his malformed face: he was scared of her. Perhaps he should be. He actually held up his hands in surrender. 'I . . . I only just got here, Sally. No one found me until this morning! You . . . you have to give me some time . . . I'll do it, I promise.'

Molly Sue piped up again. 'Now tell him he knows what'll happen if he don't.'

'Well . . . you better . . . do it . . . or you know what'll happen.' Sally tried her hardest to be menacing, but her voice sounded high and strangled.

'I know, I know! I'll break up with Jennie.'

Sally tried to keep surprise off her face. 'Good. Do it . . . nicely.' That one was all her own.

'Tell him he has until the end of the day.'

'You have until the end of the day. I . . . mean it,' she threw in for good measure.

'You might also wanna remind him what'll happen if we so much as see him put a pinky on another girl . . .' Molly Sue's voice contained an unmistakeable smirk.

'And you know what'll happen if I see you even look funny at another girl.'

Kyle nodded. He looked like he might cry. 'I . . . I promise.'

'Good,' Sally said. 'And if you tell anyone what I did . . .'

'God, I won't! Do you really think I want the whole school to know that you did this to me?' He stopped himself, no doubt scared of what she'd do. 'Can I go?'

'Yeah!' Molly Sue chuckled. 'Tell the jackass to run on home to his mama!'

'Just . . . go,' Sally said.

Kyle scuttled into the school like a mouse some cat had tired of pawing.

You and I need to talk, Sally told Molly Sue.

Sally couldn't go home because her mother would be there, but there was no way she could go back into school with such

145

a congested mind. Instead she went to the diner and squashed herself into the darkest booth in the darkest corner. At this time of day, it was pretty empty – there was one mother with a toddler and a single waitress playing on her phone behind the neon and chrome counter. With what little money she had, she ordered an Oreo milkshake in one of those metal tumblers, the way she'd seen Todd and Melody do from outside on the pavement.

What did you do to him?

'Oh, here it comes!' Molly Sue groaned. 'You're such a nag. Girl, I did you a favour.'

You STOLE my body!

'No I didn't! You told me I could take it!'

You know what I mean! You hurt him!

'You deaf or somethin'? I thought you wanted him to leave your girl alone . . . mission accomplished.'

Sally fought the urge to scream at the tattoo out loud. *I didn't ask you to mash his face!*

'What can I say? I figured askin' real sweet might not get the job done.'

Tell me what you did.

'Why?'

Sally clenched her jaw. *Molly Sue, you can't do things like that with MY body! I . . . I can't remember ANYTHING about last night. You talked to Todd! What did you say to him? What did you do? It . . . it's not fair!*

'Ya wanna talk about fair? How you wanna try being a freakin' drawing for a few hundred years?' Molly Sue broke off suddenly as if she knew she'd said too much.

A few hundred years?

She paused. 'I can show you last night if you really wanna see it.'

Of course I want to see it! It's MY body.

'OK. Just relax, darlin'. You're head's about to get real full . . .'

Boom.

Darkness. And then, colours.

It was like watching a film – passive. There were words and sounds and colours, but she was outside of the action. A hi-def, 3D movie over which she had no control. Sally was a passenger in her own head, Molly Sue in the driving seat. The first thing she saw was The Old Boat Shed – right where Molly Sue had taken over the night before. She joined the queue of people filing in.

Being in her head felt claustrophobic, like she was hermetically sealed inside a suitcase. Molly Sue was right at home, though, testing her muscles, stretching her limbs, rolling her neck, curling her fingers and toes – Sleeping Beauty awoken from her long, deep sleep.

The back of Molly Sue's hand was stamped with a red stop sign to show she was under eighteen, and then allowed in The Shed. It was cramped and sweaty and the warm-up act – Kyle's band – were already on. Sally hated them and she sensed Molly Sue did too. The instruments were so high in the mix they were crunchy and distorted, totally overshadowing the vocals – although the singer was pretty much just growling into the mic.

Hardcore fans were at the front by the stage, moshing and bounding into one another like Weebles. Molly Sue was unimpressed; Sally could feel her thoughts and she thought they were try-hards – LOOK HOW WILD WE ARE! They weren't wild, they were sheep. Girls trying to impress boys, boys trying to impress boys.

Molly Sue sidled to the bar, sashaying in a way that Sally never would, her hips swinging from side to side. When Molly Sue walked with Sally's legs she lifted her feet for one thing – one foot in front of the other, like a lady panther. She fixed the dimpled-cheeked bar boy in a vice glare. 'Double malt on the rocks.' Molly Sue's words, Sally's accent. It sounded *insane*.

The bar boy looked at the underage stamp on her hand, but she continued to stare him down with a look that said, *And what?* He went to get her whiskey without question. She paid him and rewarded him with a curve of her lips, lifting herself onto a bar stool. He couldn't take his eyes off her as she downed the drink in one huge gulp. 'Dear God, I was ready for that, you have no idea. Can I get another, cutie-pie?' He did as he was told, blushing.

That was when Todd appeared at the other end of the bar. Trapped in her own head, Sally screamed at Molly Sue – *stay away from him* – but he'd already clocked her and wove his way through the crowd. 'Hey, Sally. Didn't know you were coming tonight.'

'Well, here I am.' Sally felt Molly Sue's weariness – she had little patience for schoolboys, Sally suspected, but the last thing she wanted was to upset Todd. He looked so good tonight – he was wearing a creased Hollister shirt, rolled to the sleeve to reveal thick forearms. Enough buttons were undone to see the curve of his chest and a light smattering of dark hair. Sally liked that, it was . . . masculine.

Molly Sue must have taken pity on Sally's doomed crush because she summoned the energy to make conversation. 'Thought it'd be nice to support . . . whatshisface . . . Kyle.'

'The band are pretty good.'

'They're terrible.'

'Ha! Yeah . . . but it's better than nothing, right?'

'If you say so.'

'Wow,' Todd said as the bar boy arrived with her drink. 'Didn't have you down as a whiskey drinker.'

Molly Sue pursed her lips. 'You think you know her . . . me? You think you know me?'

Todd fumbled his words. 'I . . . no . . . I've just never seen you here before.'

'Don't sweat it, kiddo. You want a drink?'

'I can't – I drove down.'

'Well, aren't you a good boy? Where's the delectable Miss Melody Vine tonight? Washing her cauldron?'

Thankfully Todd laughed. From her vantage point behind her own eyes, Sally could have died. 'Are you kidding? Mels wouldn't be seen dead here and – between you and me – her parents won't let her come out on a school night.'

Molly Sue chuckled behind her tumbler. She tossed Sally's hair over her head, and moved a fraction closer. Closer than Sally would have ever dared. 'So, Todd Brady, prime rib of Saxton Vale High School, are you going to ask me to dance or am I waiting for a written invitation?'

He grinned. 'Oh God, I'm a terrible dancer.'

'I sure hope that's false modesty, because you know what they say about boys that can't dance . . .' Sally gasped, Molly Sue held her nerve with a sly smile.

Todd blushed. 'Sally, would you like to dance?'

'What would *Mels* say?'

'Melody isn't here and she doesn't own me.'

'Correct answer. I'd love to.'

Kyle's band had one slowie and they chose that moment to play it. 'Looks like we've entered the Erection Section,' Molly Sue mumbled out of Todd's earshot.

'I never know what to do.' Todd slipped his arms around her waist like two wet noodles.

Molly Sue hooked her arms around his thick neck. Sally looked helplessly on, wallflower at her own first slow dance. 'You just sway.'

The singer hunched over the microphone like he was in great pain, singing about bleeding out of his heart. Todd looked uncomfortable to say the least, unsure of where to look. He leaned in close to her ear. 'How am I doing?'

'You're doing good. There's nothing to it . . . just hold me tight and don't step on my feet!' He tightened his arms and the space between them shrunk. They now swayed hip to hip; her head on his broad, strong shoulder. Heat radiated from him, his shirt smelling of lavender fabric conditioner and his almost lemony aftershave. Sally blazed with jealousy. Molly Sue had stolen her moment. 'This feels good,' she muttered to herself more than Todd. 'It's been a while . . .'

Todd melted into the dance, his self-consciousness fading. They were in a sea of dancing couples, although few were as beautiful and graceful. She felt his jaw brush her hair. Molly Sue looked up to find him ready, poised, looking into her eyes. He wanted to kiss her – well, who wouldn't? Sally screamed although no noise came out. It was like being in those nightmares where you can't control your legs and they keep walking towards the edge of the cliff.

'You smell so good,' Todd whispered, licking his lips.

Molly Sue smiled a carnivorous smile, their mouths almost touching. Sally felt his breath on her lips. She cried with frustration, stuck behind her two-way mirror.

Todd pulled away, dropping his hands from her hips. 'Sorry, Sally, I can't.'

Molly Sue rolled her eyes. 'You're scared of her.'

'Aren't you?'

'No. And if you don't got the boy bits to dump that junkyard dog, you're no good to me.' Molly Sue shot him a poison glance and walked away, the crowd parting. Kyle's band finished their set to applause. She had work to do.

Todd followed her. 'Aw, come on, don't be like that . . .'

Molly Sue, wearing Sally, turned back to face him. 'Choice is yours. I'm an only child, don't do sharing. Never did play well with others – least of all Melody Vine. You know where to find me if you want to dance again sometime.' She gave him a dazzling, suggestive smile and lost herself in the crowd. Todd could only watch her go.

Now, where was Kyle? She fought her way to the front as most people headed to the bar while the next band set up. Sally guessed that they'd be packing up their instruments by now and evidently so had Molly Sue. Checking she hadn't been seen, she slipped through the stage door like she was made of silk.

The two bands met in the middle with much self-congratulatory back-slapping and high-fiving. Molly Sue hovered in the shadows. The lead singer caught sight of her, his eyes tracking up and down her legs. 'Ruh-roh, a groupie got in.'

Sally got the distinct impression Molly Sue did not like that. 'You caught me!' she said through a forced smile.

'Sally?' Kyle squinted at her. 'What are you doing here?'

'Just wanted to say well done, I thought that was . . . real special.'

'Dude, she's smokin',' the drummer muttered loudly on purpose.

She ignored him. 'You want a drink?' Molly Sue asked sweetly. 'I convinced the bar boy I was over eighteen.'

'Sure. I'll have a vodka and Red Bull.'

'Cool. How 'bout I meet you on the terrace?'

Sally saw her secure two drinks and then sneak out through a fire exit onto the terrace that backed onto the lake. It was designed that way so boaters could pull into the jetty and then get drinks or food when they were out for the day on the water. On summer days, this terrace would be packed, but right now the tables and parasols were packed away.

The indigo night was cool now, Molly Sue balanced the drinks on the safety rail and wrapped her arms around her body. She looked out over the rippling lake and felt the wind in her face. She seemed to drink in the pine-tinged air, savour it, the way Sally's dad sipped his red wines. Sally wondered how long it had been since Molly Sue had last tasted the night air. Her moment was interrupted by Kyle bursting out of the fire escape. Molly Sue forced herself to smile. 'Hey. Here's your drink.'

'Thanks, Sally. I can't believe you came to my gig. Is Jennie here?'

'No, I came by myself. Why don't we go for a little walk?'

'Sure!' The look on his face made it very clear what he thought the walk was a prelude to. The shitweasel. Although she'd have thought it impossible, Sally hated him that little bit more. The terrace led down to the jetties, the boats clinking against their moorings.

'Basically,' Molly Sue started, 'I wanted to have a word in your ear.'

'Yeah? What's up? Is it Jennie?'

Molly Sue gave him her most dazzling smile. 'There's no easy way to say this, but you're gonna break up with her.'

He blinked hard. 'What?'

The smile dropped in a second. 'You heard.'

Kyle's confusion switched to annoyance. 'What's it got to do with you? Mind your own fricking business.'

He started to stomp back towards The Old Boat Shed, but Molly Sue blocked his path. 'You made it my business when you hurt my friend.' Sally was suddenly proud of Molly Sue. Maybe she'd made the right decision after all – she could have never spoken to Kyle like this.

'What?'

'You hit Jennie.'

Kyle swore loudly, trying to step around her. 'I never hit Jennie.'

'OK.' Molly Sue rolled her eyes. 'Hurt her, then. I saw the bruises with my own eyes.'

Kyle sneered at her. 'Oh, for God's sake, chill out, woman. You don't know what you're talking about. Get out of my way.'

He shoved her out of his path, hard, almost sending her into the lake. Molly Sue grabbed hold of his sleeve and spun him back around. '*Woman*? Did you call me *woman* and then put your hands on me?'

'What?'

Through windswept curls, Molly Sue's eyes blazed. She glared at him so hard it hurt. 'I said, did you just put your stinkin' hands on my body without permission?'

He looked at her like she was speaking in tongues. 'You're not right in the head. I always knew you were mental.' He started to walk away again, the planks creaking under his feet. Molly Sue stooped to the nearest boat, a simple rowing boat, and unlatched an oar. It was an old-fashioned, wooden one; painted and chipped.

Sally held her breath.

It took her three elegant strides to catch up with him. Molly Sue raised the oar like a baseball bat and swung for the back of his head. Her arms shook as she struck him. There was moist crack like an egg breaking. Kyle, quite literally, hit the deck.

Chapter Seventeen

Molly Sue dropped the oar into the water and froze. The jetties were deserted and quiet save for the undulating bass rattling through The Old Boat Shed. The main act was now playing and nearly everyone had gone back inside. There were some voices – probably people in the smoking area, but that was out of sight around the front of the venue.

No one had seen her hit Kyle.

Sally looked on, impotent.

Molly Sue, however, sprung to life. She crouched alongside Kyle's still body and felt for a pulse in his neck. When Sally felt his blood pumping she could have wept with joy until she saw a red-black puddle pooling on the wooden slats. Without hesitation, Molly Sue hooked her hands under Kyle's armpits and reversed, dragging him along the jetty. She tugged him as far as the nearest rowing boat, which she stepped into before hauling him on board too. The little boat rocked violently, the water glugging and sloshing up the sides. Molly Sue gripped the rim to stop herself tumbling into the lake.

If Molly Sue had a plan, she wasn't letting Sally hear it. She could only watch. Was she just going to leave him in the boat for dead? Apparently not; Molly Sue wiped her blood-splattered hands on her T-shirt and cast off from the jetty. She sat in the rower's seat, taking the oars. With strong, confident strokes, Molly Sue crossed onto the darkest part of the lake, away from the lights and laughter of The Old Boat Shed. Kyle was a crumpled rag doll in the bottom of the boat, blood seeping into his grey vest. From somewhere inside his coat, a phone beeped as a text arrived.

When they were far enough out to be invisible, Molly Sue paused and rummaged through his pockets. She found the phone and, without a second thought, tossed it overboard. The image was just as Sally remembered it – the handset being sucked into the dark water with a hungry plop.

Molly Sue continued to investigate. The first thing she found was the old-school cigarette lighter. Very rock star – Kyle was such a poser. Molly Sue flicked it open and a fat orange flame leaped up at her face. 'Nice. Finder's keepers.' She slipped it in her own pocket. In his inside pocket she found a retractable blade. 'Oh you bad, bad boy. Let's put this somewhere where you can't go hurtin' yourself.' Molly Sue's own accent was slipping out now and it sounded ever weirder. She pocketed the knife as well.

She took the oars and kept rowing, using muscles Sally didn't know she possessed. Sally realised after a few minutes Molly Sue was steering them towards Cormorant Island. Before she knew it, the rowing boat was grinding against the shingle beach. Molly Sue climbed out and heaved the boat up the beach where it was in no danger of drifting away. It was a good thing Kyle lived off cigarettes and Diet Coke because he was already heavy enough. Getting his prone body out of the boat was no small feat and she kept slipping over into the slick mud. By the time she got Kyle onto land, she looked like she'd survived an apocalypse movie – it was no wonder her clothes had been in such a state; she was covered in cormorant crap.

From the boat, Molly Sue untied the mooring rope and coiled it over her shoulder. Once more, Molly Sue grabbed Kyle under his arms and dragged him up the beach and into the trees. This was harder, she had to navigate exposed, twisting roots and the slope to get him to higher ground. As soon as they were out of sight, hidden by the forest, she let him fall. Filthy and exhausted, Molly Sue dug deeper and found the strength to shove him up against a slender tree trunk. She sat him upright and twisted his arms behind the tree before tying his wrists with the rope. Worryingly, she was something of a knot expert and Sally wondered where she'd picked up that talent.

A ragged Molly Sue fell back against the opposite tree to admire her handiwork. She got her breath back before crawling over to Kyle. She tapped his face. 'Wakey, wakey, sunshine . . .' She slapped him a little harder. 'Rise and shine!' His head lolled to one side. 'Oh, don't you go and die on me, you louse.'

She felt the gash on the back of his head. It wasn't too bad, a surface wound. Molly Sue screamed 'Wake up!' in his face and this time he stirred.

'What are you doing? My head . . . oh, God . . . my head really hurts.' His eyes opened and he tried to get away, struggling against her knots. He wasn't going anywhere.

'It will do. I hit you with an oar.'

Kyle was wide awake now, pulling and tugging on the ropes. He kicked out at her, trying to rise to his feet. 'Sally, what are you doing? You have to let me go! You can't do this!'

'And yet I did.'

'God, you're a psycho!'

Sally slapped him hard around the face and he yelped in pain. 'So predictable. It's not that I'm stronger or smarter than you, it's that I'm a psycho. Guess again, buddy boy.'

'Help! HELP!' he screamed.

'I wouldn't bother. You'll only get yourself hoarse.'

'HELP!'

This time Molly Sue reached into her jacket and whipped out the blade. The steel gleamed in the moonlight. 'I said, I wouldn't bother. Quit your bawlin' before I give you something to really bawl about.'

Kyle's eyes widened. He looked terrified and Sally pitied him. She knew she shouldn't, he'd hurt her friend, but she couldn't help it – he was so helpless.

'That's better. Now let's finish that talk we started.'

Kyle was now crying. 'What do you want? P-please don't hurt me.'

'Well, now, that depends on your answers, don't it?'

'What's up with your voice?'

'I'll do the questions. Number one: what did you do to Jennie?'

'Nothing!'

Molly Sue stepped around his flailing legs and held the knife under his jaw. 'Try again.'

'OK! OK! God!' Kyle flinched away, tears rolling down his face. 'We got into a fight! We fell out about something, I can't even remember what. You know . . . you know . . . you don't know what she's like . . . she gets really angry! I had to hold her to get her off me!'

Molly Sue pressed the blade further into his face and this time it drew blood. Little red beads. 'Do you really wanna pull that thread? I know you aren't gonna try to pin this on a girl who weighs the same as a prairie rat.'

'I'm not! I'm not! I'm sorry! I . . . I shouldn't have . . . I didn't mean to . . .'

'Didn't mean to what?'

'I didn't mean to hurt Jennie.'

'But you did.'

'I know! And I'm sorry.'

'Did you tell her that?' His silence said that he had not. Sally wasn't thrilled with her method, but Molly Sue was getting the job done. 'OK, so now we just gotta work out what the punishment's gonna be.'

'What?'

What? Sally thought. *You've got what you wanted – he admitted it! Now let him go!* She had to cling to the fact she'd seen him alive and well – or well-ish – that morning at school.

'You didn't think I was going to let you get away with hurting that girl, did ya?'

'Please . . . please, Sally, you don't want to do this.'

Molly Sue's face twisted into a manic grin. 'Oh, but I really do. See, I think there's way too many parasites like you getting away with it every single day. Boys who think it's OK to beat on girls half their size. Tell me, Kyle, did it make you feel like a big man?'

'No!'

'Did you like the power Kyle? Did you feel all manly?'

'Please, just let me go!'

Please, just let him go, Sally echoed.

Molly Sue let the hand with the knife fall to her side. She ran the tip of the blade oh-so-slowly up his inside thigh, heading straight towards his crotch. 'Maybe I should turn you into a girl,' Molly Sue mused airily. She gritted her teeth and jabbed the knife through the denim. Kyle cried out with horror, now sobbing with fear. 'Maybe then you'd know how it feels. How it feels to walk down the street and have men gawp at you, thinking you're something they can buy and own. How it feels to be hungered and ignored at the same time. How it feels to be disposable. Maybe then you'd know how it feels to have men look at you and see you as somethin' *less* than they are because you don't got this dangly bit of meat between your legs.'

'Please!' Kyle's scream shook the birds out of the trees. 'Please, stop!'

Molly Sue smiled and retracted the blade. 'Lucky for you that's not what a woman is. We aren't lacking anything, hon. We're not men without dicks. We're not holes for you to fill.'

Kyle's eyes were wild and wide with fear. 'I know. I . . . I don't hate girls. I don't!'

'You won't now because you ain't going anywhere near one. Got that? If I even see you within two metres of a girl at school, I will hurt you in ways you can't even imagine. That clear?'

'Yes. Yes . . . please . . . just let me go.'

Molly Sue assessed him pityingly. 'No.'

'What?'

'Big clever man like you should be able to make your own way home. It'll give you some time to think about how you treated my little friend.'

Kyle looked at her incredulously, testing Sally's sympathy. 'You can't . . . you can't just leave me here.'

Molly Sue walked away, treading over the roots towards the shore. She tossed the dagger into the lake. 'You have twenty-four hours to break up with Jennie.'

'If you leave me here, I'll die!' Kyle cried.

Molly Sue just shrugged. 'Oh, shucks. Either way, you won't be with Jennie.' She steered the rowing boat to the water's edge and climbed aboard. She cast off, smiling so widely, her cheeks ached.

'Can I get you anything?' the waitress loomed over Sally in her booth at the diner.

'W-what?'

'I said, do you want anything else to drink?'

Sally blinked, readjusting to the real world. 'No. No, thanks, I'm fine.' The waitress gave her a stinky look before skulking back to the counter.

Oh my God, he could have died out there!

'But he didn't. We just saw his sorry ass,' Molly Sue said far too casually.

That's not the point – you had no way of knowing! What were you thinking? That was TOO MUCH! If he'd died, it would have been me who went to jail!

161

'Girl, where you go, I go. But it don't matter now, does it? He's fine. A little beat up, but fine. I think he learned his lesson.' She sounded almost gleeful.

Sally's mouth was desert dry. It was more than that. It had gone so much further than teaching Kyle a lesson. Molly Sue had *enjoyed* torturing him.

Chapter Eighteen

Not wanting to attract any more attention to herself than necessary, Sally was about to return for her afternoon lessons when her phone rang. The display said it was Jennie. 'Hi, Jen —' Sally was cut off by what sounded like whale song. 'Jennie, are you OK?'

'He broke up with me . . .' Jennie managed to get the words out between sobs. It was like she'd been winded, gasping for air.

Sally stopped outside the school gates. He'd done it. He must have done it at lunchtime. Some of the guilt was replaced by validation. Molly Sue had done it the wrong way but she'd got the job done. Sally inhaled deeply, relief washing through her. In time, Jennie would thank her, she was sure of it. 'Oh, Jennie, I'm sorry.' There were fresh wails down the phone and Sally had to hold the handset away from her ear. 'Where are you?'

'I couldn't stay at school. I'm on my way home.'

'Do you want me to come over?'

More wailing. 'Yes, please.' Sally continued past the school gates and walked in the direction of Jennie's. This new plan worked: her mum still wouldn't know she'd skipped school, and by the time she finished at Jennie's, school would most likely be over. Tomorrow was a new day – no more skipping lessons, she vowed. Teachers were bound to notice sooner or later.

Jennie lived a few streets away from Sally's house, not too far away from Todd now that she thought about it. All the streets in Mulberry Hill looked alike, the only difference being the number plates of the BMWs on the driveways. If you didn't know where you were going you could get lost in a labyrinth of Happy Meal houses.

Her friend appeared at her front door in a state. Jennie's face was red, puffy and snotty. She looked like a baby bird that had prematurely crashed out of a nest. Sally embraced her tightly. Jennie's body shook against hers as tears soaked into her shirt. 'Aw, you poor thing. Tell me all about it.'

Sally led her upstairs to her bedroom. Kyle's band was playing out of Jennie's laptop on her bed. *Ooh, this was going to be some heavy emo chat,* Sally sensed. Jennie curled up on her pillow. Sally sat beside her and turned the music off. 'That's not helping.' She stroked her friend's hair and handed her a tissue. 'Come on, tell me what happened.'

'I can't!'

'You can! You and Kyle are pretty up-and-down . . .'

'This was different. He meant it this time.'

Good. 'Why? What did he say?'

Jennie blew her nose noisily. 'He said it was over.'

'Well, why?' Sally hoped her performance was convincing. She had to act clueless while at the same time burning to know if Kyle had kept his promise to 'do it nicely'.

'I don't know! He actually said, "It's not you it's me"! That he wasn't in love with me any more and needed to be by himself.'

Molly Sue chipped in, sounding extra smug. 'Hate to say I told ya so . . .'

Go away. 'Oh, Jennie, I'm sorry. I don't know what to say . . .'

'I just don't understand. I thought we were in love.' She sobbed afresh.

Sally shushed her and continued to smooth her hair. She wasn't known for her tough love, that was Stan's department, but she couldn't sit here and watch Jennie weep over that bumface. 'Look, I probably shouldn't say this,' she started, 'but it didn't look like you were having much fun . . . you fell out all the time.'

'No, we didn't!'

'Jennie, come on . . . you bickered constantly.'

'You don't know what it was like . . .' This time she didn't seem so certain.

'Were you going to marry him? Seriously? A guy from school? What were you going to do when you went to university? Follow him?'

'I don't know,' Jennie said sulkily.

'I'm just saying that even though it feels awful now, this might not be such a bad thing . . .'

'BUT I LOVE HIM!'

'I know, I know.' Sally could see that logic wasn't going to get her very far on this occasion. She supposed there was a time for tough love and a time for *there, there*. She resigned herself to a couple of hours of hair stroking. Internally, she was giddy. Kyle had done exactly as Molly Sue had said and Jennie, although upset, was safe.

She wasn't ready to forgive the tattoo just yet though. None of this excused what Molly Sue had done. The tattoo had *used* her body.

After a couple of, frankly damp, hours, Jennie pulled herself together. She didn't want to have to explain it all to her dad (the sternest parent Sally had ever met, he made her dad look quite laid back) so she'd dried her eyes. Sally, satisfied Jen wasn't going to throw herself down the stairs, headed home for dinner.

As ever, she and her parents sat in their designated places at the table. The Carpenters greatest hits played quietly in the background. Sally always thought that although the songs were saccharine, the singer sounded so, so sad.

'Your report arrived today,' her mother said as she served a pungent fish pie alongside some soggy broccoli. There wasn't a vegetable on earth her mother couldn't over-boil.

Her dad sipped his wine. 'Are we still doing well?'

Who's we?

Her mother sat down. 'It was a wonderful report, Sally. All A-grades.'

'Excellent,' her father said. 'Keep it up.'

Sally blushed. Her mother went on. 'Your teachers do say you need to participate more, though. You must join in, Sally.'

'That's just what they say when they can't think of anything else to put,' Sally told them.

'If that's what they're saying, you make sure you do it. Don't get too big for your boots, young lady,' her dad said. 'There's no point in being a brainbox if you haven't got common sense, is there? We get these cocky graduates at the bank, qualifications coming out of their ears, and half of them don't even know how to tie their shoelaces.'

'Yes, Dad.' She poked at the fishy potato blob, appetite destroyed. Whatever she did, it was never going to be enough. Maybe she should just stop trying.

After dinner, she tried to focus on her homework in her bedroom but maths problems turned to images of the previous night no matter how hard she tried to concentrate. She couldn't get the memory of Molly Sue swinging the oar at Kyle's head out of her mind. Worse, the glee she'd felt while doing it. The bloodlust as she'd run the knife up Kyle's thigh.

She closed her textbook and slumped over her desk.

She was scared and she didn't know how to hide it from Molly Sue. The more she tried to not think about it, the more she did. She felt so guilty. Was there still blood all over the jetty? What if Kyle told the police?

Molly Sue snapped at her. 'You're not still gripin' about last night, are ya? Didn't you get what ya wanted? I put the dog down.'

'Please, just stop,' Sally said aloud, confident her parents couldn't hear. 'For God's sake, leave me alone.'

Feeling too hot and like her skin was on too tight, Sally pushed herself away from the desk, crossed to the window and pulled it open. The night air did nothing to take the edge off her queasiness. There was a whole town, a whole world outside the window, but wherever she ran, Molly Sue would be on her back. Literally.

Leaning on the windowsill, sudden movement from Stan's house drew her gaze. Through his window, she caught a glimpse of naked flesh and recoiled back into her room. *Why is he walking around in the buff?* Not wanting to see her friend in all his glory, but oddly unable to resist, she peeked out again. This time she saw that he wasn't naked, thank God, just walking around shirtless. He had headphones on and was dancing around his room. Safe to say he wasn't a natural dancer – he looked a lot like he was having a seizure. Sally suppressed a giggle. He'd die if he knew she could see him.

'Wow,' Molly Sue purred. 'Check out the six on your boy.'

Sally squinted to get a better look. Stan was looking surprisingly good. Under all those baggy T-shirts, his body had totally changed: the puppy fat was gone and his chest was round and firm. Molly Sue was right; his abs were amazing. He had those hot muscular line things running over his hips. Boy lines? When had that happened?

'Someone has been doing his crunches,' Molly Sue went on. 'Maybe you should call him up for one of your little sleepovers.'

Sally got up and drew her curtains across the window. She covered her ears with her hands. 'Stop it! That's disgusting!'

'What? He's hotter than all get out!'

Sally ignored her and went to the bathroom. She twisted the taps on full power, water gushing into the sink.

Molly Sue wouldn't stop. 'Oh, baby girl! You gotta lighten up, honey! He's a cutie pie and he thinks you're swell!'

Sally plunged her face into the icy water and it felt like a slap she badly needed. Bubbles rippled against her cheek. She closed her eyes and held her breath, blocking out the voice in her head. Maybe she should just hold herself under, make the noise go away. She remained underwater until her lungs were ready to burst. Gasping for air, she pulled her head back and reached for a towel. 'Just stop,' Sally said. 'I've had enough.'

'Fighting talk,' Molly Sue said. 'You know, now that we're friends, you don't wanna go pissin' me off, darlin'.' There was steel under the sugar coating of Molly Sue's voice.

Sally swallowed the painful lump at the back of her throat. She believed every word.

Chapter Nineteen

On Tuesdays, Sally had a free period first session while Jennie and Stan were in sociology. She hadn't been allowed to take that option because her dad didn't think it was a proper subject. Students were *supposed* to register as normal, but only two or three of the strictest teachers applied that rule – you just signed in at the office when you arrived.

Sally waited in bed until she heard her mother shut the front door. On a Tuesday, her mother helped out at the church coffee morning and wouldn't be back until almost lunchtime. Hopping out of bed, Sally threw on whatever clothes were nearest and hurried downstairs to her father's study.

Being a bank manager, Sally's father didn't believe in credit cards, but they did have one they used to book holidays so they'd be protected if the holiday company went bust. Her dad assured her that this was good practice. This sole credit card was kept in the same drawer as her own forbidden bank card. For whatever reason, the PIN number – 0711 – had stuck in her head as the time she dragged herself out of bed on a school day.

The time had come. She'd spent all night thinking this

through – she just hoped that Molly Sue had caved to sleep before she had. She slipped the gold card into her pocket.

She got the bus into town – not Saxton Vale, the big town centre. It was a thirty-minute bus ride, but there was nowhere local that could help her. Every minute she sat on the bus she grew more anxious. Molly Sue was uncharacteristically silent. Was she sleeping or merely waiting?

Sally was starting to wonder if there was a bunker in her mind where Molly Sue didn't have access to her thoughts – somewhere behind all the noise in her head there was a locked door. Perhaps some thoughts were remaining private. If Molly Sue could see what she was thinking now, there'd be hell to pay.

The bus rolled through the twee, touristy part of town before heading past the billowing chimneys of the warehouses and factories until it finally reached the drab, entry-level purgatory that was the bus depot. It was a haven for street drinkers, directionless foreign students and angry pram women from what Sally could tell.

Using maps on her phone, she found her way into the town centre and to the right place – a modern-looking building called The Laser Centre. In the window, a picture depicted a blonde woman lovingly stroking her blemish-free skin next to the words *LASER TATTOO REMOVAL, TEETH WHITENING, HAIR REMOVAL*. By the looks of it, she'd had all three.

It didn't matter how much it was going to cost any more. There was a slim possibility her dad didn't even check the card's balance, they used it so rarely. It was pretty crystal now: Molly Sue was capable of doing terrible things. It was a wonder Kyle had survived. However skanky he was, Molly Sue had left him for dead. Sally couldn't control what was happening to her body and it scared her all the way to the bone. So, she had to go. Taking a deep breath, she entered the clinic.

A receptionist in a futuristic, white smock-dress greeted her. 'Good morning, how can we help you?'

Sally drew herself tall, trying to look older than she was. 'Hi, there. I need to speak to someone about getting a tattoo removed . . .'

One second she was looking at the receptionist, and the next she was looking down at a car park. From a great, great height.

Sally yelped as her legs wobbled and she teetered over the edge. Dizzy, her knees gave way. She was standing on a narrow concrete ledge. All Sally could do was grip it and hold on for dear life. Now on her knees, she was more stable, but she fought the urge to vomit. Vertigo messed with her eyes, the ground seemed to whoosh up at her.

Oh God! How? She dug her nails into the ledge, whimpering uselessly. It was so windy at this height. One strong gust and she'd be blown off the ledge.

The fall would kill her. She'd be splattered on the tarmac.

To her left was a shorter drop. Sally took in her surroundings. She was on top of a building or something. No wait . . . she recognised this. It was the car park – the big multi-storey car park in the city. Her dad parked in here if they ever came shopping.

Sally rolled to her left and flopped about a metre onto the concrete. She lay there amongst leaves and cigarette butts for a moment, relishing the sensation of solid ground underneath her body. She hugged herself tight. *What the hell is going on?* She'd been in the clinic one second . . .

'You dirty little rat,' Molly Sue said, her voice grave. 'That was a real low stunt to pull, Sally Jane Feather.'

Sally screwed her eyes shut to hold back tears. Wind howled across the exposed top storey. There were only a couple of cars parked up here. She searched for someone, anyone, to help her, but she was all alone. 'I'm sorry,' she breathed.

'*Sorry?*' Molly Sue barked, her voice gravel. 'You're coming at me with *sorry*? Don't think *sorry*'s gonna cut it, sugar.'

Sally rolled onto her back and looked up at some stern, steely clouds. They seemed to echo Molly Sue's mood. 'What else can I say?' Sally said.

'You were gonna blast me off your goddamn ass!'

'I'm sorry!' Sally shouted, her voice rattling around the empty car park.

'I'll give you sorry, you little bitch. You really think that was gonna work? That I'd let ya go through with it? You're *weak*, Sally Feather. You couldn't stop me if you tried.'

Sally realised that Molly Sue must have seized control of her whole body the second she'd stepped into the clinic. The journey from the clinic to the car park was another black void in her memory, just like the trip to the island had been. Sally sat upright, her back against the wall. She still didn't feel altogether whole.

'Let's get this straight. If you ever pull a stunt like that again, you'll live to regret it. Girl, I will cut me some willow, so help me God.'

Sally didn't know what that meant, but it didn't need clarifying. But then a new thought occurred to her. Molly Sue could hurt her all she wanted but she couldn't *kill* her. She'd said it herself – *where you go, I go*. 'You can't hurt me. You'd kill yourself.'

'Nice try, small fry. There's some twenty fingers and toes you'd miss.'

'You wouldn't.'

'Don't test me, girl.'

Fingers and toes. Sally imagined taking her mum's secateurs from the garden shed and snipping above her knuckles . . . she shuddered. An image drifted into her mind. Amputation . . . arms and legs . . . this all felt very familiar.

The homeless guy who'd been killed outside school staggered back into her memory for the first time in weeks. His manic, rolling eyes. *It's . . . it's inside me. Get it out. GET IT OUT.* Get what out? Get *who* out? There was no way . . . both hands *removed* so he couldn't hurt himself. Or where she'd punished him. *Oh, God, no.*

'Well done, darlin'. You figured it out.'

'It was you. It was you that night.' The eyes . . . those feral eyes.

'Sure was.'

Sally hugged her knees to her chest. 'How? How did you do it?'

'Ah, that'd be telling. Like I told ya . . . I'm a wanderer. I been around a long time, darlin'. Gonna take more than a car to stop me.'

Sally rose to her feet and looked out over the concrete sky merging with the concrete buildings of the city. Cars so small they were like shiny beetles far below. 'What about a fall?' Sally lifted herself back onto the ledge. She knelt, too scared to stand.

'Girl, get your ass down.'

'No. You need me, Molly Sue.'

'Ha! I don't need no one.'

'Where will you go? There's no one around.' She'd been the closest. When the tramp got hit, she'd been the nearest – and the one he'd fixed in his gaze. God, that was it. The other homeless guy had steered her deliberately towards the House of Skin but Molly Sue had already infected her – planted enough of a seed to make her think a tattoo was a good idea. *I've figured you out . . .*

She had to act quickly in case Molly Sue grabbed for control again. Sally rose to her feet. The wind was stronger than ever. It could so easily carry her over the edge. She wondered how long it'd take to hit the tarmac. Not long at all. She doubted she'd even feel it. It'd all be over: Molly Sue would be finished. Whatever she was, she'd been gone for good.

'Go on then,' Molly Sue taunted. 'Do it.'

Sally inched her toe over the edge. Her hair blew about her face, blinding her.

'Girl, we both know you don't got the stuff. What yo poor mama and papa gonna do? Go to church and talk about their little girl who committed suicide? What about Stan and Jennie?'

A little voice in her head questioned if her parents might even feel unburdened if she were to die. As for Stan and Jennie . . . well they'd have each other. 'They'll be fine.' Sally balled her hands into fists, geeing herself up to take the final step. *It'll be just like flying . . .*

'No, they won't and you know it. Let's paint us a picture. Without you, Stan fails all his exams, can't get into college, ends up working at a deli in town for ten years or so before he gets himself a nice little problem with liquor. Grief can really mess people up.'

Sally screwed her eyes tight. 'Stop it.'

'With you gone, Jennie gets back together with that there Kyle. Back to business as usual. He beats her and he rapes her . . .'

'I said stop it!' Sally screamed and stepped down off the ledge. Molly Sue was right. She couldn't risk hurting them – even if it meant Molly Sue hurting others.

'See what I mean?' Her voice was even, matter-of-fact. 'You are so weak, you can't even kill yourself right. Now, listen up, girly . . . we ain't gonna have this conversation again.'

Sally nodded. She had nowhere to go.

The inside stairwell of the multi-storey car park smelled so powerfully of urine, it burned Sally's nostrils. It didn't matter. At that moment, nothing mattered much. Sally felt like she was turning to cement, each heavy footstep towards the elevator was exhausting. At least Molly Sue had shut up.

You are so weak, you can't even kill yourself right.

Sally sensed she wasn't alone. Was that footsteps? She looked around and saw a figure duck around the corner at the furthest end of the fourth level. She only got a glimpse, but it was enough to recognise the kilt and wimple. It was

Sister Bernadette. 'Sister Bernadette!' Sally called without thinking. 'Wait!'

There were staircases at both ends of the car park. Sally darted across the fourth level, past the few cars that were parked and reached the left stairwell. She pushed through the doors and hurried past the Pay And Display booth. 'Sister Bernadette! It's me, Sally!'

This staircase was no less pungent than the other. Below her, Sally heard footfalls slap down the stone steps. Looking down the central shaft, Sally saw the top of her head spiral down the stairs. The nun, evidently, was in a hurry. Hadn't she seen her? Or didn't she want to be seen watching her? Sally chased after her, taking the steps two at a time. She almost fell, tripping over her feet, and had to grab the rail for support. 'Please wait!' she repeated.

As she reached the ground floor, Sally saw the main exit closing. The sister couldn't be far ahead. Sure enough, once Sally was outside, she saw Bernadette walking briskly across a dreary courtyard of cracked paving slabs and pebbledash bollards. Sally tore across the yard and grabbed her shoulder. Sister Bernadette gave her a shy glance, almost embarrassed. 'Oh, Sally . . . I didn't realise that was you. I thought it was . . . well I didn't know who it was.'

Sally didn't buy that – she must have heard. 'I called your name. What . . . what are you doing here? Are you following me?'

Sister Bernadette looked around the concourse. They were alone. Except, of course, they weren't. 'Very well, I lied. Something for confession later. I saw someone standing on the edge of the car park and I was compelled to help.' Well that was quite the coincidence. Sally went to call her on it, but the nun spoke again. 'What were you doing up on that ledge, Sally?'

Now it was Sally's turn to be embarrassed. 'Oh, nothing. I . . . I just like the view from up there.' Sally looked at her feet shiftily. Only a total imbecile would buy that.

'Ah that makes sense,' she said with that familiar kindness in her eyes. 'See, I thought there was someone up there about to make a terrible mistake, but I was wrong.'

'Oh I wouldn't ever . . . '

'I know, Sally. You're too strong for all that.'

Molly Sue wouldn't agree, Sally thought to herself.

Sister Bernadette gave her hand a squeeze. 'I have to go, but we shall meet again – when the time comes.'

'What?' Sally blinked, not sure she'd heard correctly. 'I don't understand!'

'You will. Remember, Sally, do no harm: not to others and not to yourself.' And then she leaned in and whispered in her ear. 'There's a place where she can't hear you.'

Sally snapped her hands back. 'What did you just say?'

Sister Bernadette tucked Sally's hair behind her ear and stepped into the road, darting to the other side. Sally took off after her, but a horn wailed and she leapt back in time to feel the whoosh of a Royal Mail van miss her by about a centimetre. Woah that was close. A bus followed the van and once Sally got over the road, Sister Bernadette was gone, lost in a crowd of school kids, charity workers and old ladies with shopping carts.

Chapter Twenty

Over the coming days, the weather broke. The humidity built and built like a fever. At night, Sally cast off her nightdress, laying naked on top of her sticky sheets, burning up and unable to sleep a wink. On the fifth day, like a water balloon, the sky burst into a downpour, accompanied with rumbles of thunder and sheets of lightning. Murky brown streams gushed along the gutters, the drains clogged and overflowing. The corridors and common rooms of Saxton Vale High became packed with ripe bodies rubbing portholes in steamed-up windows.

Neither Sally nor Molly Sue spoke about the rooftop incident again. Sally behaved herself, not even *thinking* about tattoo removal and so Molly Sue left her alone. If anything, she was quieter than she'd ever been, allowing Sally to carry on with her life. It felt like they'd reached a truce, albeit an uneasy one. In her skull, the *presence* remained; the pea under the mattress, the pebble in her shoe.

If Molly Sue knew what Sister Bernadette had said, she didn't let on. What did the nun mean? Was there a *physical place* where Sally could have privacy, the church perhaps, or did she mean *somewhere inside*? The encounter had added another level of

Dali-like weirdness. It wasn't a coincidence, Sally was sure of it. Bernadette had followed her to the car park, but why?

The whole thing was starting to piss her off – an evil tattoo and an enigmatic nun. Bernadette had said there was no such thing as black and white, but it was looking pretty clear cut: good and bad. *Are these my options?* Sally thought, *sexy bad gal or chaste sister? Virgin or vamp? How is that fair?*

There was plenty to keep Sally busy and it was impossible to stress about Molly Sue twenty-four hours a day. As opening night crept ever closer, rehearsals for *Little Shop* intensified – they now had after-school sessions on Tuesdays and Wednesdays *and* singing workshops on a Wednesday lunchtime. Sally found herself immersed in Chiffon and the world of Skid Row.

Stan had taken on Audrey II, or rather the model of him, as a project and was working with Mr Peterson, the art teacher, to construct the giant plant. There were to be four versions of it: two baby ones (which would be glove puppets operated through a hole in a table), an intermediate one and then the giant one for the second act which had to be big enough for the cast to crawl through when they got eaten.

Sally was pleased to find they were doing the original version, in which pretty much the whole cast dies, not the schmaltzy movie version which had a happy ending. It felt more honest somehow.

Two good things happened at rehearsal the week after the car park incident. Mr Roberts gave her the opening lines of 'Skid Row' to sing as a solo. It was a really beautiful section and she got to make big, sad eyes and really emote. Although wary of the spotlight, Sally agreed.

'You could do this in your sleep.' Molly Sue spoke for the first time in a couple of days. 'The notes aren't even that tough.'

As Sally sang the part, she saw Stan watching her, covered in enough paint to resemble the Jolly Green Giant. He grinned and gave her a somewhat lame thumbs up. Song over, she smiled back, allowing herself a minor victory.

Secondly, Mr Roberts was pleasingly tough on Melody, who wasn't exactly nailing Audrey. The thing with Audrey, Sally felt, was that she's a tragic figure (she is, after all, in an abusive relationship with a 'semi-sadist') and Melody was playing her like . . . well, a bit like Molly Sue. Too strong, too sexy. What's more, Sally was starting to think she had the edge when it came to singing; Melody's top line was reedy at best. Her American accent also sucked.

Sally was surprised how much she was enjoying the production. Keira had a major crush on Duncan Curtis, who was playing the dentist and Sally was enjoying being her wingman.

'Are you coming to the Year Twelve dance?' Keira asked, her arms in the air as her bust was measured by Mrs Greene, the textiles teacher. They were being fitted for their fantasy gowns, the costume they wore for most of the production.

Sally wondered if she was hearing things – again. It sounded a lot like Keira Stevens had just invited her to a party. 'Erm . . . no, I don't think so.'

'Aw, why not? It'll be fun. Everyone's going.'

Sally squirmed. 'It's just not really my thing,' she said before adding, 'And no one's asked me, anyway.'

Keira laughed. 'Jesus, Sally, this isn't 1950! Just come with us girls.'

'Aren't you going with Duncan?'

'He hasn't picked up on the first six hundred hints, but fingers crossed. Anyway, you could take your pick. I know Lucas Greer thinks you're hot.'

Sally rolled her eyes. 'Well, I'm female and have a pulse, so that's not a surprise.'

Even Mrs Greene stifled a chuckle at that as she measured Keira's hips. 'What's the story with you and Randall?' Keira checked to make sure no one was listening. 'Haven't you been together since you were three?'

'No! We're just friends!'

'That's a shame. You know, we were just saying the other day that Stan is like the third hottest guy in the year.'

'What? *Stan Randall?*'

'Totally! He's super hench! Puberty massively agreed with him. If Duncan takes someone else to the dance, I was thinking of asking him . . . if it's OK with you?'

Sally was speechless. *Stan and Keira? No way!* For some reason even the concept made her uneasy. He *hated* her. *Stan and Keira?* Sally shook her head. 'Well . . . erm . . . Stan's not my boyfriend . . . it's just not like that.'

'Mayor of the Friend Zone?'

Sally shrugged, feeling clammy-palmed all of a sudden. 'I guess.'

Keira grinned. 'You have a crush on someone else! I can tell! Who is it?'

'I don't!'

'You do, you're blushing!'

'I am not!' *You definitely are.*

'Oh, come on, you can tell me! Unless it's Duncan, in which case I'll have to nut you.' At that moment, because the universe is cruel, Todd entered at the back of the hall, no doubt coming to collect Melody after football practice. He was still in his short shorts and Sally couldn't help but stare. 'Oh my God!' Keira gasped. 'Is it Todd?'

'No!'

'Duh! Of course it is; I saw you dancing with him at the gig.' Sally's heart plummeted. 'Did you tell Melody?'

A wry smile. 'If I had, do you think you'd still be breathing?'

'Good point.' Sally smiled her a thank you.

Mrs Greene stood up, her knees creaking. 'OK, Sally it's your turn.' She moved over to her and Sally lifted her arms obligingly.

Keira leaned in conspiratorially. 'You wanna know a secret?'

'What?'

'Todd told Lucas that he's going to break up with Melody.'

Sally almost knocked Mrs Greene out with her elbow. 'What?'

'I thought you might like that. I thought it was just Lucas stirring, but maybe not. What did you say to him last week?'

Sally shrugged. 'I told him if he didn't have the balls to dump Melody I wasn't interested in him . . .' Well, it was *sort of* true.

'You didn't!' Keira looked like a scandalised Victorian maid. Sally nodded. 'Oh my God, that's hilarious! It must have worked.'

Sally looked over to where Todd was waiting. Melody was ignoring him, trying to engage a frazzled Mr Roberts in a conversation about her performance. Maybe it was true . . . Todd must be sick to death of Melody, but Sally couldn't believe he'd taken their conversation at the gig seriously. Well, taken Molly Sue seriously.

He looked over and caught her eye. With a subtle nod he gave her a half-smile that was almost more than she could stand. She fixed her eyes on her feet but every square inch of her skin felt like it was glowing.

Sally and Stan took it in turns to babysit Jennie. She wasn't sobbing and wailing any more, but she couldn't tolerate a moment by herself, as if she couldn't stand to be alone with her own mopey thoughts. On the Saturday night, they all got together at Stan's and did a recap of all the season four episodes of *Satanville* so far. For some annoying reason, new episodes were 'on hiatus' for three weeks before the last three finale episodes. Why did American shows always do that? It was SO frustrating.

'They've confirmed season five, right?' Jennie said. 'So there's no way they can kill Dante?'

It was good to see her chatty and engaged again. Sally was beginning to worry she'd permanently damaged her friend.

'I don't know,' said Stan. 'They haven't confirmed who's coming back.' Rumours circled the forums that one of the major characters was to be killed off in the finale.

'They can't kill Dante,' Sally agreed. 'If any of them dies, it'll be Angela.'

Stan's face sank. 'No way! I'm never watching it again if they kill Angela!'

'You liar!' Jennie laughed.

It was weird. Now that Sally had seen Stan without his shirt, she couldn't see him in the same way any more; she found herself trying to sneak peeks at his abs. It was freaking her out, but she couldn't stop herself. He wasn't *safe* any more – as stupid as that sounded. This was all Molly Sue's fault; she'd made her see him differently – he was a man with a manly body and man bits. She couldn't help but compare him to Todd; Stan was bigger and broader than Todd, although Todd was more athletic.

She wished she'd never seen him. Now things were messed up.

'Thanks for entertaining me, you guys,' Jennie said. 'I know I'm being a nightmare.'

'No way! You're not!' Sally snapped out of her boy trance.

'I'm feeling a lot better now,' Jennie said, *almost* convincingly. 'I can do better than Kyle.'

'Oh, God, you can do a hundred times better! That guy is a wang.' Stan said, possibly too enthusiastically. Sally shot him a look. No good could come from telling Jennie what they really thought about Kyle . . . they might still wind up back together – despite Molly Sue's warning.

Jennie wrapped a liquorice lace around her finger. 'Well, right now I agree. I hope he gets herpes and dies.'

'I don't think you die from herpes,' Sally said. 'But he has it coming.'

'Being single isn't too bad. I just have all this time on my hands. It's weird.'

'More time to hang out with us,' Stan said. 'And you can help me build this bloody plant.'

'Sure!'

'And all's well that ends well,' Molly Sue chipped in. 'Told ya so.'

Sally just ignored her.

The next day started very well indeed. Sally woke up to a Facebook friend request from Todd. Her eyes were so fuzzy when she checked her phone that she had to do a double take to check she wasn't dreaming it. But sure enough there was a little red flag. She added him at once, only to then wonder if that seemed a bit desperate. She sat up in bed and thought about Melody. She'd be able to see all this so Todd was either very brave or very stupid.

There was a knock on her door. 'Sally, dear.' It was her mother. 'Are you ready? We have to leave for church in fifteen minutes.'

'I'm not going,' she groaned.

Her mother entered her room. 'Why not? Are you feeling ill?'

Sally pulled the duvet over her head. 'No. I just don't want to go, Mum.'

'Well, you're coming and that's that.'

'I'm not.' Sally pushed the covers back and looked her in the eye. Her mum gawped at her like she was waiting for the punchline. 'I'm not. There's no one else my age there and I feel stupid.'

'Oh, I've never heard such nonsense.'

'I'm not going.'

'You are.'

Sally didn't know why today was the day she decided to fight back, but she wasn't going to cave in. 'I don't see how you can make me. What are you going to do? Drag me into church? That'll look great.'

Her mum looked so wounded, Sally wondered if she'd gone too far. 'What will your dad say?'

'I don't care. Just go without me. I'm seventeen years old; I can stay here by myself. I'm not a baby.'

'Sally . . . I thought you liked coming to church.'

'Well, I don't. You've never asked what I thought, Mum. I don't even believe in God. I think it's all a load of brainwashing.'

Her mother was speechless for a second, like she'd been slapped around the face. 'Sally Feather, that is a despicable thing to say and I know you don't mean it.'

She shrugged. 'I do.'

Her mother's bottom lip trembled. 'What has got into you?'

That hit Sally just as hard because she had a very specific answer to that question, but with no comeback, she just rolled away from her mother to face the window.

'Where has my Sally gone?' Sally felt her mother smooth back her hair, but ignored the gesture.

Sally waited until she heard the car pull out of the driveway before daring to surface for her breakfast. She padded around the house barefoot, feeling triumphant – but with a side order of guilt.

'You sure told her,' Molly Sue said.

I don't need your opinion. Stay out of it.

'Girl, you're gettin' a little feisty. I like to think that's me rubbin' off on ya.'

Sally didn't like to admit that Molly Sue was probably right. She made a cup of tea and chopped a grapefruit in half before returning to her bedroom. Sitting at her desk, she flipped open her laptop to properly stalk Todd's Facebook page. She'd only flicked through the first few pictures, all of which were contaminated with Melody's face, when a message box popped up.

TODD: HEY!

Sally squirted grapefruit juice over the keyboard. 'Crap!' She quickly mopped it up with her sleeve. What was she meant to say?

'Start with "Hi",' Molly Sue said dryly. 'I hear it's a classic.'

Thank you, I don't need your help. She typed, HEY, THANKS FOR ADDING ME.

She didn't have to wait long for a reply. NO WORRIES. WHAT U DOING?

SALLY: EATING GRAPEFRUIT.

'Wow. Sexy stuff,' Molly Sue put in unhelpfully.

TODD: GROSS. YOU NEED A BACON SANDWICH LOL.

She wasn't sure what to say to that.

SALLY: WE DON'T HAVE ANY ☹

There was a pause.

188

TODD: Are u home? I'm bringing u a bacon sandwich!

Sally almost fell off her chair. 'What?'

SALLY: Don't be daft!

TODD: Too late! I'm on my way!

'Oh my God! What do I do?'

Molly Sue was silent.

'Molly Sue! Todd is coming HERE!'

'Oh, *now* she wants my help,' Molly Sue said, floating down her exposed arm and coming to a rest. She had her hands behind her head and kicked her feet as if she was floating on her back in a Hollywood pool.

'Please don't give me a hard time, just tell me what to do. He can't come here!'

'Well, for starters get your ass dressed. He don't need to see you in this.' She motioned at her frilly nightdress.

'What should I wear? I haven't got anything.'

'OK, baby girl, take a big breath. S'all gonna be fine. Wear that skirt you hate. The flowery one.'

'It's grotesque! I can't wear that!'

'Sure you can. Wear that and the big black T-shirt you sleep in sometimes.'

'Are you actually kidding?'

'Just do it, for cryin' out loud.'

Sally did as she was told, and somehow her tattoo was right yet again. The huge, slouchy T-shirt took the prissiness out of the floral skirt. She rolled the sleeves of the T-shirt up, the way Angela sometimes did on *Satanville*. Molly Sue told her how to do her hair and she just had time to apply some eye-liner when she heard a horn toot outside. She looked out of the window and saw a car waiting at the end of the drive. He'd driven here. That was a) kinda cool and b) gave her a getaway vehicle.

She hurried out to greet him as he was climbing out of the car. It was a shiny silver hatchback – his mother's, she guessed. 'Morning!' he said. 'I really did bring you a sarnie.'

'Can we go somewhere?' Sally asked, her nervous voice girlishly high-pitched.

'Sure, why?'

'If my parents came back and found you in the house . . . well, they'd burn me at the stake.'

Todd snorted and she was pleased with her little joke.

'Good,' Molly Sue whispered. 'Keep it up. I'll help if you can't think of stuff to say.'

Sally got into his car, which smelled strongly of bacon. 'I can't believe you made me a sandwich! Thank you!'

'I even brought a choice of red or brown sauce. Now, where are we going?'

'Anywhere. Somewhere Melody won't see us.'

'Good point.' He reversed the car out of the drive, craning to look over his shoulder. 'Although on a Sunday she religiously visits her grandmother – she gets a twenty pound note just for turning up.'

That put Sally's mind somewhat at ease although this still felt very, very risky. They drove up into the hills towards the lake, Todd all the time talking about the politics of the football team. Sally had no idea boys could be so bitchy. 'Granger plays like a total gimp but he brown-noses Mr Hussain so much he never gets put on the bench. It drives me mental. I swear he's got one leg longer than the other or something.'

She didn't care about football in the slightest but it was giving her precious time to adjust to the impossibility of the situation. In many ways, this was less probable than the enchanted tattoo. She was in TODD BRADY'S CAR. She had fantasised about this, but never for a second dreamed it might one day come true. And yet, here she was. In the fantasy version, it had all had that same Vaseline-lens gloss as her American TV shows. In reality, it was surprisingly normal. She was in his car, picking at a bacon sandwich.

She was nervous as hell.

They parked up in a layby on the furthest side of the lake – the quieter side without the restaurant or The Old Boat Shed. A maze of oaks and firs blocked out the light, smothering the winding lane in an emerald haze. It felt private out here, sealed-in even, but it was only a short walk through the woods to the lakeside. Here, there were lots of little coves for them to choose from.

'I sometimes come up here with Jennie,' Sally said as they tramped through the undergrowth. Many feet over many years had worn dirt paths down to the water's edge. 'We bring a picnic and just read for a whole day.' She regretted that at once. It made her sound so nerdy.

'Sounds good,' Todd said and she breathed a sigh of relief. 'I can't remember the last time I just read a book. I've always got so much to do.'

Sally didn't need to tell him that she didn't really have a life to speak of. They emerged into the little cove. Sally knew this one well. 'This is it.'

'Oh, wow.' Todd admired the view. 'You can see The Old Boat Shed from here. It looks so far away.'

'I always forget how huge the lake is. You can't even see it all from here.' It could be easily an ocean if it weren't so utterly still. Sally sat down on a familiar boulder jutting out of the landscape, already absorbing the tranquillity of the lake. After all the storms, the beach itself was too damp to sit on. With no other choices, Todd sat behind her, a little higher up the rock.

'It's so peaceful. I can see why you come here.'

Sally was struggling for something to say. 'It's deep too. Deeper than you think. That's why they tell you not to swim in it. It gets deep so fast that the temperature in the middle of the lake is loads colder than at the edge. If you swim out too far, your muscles cramp with cold and you drown.'

Todd chuckled. 'Wow. Morbid.'

'Jesus, girl!' Molly Sue scolded in her ear. 'Did you bring him out here to kill him? Lighten up on the drownin' talk.'

'Sorry! I'm full of fun facts,' Sally said. 'I bet Melody doesn't talk about drowning.'

Todd slid down to join her on her level. 'No.' He paused for a moment. 'Melody mainly talks about Melody. Look . . . what you said the other night . . .'

Sally flustered, covering her face with her hands. 'God, I know. I'm so embarrassed. I shouldn't have said anything. It's really none of my business.'

'No, no, I'm glad you did. You were right.' He looked out over the lake, his eyes the same colour as the water – steely blue. 'The reason I'm with Melody is because I'm scared of what she'll do if I break up with her. How freaking sad is that? It's just . . . easier. Well, I've had enough. I'm so tired of people thinking I'm her pet, like one of those frouffy little dogs in a handbag.'

'Why did you go out with her in the first place?'

He looked to his feet. 'I didn't have a lot of say in the matter. You know what Melody's like; I was steamrolled into it.' He paused again, considering his words. 'In a weird way she looks after me too. She makes it easy for me – she tells me what to do, what to think. All I have to do is turn up and smile.'

Sally wasn't sure whether to pity him. 'Is that enough for you?'

'No, it's not. Despite what you think, I do have balls. I just needed a reminder.'

Sally felt her cheeks blaze. 'Again, I'm sorry I said that.'

'No, it was the kick up the arse I needed. That night . . . when we danced . . . I felt something I hadn't felt in ages.' He then looked at her the way she had always dreamed he would. He looked *right* at her, his eyes meeting hers and continuing on into her soul.

There was a lump the size of an apple in Sally's throat. *It wasn't me who danced with him. It was* her. 'H . . . How did you feel?'

'Like I really, really wanted to kiss you.'

Sally froze as he leaned in towards her. When she didn't meet him in the middle, as she suspected she was supposed

193

to, he cupped her face in his hand and turned it towards his. She closed her eyes as his mouth met hers. Unable to breathe, she felt his warm, soft lips brush against her own.

I am kissing Todd Brady.

She did it the way she'd seen on TV, and it seemed to work, thank God. It felt *amazing*. He was so warm and so close and his skin on her skin felt so good.

But it was wrong. *Stupid morality.* She pulled back. 'You have a girlfriend,' she said sadly.

Todd looked guiltily at the lake. 'I know. But not for long. I'm ending it with Mels. I am.'

Sally nodded, saying nothing. It was too scary to verbalise. He was going to dump Melody and then what? They'd be an item? It was all she'd thought about for years but now that it was sitting right in front of her it was a terrifying thought. Her whole life would be tipped upside-down and everything would change. The idea alone made her head spin. No one likes change . . .

She did want to do more kissing, though. That had been good. Todd was looking at her. 'What?' she said.

'You. How you were the other night and how you are now. You're like two totally different people.'

You have no idea. Sally couldn't meet his gaze. 'I . . . I was just a bit drunk.'

'I like it. You've got a dark side.'

Yeah, and she's called Molly Sue. 'Doesn't everyone?' Sally said, hoping to end the conversation.

'I guess.'

He was only ever interested in you, Sally told Molly Sue. *He doesn't want me at all.*

194

Molly Sue tutted. 'Girl, we don't know that. He just kissed you, didn't he?'

Foreboding black clouds were gathering over the hills. A storm was brewing. Sally turned to Todd. 'I should really get home before my parents finish church. They'll be worried if I'm gone.'

Todd nodded although looked disappointed. 'Sure. Can we do this again, though?'

Joy or panic, she wasn't sure which, turned her tummy. 'Yeah. I'd really like that.' It was sort of like a horror film – scary, but she wanted to put herself through it.

Todd stepped down from the boulder and offered her a hand, which she took. They held hands all the way back through the woods.

Chapter Twenty-One

Sally knew there was something wrong as soon as she got to school on Monday. People were talking about her and she was sure it wasn't paranoia. To be more specific, people *weren't* talking to her. As soon as she entered a building or corridor, people stopped talking altogether – a sure sign gossip was afoot. 'What's going on?' she said as much to herself as to Jennie and Stan as they walked together into the sixth-form wing.

'I dunno,' Jennie replied. 'Everyone's still talking about your makeover. You do look awesome today.'

Molly Sue had suggested cutting some of her old jeans into shorts. It did look kinda cool. 'Thanks,' Sally said, but wasn't convinced. People were staring at her. Maybe it was in her head, but she swore some onlookers were stifling giggles behind their hands. *I think I preferred being invisible.*

'What?' Stan snapped at the crowd of Year Thirteen girls gathered by the noticeboard. They just looked at him and, this time, definitely giggled. 'God, I can't wait until we can leave this place for ever.'

'I second that.' Sally believed him – there were fat black Xs counting down the days on his *Satanville* calendar. May was a pretty good month: Taryn and Dante standing in a crypt, with Dante's shirt wide open.

All through registration, Sally still couldn't shake the creeping feeling that there were eyes on her back. She definitely caught one girl giving her a none too subtle side-eye. Register over, they trudged towards Monday morning, period one. 'Meet you outside the library at break-time?' Stan asked and she agreed. She walked to maths with her head down; without the others she didn't feel nearly as secure.

At least maths held the promise of Todd. She was excited and nervous to see him. It already felt like their trip to the lake had been a lovely weekend dream and this morning he'd deny it ever happened. As ridiculous as it sounded, the outing was also 'their little secret' and that made it special. She hadn't even told Jennie, and certainly not Stan. She didn't need Molly Sue's opinion to know that was a bad idea.

Todd was already in his seat when Sally arrived at her classroom. Unfortunately, Mr Pollock was already there too, so there was little she could do except give him a smile and brief greeting, which he readily returned. His whole face lit up when she walked in. A shampoo ad cliché, yes, but definitely a good sign. Inner smugness ensued.

Sally sat next to Dee as usual and pulled her things out of her bag. A movement outside caught her eye. At first she though she must be imagining it, but she squinted out of the window and saw it wasn't her mind playing tricks on her. At the furthest edge of the school grounds, beyond the railings, stood Sister Bernadette. Once again, she wore the same simple clothes and wimple.

Blossom rained down from the trees around her, barely pink petals twirling like confetti. The rise and fall was hypnotic and Sally was unable to look away.

Bernadette seemed to be watching her. Even from so far away, her serene gaze fell on Sally. The nun's hands were clasped in front of her chest, like prayer but stronger. Her lips looked to be moving but, of course, Sally couldn't hear what she was saying.

She *was* following her! Sally instinctively rose out of her chair, ready to go after her.

'Miss Feather? Are you going somewhere? Do you have plans?' Mr Pollock glared at her over his glasses as he took the register.

'Sorry, no . . . I . . . there was a wasp.' Sally turned back to the window as soon as she could discreetly do so. When she did, she saw that Sister Bernadette was gone.

We'll meet again – when the time comes.

After school there was an extra singing rehearsal for *Little Shop* – according to Mr Roberts, 'Skid Row' sounded like a bag of cats being swung against a wall. Sally's last lesson had run over, she was late, and to top it all, it had started raining during the last period. A fine drizzle clung to the air and Sally darted across the courtyard to get to the hall. She shook her umbrella off and took the stairs two at a time, not wanting to incur Mr Robert's wrath. She was sticky and out of breath by the time she slipped into the hall. Luckily they didn't look to have started yet. Once again, however, as Sally entered the room, there was a wave of twittering, the girls turning into bitchy sparrows and muttering to one another.

She didn't see Stan until he grabbed her by the elbow. 'Ow! Stan, what are you doing?'

He dragged her to one side. 'Is it true?'

'Is what true?'

The anger fell out of his eyes, but he was still wary of her. He lowered his voice and tried to appear casual. 'Everyone's saying that you've been sending pictures to guys on the football team.'

'What?' Sally's mouth fell open.

'You know . . . like nudey pictures.'

Sally honestly didn't know whether to laugh or cry. 'Stan! Of course it's not true! Hello!'

Stan softened. 'OK. That's what I said but no one believed me.'

'Is that why everyone's been staring at me all day? Who's saying that?'

'I dunno. I heard it from Annabel Sumpter.'

Figured. 'Well, who told her?'

'I have no idea.'

Sally looked over her shoulder to see Melody and Eleanor giggling to one another. 'I think I have an idea.' Sally quickly located Keira, who was trying to cram in her homework before rehearsal started. 'Hey, Keira.'

'Oh, hey.' Keira looked very much like she didn't want to be seen talking to her. Unpopularity is like a virus – no one wants to get infected.

'Look, I know what people are saying about me and it's not true. Do I look like the sort of person who sends pictures like that?'

Keira pouted and eyed her denim shorts. 'Erm, a little bit, yeah.'

'Well, I'm not! Who's been saying that I have?'

'Sally, I've seen the pics. They're on Facebook.'

'What? Show me!'

Rolling her eyes, Keira opened her phone and handed it to her see. The photo was just of a pair of breasts with a suggestion of blonde hair. 'For God's sake! They're not mine. I wish they were; they're at least three cup sizes bigger!' Unsurprisingly, the original poster was Eleanor Ford and the caption read *Guess someone didn't tell Sally Feather pics can be screen-grabbed LOL*.

The clever little bitch. Sally didn't for a second believe Eleanor had distributed the pictures. Melody had ensured once again there was no paper trail back to her.

'Oh, that bitch needs to pay,' Molly Sue growled in her ear.

Keira examined the boobs and then examined Sally's. 'I see what you mean . . .'

'Get Eleanor to delete it. Please.'

Keira looked about halfway sympathetic. 'I'll try . . . but if this was a Mels thing, you know she won't. Trust me, it'll blow over like that time everyone saw my camel toe in PE. Hell, you might even be more popular with the football team . . .'

Sally said nothing but marched towards the stage to get ready. She didn't feel embarrassed any more; she felt Molly Sue's anger and doubled it.

'Good girl,' Molly Sue purred. 'But don't get mad . . . get even.'

Sally channelled her anger into her singing, the one power she had over Melody. Not content with nailing the opening lines of 'Skid Row', she made a swing at a death punch. 'Mr Roberts,' she said after they'd been through it a couple of times. 'Could

I have a go at the Audrey part?' She looked dead at Melody. 'You know, just in case?'

'Yeah, sure. That's not a bad idea, actually.' He called for the Seymour understudy to also fill in. Melody gave her a poisonous glare but it only spurred her on. Audrey had only a few solo lines in the song, but two very big notes.

Mr Roberts rearranged the song quickly, getting Keira to do the big opening line. When the time came, Sally *was* Audrey. She started off small, coy and shy – her voice cracking on purpose, building up to the big note, which she belted for all she was worth. As Seymour's solo took over, she saw Mr Roberts nod, clearly impressed. Melody could only sulk at Eleanor, although even her winged monkey couldn't deny it was impressive. *How do you like me now, bitch?* Sally thought.

'Someone needs to teach her a lesson,' Molly Sue said and Sally agreed.

It was a relatively short rehearsal and Mr Roberts dismissed them at about four fifteen. Sally made a beeline for Melody.

'Do you want me to take over?' Molly Sue offered with a sly breeziness.

No. Sally was sorely tempted, but didn't want to risk a repeat of last time. 'Hi, Melody, can I talk to you, please?'

With a swish of her hair, Melody turned to face her. 'No. I don't talk to sluts,' she said so quietly no one would hear her.

Sally felt oddly empowered. 'Cyberbullying could get you suspended, you know.'

Melody cocked her hip. 'Are *you* threatening *me*?'

'I just . . . want you to take those pictures down, OK? We both know they're not me. To be honest, it's pathetic. Some

201

boobs? Is that really the best you can do?' Sally wasn't scared of her any more. Suddenly her towering presence seemed little more than hairspray.

Eleanor hovered at the hall exit, waiting to leave. 'Melody, I need to run. My dad is outside.'

'Oh, just go, then!' Melody dismissed her. A steady stream left the hall until they were alone with only the cleaner. 'I don't know what you mean. I had nothing to do with those pictures. Maybe you should be more careful who you send your tits to. Not that you've got much to show off in the first place.'

Sally closed her eyes and mentally counted to three. She wouldn't sink to that level. 'Just take them down or I'll go to Mrs Flynn, I mean it.' Sally headed for the door, trying Molly Sue's confident strut on for size. It probably didn't come off.

As she reached the corridor, Melody grabbed her arm. Looking around, Sally saw they were now all alone. All the students had long since gone home and God knew where all the teachers were. Her throat tightened. If Melody tried to fight her, she didn't stand a chance.

'Just let me take over,' Molly Sue urged.

No!

Melody didn't let go of her arm. 'I'll take those pictures down if you leave my boyfriend alone.'

'What?'

Melody's face wasn't nearly as pretty when it was screwed up and full of spite. 'Oh, don't bloody play all innocent. I know what you did.'

Sally choked up further. 'I don't know what you mean.' She could hardly force the words out.

'Drop the act! I know you went off with Todd in his car yesterday.'

Sally pulled her arm free and hurried for the stairs. *How does she know?*

'Did he drive you somewhere quiet? Did you have a little backseat session?'

Sally whipped back around to face her. 'No! We just talked!'

'Oh, I bet you did.' Cool as ever, Melody slithered to join her at the top of the steps. 'I bet you *talked* all night.'

There was no comeback. She shouldn't have been in Todd's car and she certainly shouldn't have kissed him. 'Look. You need to talk to Todd about —'

'I'm not stupid. I know he's going to break up with me, but I'm not going to make it easy for him. If you think I'm gonna let him leave me for *you*, you're insane. I mean, how shameful would that be? Getting dumped for *you*?'

That stung. 'How did you find out?'

Melody smiled. 'That's the best part. Your next-door neighbour saw you . . .'

What? No way . . . 'Stan?'

'The poor boy. I think you broke his heart. God knows what he sees in you,' Melody sneered. Tears glazed Sally's vision. She couldn't believe Stan had sold her out. 'You know, good job on the makeover, but you're still a frigid little virgin with no tits. If you think you're stealing my boyfriend and my role, you're freaking mental.'

It was like a siren pealing in her head. Everything went blood red and then pitch black. It was just a split second, but it was enough.

Sally heard Melody gasp and felt her hand thrash out at thin air. A shoe squeaked on the wet floor before the terrible, moist crack when Melody hit the stairs. It was so fast. She clanged and bounced and ricocheted off the rails, tumbling head over heels. Melody unfurled at the bottom like a battered rag doll, her arms and legs bent all wrong.

Sally's hand flew to her mouth just in time to stop the vomit from spewing everywhere. She swallowed back a bitter mouthful. 'Oh my God, Molly Sue! What did you do?'

Melody lay very still at the foot of the stairs. Sally couldn't even tell if she was breathing.

'Baby girl, I didn't do nothin'. That one was all you.'

Chapter Twenty-Two

No! That was you! It was you! Everything went black!

''Fraid not, darlin'. I guess you done saw red. Anyways, is this an argument you wanna be havin' right now?'

Molly Sue was right. Sally was halfway down the stairs when Mr Roberts appeared at the bottom, apparently heading back to the hall. He dropped his pile of marking and kneeled at Melody's side. He looked to Sally. 'Jesus! What happened!'

'You better lie real good,' Molly Sue told her.

'She just slipped. The floor was wet . . . she must have slipped.'

He seemed to buy it. 'Did you call an ambulance?'

'No, it just happened like a second ago.'

Stan appeared in the fire exit door too. For an instant, Sally was reminded of his betrayal but, again, this wasn't the time. 'Stan, call an ambulance!'

On seeing Melody, he pulled out his phone, dialled and turned his back to them. Sally couldn't drag her gaze from Melody's twisted limbs. 'Is she . . . ?'

Mr Robert's tentatively felt for a pulse. 'I don't think so.' His face was an ashy grey colour. 'But I don't want to press too hard in case her neck is broken.'

Tears streamed down Sally's face. *What have I done? I pushed her down the stairs.* From outside, she could hear Stan giving instructions to the 999 operator. There were footsteps too, more teachers running to see what the commotion was. The world was tipping . . . *no, wait* . . . Sally felt her legs dissolve, her vision black out and she sank down against the wall.

The rest was a blur until her father got her home. There were snippets – brief snapshots of Melody being stretchered away, the paramedic checking Sally over for shock, Mrs Newell, the Head, trying to work out what had happened. In the end they'd called Sally's dad to come and get her, as it was quite clear they weren't going to get any sense out of her.

By the time she was home, she felt more like her feet were on solid ground. She excused herself and went straight to her room. She didn't want Stan looking over either, so she pulled the blinds down and put some music on to block the sound. Finally, Sally pulled her T-shirt off to see Molly Sue. The tattoo waited, coolly balanced on her hip.

'I know you pushed her,' Sally said. In the mirror, she saw how pale her own face was, her lips grey, corpse-like.

'Not guilty, sweetheart. I'm a-tellin' ya!'

'No! I . . . I don't remember pushing her! Everything went black, just like before.'

Molly Sue shrugged, holding her hand open. 'Then I guess you blacked out or whatever. You were pretty pissed-off, darlin'.'

'I didn't push —' She lowered her voice. 'I didn't push Melody down the stairs.'

Molly Sue stood and paced across Sally's stomach. 'Whether it was you or me don't make a difference. They got CCTV up in there that'll show one of us pushing her. Oh . . . no . . . wait . . . it'll just show *you* pushin' her.'

Her head spun. 'Oh my God! CCTV! I didn't even think of that.'

'That's why *I* wouldn't have pushed her down the stairs in full goddamn view of a camera.'

Sally tugged back her hair. 'What am I going to do?'

'You are so lucky you got me, darlin'. I'm gonna take care of it.'

'OK, what are *you* going to do?'

'I'm gonna save your sorry hide and you ain't gonna ask questions, got that? Let me take over again.'

Sally hated it. Hated the idea of Molly Sue taking control again, but she also couldn't see how things could possibly get any worse. If someone saw that . . . it'd be murder. If Melody died, it *was* murder. 'OK,' she said. 'Just do it.'

'We wait until midnight.'

This time Sally was more aware of Molly Sue's movements with her body. She wore androgynous, baggy clothes and a winter parka with a hood and took an insane route to school. They crossed through back gardens and across fields for an hour until Sally realised they were walking through the woods at the back of the football pitch. They'd avoided every CCTV camera in town.

Sally had no idea what the security was like at her school, but this was Saxton Vale, not London, so they weren't likely to have guards with ferocious Alsatians or anything. In fact, once they arrived on site, it was as still as a crypt. Like a shadow, Molly Sue stuck to the external walls of the school blocks, wary of the lamps on the pathways. She went from window to window looking for one that was open. Sure enough, after about sixty windows, she found one that hadn't been properly shut for the night. It took some effort, but she wrenched it open and slid inside like a snake.

There were no cameras in the classrooms, there was some legal reason about filming teachers, but they couldn't stay out of the corridors forever. Sally saw a burglar alarm above the door, blinking like a red eye. They'd been spotted and if she knew, Molly Sue knew too. Sally had no idea how the security worked, but some kids once set off a fire alarm and the brigade were there in minutes *automatically*. Molly Sue moved like a cat, darting through the corridors with the type of agility Sally would never have.

The offices were by the main entrance. All these weeks, Molly Sue must have been watching *everything*, taking it all in; she knew exactly where to go. She dived over the reception desk, dropped to the floor and pulled Sally's father's axe from her rucksack. It was a short, sturdy hatchet, the one they used for firewood. Putting it to good use, Molly Sue gained access to the admin offices and instantly located the cabinet housing the security unit. Inside, it was like a huge DVD player with a small flat-screen TV on top. Wasting no time, Molly Sue took the axe to the recorder, making light work of it. She couldn't hear an alarm but that didn't mean one wasn't going off somewhere. A security team, or even the police, were probably already on their way.

What if they already checked the CCTV tonight? Sally asked.

'I didn't see no police on your doorstep, so I'm guessing they didn't,' she hissed impatiently.

The CCTV system in scraps, Sally was horrified when Molly Sue didn't head back to the window they'd climbed in through. Instead, she went to the communal library space in the foyer, making a mess as she went; tipping bookcases and chairs over. She located the cabinet in which the research laptops were kept and smashed the padlock off with the axe. Molly Sue slung the rucksack off her shoulder and started ramming computers into it.

Sally figured it out; she was making it look like a robbery. She had to hand it to her, Molly Sue wasn't anyone's fool. She could fit four of the notebooks comfortably into the bag. Swinging them onto her back, she pelted back to their break-in point.

They had been in the school for less than ten minutes.

Chapter Twenty-Three

There were so many lies on top of lies on top of lies that Sally felt like her life was a game of Jenga, and a precarious one at that. All she could do was pretend everything was normal but she lacked faith in her acting ability. Molly Sue had to coach her just to make it to the shower and get dressed, but she knew that the only way they were going to pull this off was maintaining wide-eyed innocence.

She couldn't even confront Stan about his blabbing to Melody or he'd know they'd spoken right before the fall. So as she, Jennie and Stan walked to school, Sally had to carry on as if everything was fine between them, laughing at his jokes and sympathising about the new-born baby about to invade his nest. It blew her mind: how could he have been so spiteful? Was he that keen to see her miserable? Sally was so, so angry – more angry than she'd ever been about anything. The anger was the only thing stopping her from completely unravelling over what had happened to Melody – the anger kept her earthed somehow. It sounded melodramatic, but Stan had truly *betrayed* her.

'Have you heard how she's doing?' Stan asked.

'No,' Sally said, fighting to keep her tone civil.

Jennie was better informed. 'I'd heard that last night the doctors put her in a coma because they were worried about brain damage.'

'Whoa,' Stan said. Sally pinched her nose. She'd come to learn you can hold back tears that way. 'I guess karma finally caught up with her,' said Stan.

Sally instinctively swiped at his arm. 'Stan!'

'That is literally the shadiest thing you've ever said!' Jennie gasped, although there was a faint smile on her lips.

'Oh, come on, you were thinking it too.'

'It's way, waaaaaay too soon for jokes. She might die.' Jennie did love to be the bearer of bad news.

'Whatevs.' Stan shrugged it off. 'There's no way Melody Vine would miss all this free attention. She'll be back from the brink and on morning TV talking about her survival miracle before you know it.'

School was a revelation. Sally quickly learned how fortunes can change. In twenty-four hours she'd gone from being the boob-flashing Whore of Babylon to centre of attention. The topless pictures were forgotten as everyone clamoured over her to get the eyewitness account of Melody's fall. Outside the library, people she'd never met seemed to know her name.

'Sally, did you really see her neck snap? Did her head go right round?' one slavering ghoul asked.

'No! God!'

'Was there loads of blood?' asked Dee.

'No. Hardly any.' Her own head was spinning.

'Did the bone poke out of her leg?' someone else put in.

Keira and Eleanor pulled her out of the barrage and each gave her a hug. 'Are you OK? It must have been *awful*? I heard you fainted.' Keira seemed genuinely concerned.

'Yeah, it was pretty intense. Is . . . is she OK?'

Keira half shook, half nodded her head. 'It's way too early to tell. The girl broke her actual neck.'

'And both her legs,' Eleanor added with a little too much relish. 'Well, I guess you'll be Audrey now.'

In all the chaos, Sally hadn't even processed that. 'I . . . I don't know if the show will even go ahead . . . I mean, with what's happened.'

Kyle made his way towards the quad with some of his bandmates. As he passed her, he gave Sally a grim look. A grim, suspicious look. She didn't flinch; she didn't dare.

'He can't prove a goddamn thing,' Molly Sue whispered. 'Don't you worry about him.'

At the same time, a trio of uniformed police offers walked down the main drive towards a patrol car parked outside the gates. 'Are they here about Melody?' Jennie asked, reading Sally's mind.

'No,' Annabel Sumpter chipped in. Her mum was a geography teacher so she was always the first with inside knowledge. 'Last night there was a break-in! I know, right?'

'What?' Sally said, playing dumb.

'Oh, just some kids probably. They trashed the Resource Library and took a couple of laptops.' Laptops which were now at the bottom of the river about half a mile behind Sally's house.

'Wow.' Stan ruffled his hair. 'All the dramz at Saxton Vale High School yesterday.'

Sally breathed a sigh of relief. For now, no one seemed to be suggesting that Melody's fall had been anything other than a nasty accident. The crushing sensation lifted slightly from her shoulders and she realised, shamefully, that it had been worry more than guilt.

By lunchtime, Mr Roberts sent a message for her to meet him briefly in the drama studio. In the five minute meeting, Mr Roberts, looking somewhat harassed, told her that he had no idea what was happening with Melody, but that the show must go on and she would fill in as Audrey until further notice. 'Do you think you can handle it?'

Sally never thought she'd have wanted the glare of the spotlight, but so far she'd loved being Chiffon and Audrey had much more to say. Also, she'd watched Melody make a mess of it so was pretty sure she couldn't do a worse job. 'Yeah, I think so.'

'And can you learn the lines in a couple of weeks?'

'I've sort of been picking them up anyway,' Sally admitted. 'But I just feel really bad for Melody,' she added for good measure. It was true, the truth was rotting shipwreck at the bottom of her stomach.

Her weary teacher ran a hand over his buzzed hair and swallowed a huge gulp of coffee, clearly still unsure of how to proceed with the production. 'Who knows, maybe there'll be some sort of miracle and she'll be OK, but it's not looking good.'

Sally just nodded. There was nothing else to say. *Did I do it? Did I push her?* She hadn't wanted this, she hadn't . . . she'd just wanted her to take the pictures down. That was all. But now she was Audrey and Melody was in a coma.

'Girl, don't blow it now. Just leave the room,' Molly Sue breathed.

'I'll see you at rehearsal later.' Worried the guilt was all over her face, Sally left the studio as fast as she could.

Amidst the bustle of students either heading towards the cafeteria or eating their sandwiches in the hall, Sally saw the familiar shape of Todd hurrying towards the exit next to the boys' toilets. She hadn't seen or heard from him since the fall.

'Todd!' she called and took off after him.

He turned and she saw he looked shattered, like he hadn't slept a wink. That morning, he'd forgotten to put any product in his hair so it was fluffy like a baby owl or something. 'Oh. Hi,' he said, a little impatiently.

Sally caught up with him at the exit. 'Are you OK?' She followed him out onto the path. It was quiet at this time of day; students weren't allowed to eat lunch out there.

'Honestly, no. I'm really not.'

'How is she?'

'A mess. She's stable, but she's a mess. I went to the hospital last night but I wasn't allowed to see her. They took her into surgery just as I got there.'

'God, I'm so sorry.' Sally slipped her hand into his but he pulled it away at once and checked if anyone was looking.

'What are you doing?' he snapped.

It hit Sally like a fist. 'Nothing . . . I . . . wanted to make you feel better.'

'I'm fine. I just need to get to the hospital. OK?'

214

Sally nodded, feeling a lot like a crumpled, discarded tissue. 'Sure. I hope she gets better.' She was dying to hug him, to recapture the closeness they'd had at the lake. She longed to grab him and scream *'WHAT ABOUT ME?'* but knew she couldn't. All Sally could do was watch Todd walk away.

Oh wow. It turned out there was something stronger than guilt after all . . . and it was envy. It punctured her chest in red hot needles. *Great! I've driven Todd back towards Melody!* The sheer wickedness of the thought, and the readiness at which it entered her head, shocked her. Melody was broken, maybe even dying, and all Sally wanted was her hands back on Todd.

'Relax, darlin'. Just give him a little time.' She felt Molly Sue slink around her torso. 'And if that don't work, we can always put Melody out of her misery.'

Chapter Twenty-Four

Guilt is such a heavy thing to drag around. Rehearsals carried on, now with Sally filling in for Melody and Eleanor thrilled to be Chiffon, but she was wading through glue. Every time she closed her eyes, Sally saw Melody's tangled body at the foot of the stairwell. It was like wearing chains and it was affecting her performance – she could already see Mr Roberts starting to fluster. He was pounding coffee after coffee and creeping out every twenty minutes 'for air'.

She was getting to grips with the accent (she had, after all, watched enough American TV) but she couldn't remember her lines at all. It was embarrassing. 'Sorry,' she said. 'They will sink in, I promise.'

'Don't worry, it's a lot to remember. Stick to the script for the next couple of rehearsals,' Roberts said. No one else was still using their script. 'Let's call it quits there for tonight.'

There were cheers as the rest of the cast climbed down off the stage and started collecting their bags and jackets.

'Hey.' It was Keira. She fell into step alongside Sally. 'We're gonna head to the diner and get chilli dogs or something. Wanna come along?'

Whaaaaaat? Sally's immediate response was wondering if this was a practical joke. They'd probably lead her there and then lock her in the toilet or pour pig blood on her head or something. Only then she reminded herself that she was now the lead in the school play and Keira had been nothing but nice for the last few weeks. 'Erm . . . who's going?'

Keira fluffed her hair. 'Oh, only cool peeps. Me and El, Duncan . . . and I think Todd.' Well, that made all the difference. 'Come, come, come. It'll be fun.'

Sally looked around the hall. She couldn't see Stan or Jennie anywhere – they were probably painting the set walls in the art room. The coast was clear. After the rubbish rehearsal, she could use cheering up. 'Yeah, OK. Why not?'

She, Keira and Eleanor walked to the diner together. This was surely a parallel world. There were still six legs parading down the path out of Saxton Vale High School, but now two of them belonged to her. Sally wondered if it always felt like this when they moved as a pack, like they were supermodels in a personal slow-motion catwalk show. As awful as it was to admit, walking alongside Keira and Eleanor made her feel prettier than she ever had before.

Sally saw a few students filtering out of other after-school clubs. And they were *staring* at them. They were staring at her. Something became very clear to Sally. It wasn't that these girls were intrinsically powerful, it was that the rest of the school gave them power. And it felt nice.

A pair of tiny Year Seven girls struggled with cellos as they emerged from the music room. Their sweet, opal eyes followed Sally as they crossed the courtyard.

Molly Sue chuckled. 'They wanna be just like you when they grow up . . .'

That didn't make Sally feel as good as it probably should have done. *They wouldn't if they knew*, she thought.

'Oh, girl, can't you lighten up for a single cotton-pickin' minute?'

When they reached the diner, Todd and Duncan were already seated in one of the vinyl booths. It was busier than ever, the air thick with grease and Elvis. Once more, as she, Keira and Eleanor strutted across the restaurant there were awed glances – the A-List had arrived. Sally knew she wasn't truly A-List; she was an infiltrator, bound to be exposed at any moment. Salanora was *not* going to be a thing.

'But it could be . . .' Molly Sue told her.

'Hey!' Duncan said, shifting over to make room for them. Duncan was one of those simply lovely guys who traversed the social ladder with ease. He was as well liked by the geeks as he was the music crowd as he was the football team. He'd won the Head Boy election in a landslide last October.

Keira slid into the booth next to him and Eleanor next to her. That meant Sally had no choice but to sit next to Todd. 'Hey,' she said.

Todd looked up at her from under his brow. 'You OK?' he said.

'I'm fine.' This was awkward.

'Look,' he said, under his breath. 'I just wanted to say sorry for the other day. I was pretty stressed out and I shouldn't have taken it out on you.'

'That's OK.' Sally's mouth was dry.

'No, I was a dick.' Under the table, Todd rested a warm hand on her thigh. Sally shivered, but a good shiver. Which version of her did he want today? The vamp from the gig or the virgin from the lake? He ran his hand higher up her thigh until she halted its progress with her own. Sorry mate, *virgin* today. It was too much for her.

There was a warm, amber glow in her chest, but she fought it. This wasn't fair when Melody was laying in a hospital bed across town. 'How is Melody?'

Everyone at the table stiffened slightly. Perhaps they were all feeling guilty hanging out in a diner when they should have been visiting. 'I heard she's doing better,' Eleanor said, twirling a lock of hair around her finger un-ironically.

'Have you been to visit her?'

'Not yet . . .' Keira said. 'I didn't want to get in the way, you know.'

'Or,' Eleanor added, 'if we, like, went and gave her a cold or something, she might die. We'll go when she's a little better! You guys, do you think we should share nachos?'

'Chilli nachos!' Keira exclaimed.

Sally couldn't quite believe what she was hearing. All talk turned to food and Melody was conveniently forgotten.

But Sally couldn't forget. After they'd finished at the diner, Sally boarded a bus to the hospital. She had no idea why, but she just needed to see what she'd done. If she was honest, she reckoned she didn't feel bad enough about it. Apparently the dentist wasn't the only sadist in the play and she craved a little salt for the wound. Seeing would be believing.

'I get it! You're guilty! Do we really have to do this?' Molly Sue complained.

It's the right thing to do.

'Why put yourself through it? Heavens to Betsy, you're a real downer, ya know that?'

The hospital was a grey, pebble-dash cube with rows and rows of uniform square windows. It had an almost military feel to it and was a labyrinth. It took Sally almost half an hour to find the correct entrance to the intensive care unit.

Sally bought a card at the gift shop, knowing that flowers were a banned infection risk. It was such a feeble gesture and Hallmark don't make an *I'm sorry I almost killed you!* card. Visiting hours were on, and an orderly showed Sally where she had to go. The fourth floor smelled so much of alcohol hand gel it caught in the back of her throat. Her footsteps were accompanied by arrhythmic bleeps from competing heart monitors. It was robotic, sterile.

As she walked away from reception, the ward grew eerily still; no doctors or nurses bustled around the long, empty corridors. The orderly had told her Melody was in Room 412. Sally found the correct door and tapped gently. It swung inwards and Mrs Vine's head turned to see her. Melody's mother was Melody in twenty-five years' time – same hair and, with the help of a lot of botox and a rumoured brow lift, more or less the same face. 'Hello?'

'Hi. My name's Sally. I just came to drop off a Get Well Soon card from the *Little Shop* cast.'

Mrs Vine was immediately disinterested. 'Oh. Thank you. Would you like to leave it with the others?'

'Thanks.' Sally entered the room properly. It was a twin room, with stations at both sides of the room, only, the opposite bed was empty and stripped.

Edging closer, Sally got a proper look at Melody and flinched. Melody was in a bad, bad way. Her eyelids were taped shut and a tube curled out of the corner of her mouth. Her face was grey, squashed up by the neck brace. She was a far cry from the invincible goddess who'd stalked SVHS; she was a broken doll that glue and sellotape weren't going to fix.

Sally swallowed back tears as reality finally hit her. This knife to the gut was what she'd come for. *What have I done? I'm so, so sorry.* This disgust, this repulsion, she felt at herself was never going to go away and she deserved nothing less. Her bottom lip trembled.

'Get it together, you goddamn pansy! You want her mama to get nosy?' Molly Sue barked. 'Get. It. Together.'

'I'm so sorry,' Sally muttered to Mrs Vine, her voice unsteady.

'Thank you,' she replied. 'She's comfortable. She's not feeling any pain.'

That didn't matter. It would be a long, long time before Melody was a triple threat again. 'Is she going to be OK?'

Mrs Vine let out a long, shaky breath. 'Yes, thank God. The swelling in her skull is going down and they've put pins in her neck. They think she'll be fine. They're waking her up tomorrow or the day after. My poor baby . . . you know, she had cancer when she was a little girl. She's a fighter.'

Sally breathed her own sigh of relief and released some of the guilt from an imaginary valve deep inside her. 'Oh, thank God.'

'What did you say your name was?'

'Sally.'

Her eyes narrowed. 'I don't think Melody's ever mentioned you.'

'We're not really that close.' They'd been in the same class for ten years, she'd just never been invited to Melody's birthday parties. 'We're in the play together.'

'Would you do me a favour? Would you watch Melody while I nip to the ladies'? I don't like to leave her alone.'

Sally hesitated. 'I . . .'

'In case she stirs? If she does, just press the button for the nurse.'

How can I refuse? 'Sure. No worries.'

'You're a star.' Mrs Vine planted a tender kiss on Melody's forehead (that nearly floored Sally) and hurried out of the room.

The second the door closed, Molly Sue spoke. 'OK, we need to finish her off. I mean how hard can it be? She's pretty much a cabbage.'

What?

'God, you really are as dumb as a soup sandwich. What happens when she wakes up and tells someone what happened?'

Sally hadn't thought that far ahead. 'I . . . I don't know . . .'

'You gotta finish the job. Just put a pillow over her head. It'll take less than a minute.'

'But . . . but . . .'

'Oh, if ifs and buts were candies and nuts we'd all have a merry Christmas! Get on with it! Her mama'll be back in a second.'

'I can't! They'll know it was me!'

'C'mon! Take a look at her, a sneeze'd kill her right now. They'll think it was natural causes or whatever.'

'No!' Sally said through gritted teeth. 'I *won't*.'

'And just what makes you think I'm giving you a choice?'

Sally's hands reached out for Melody's pillow. They moved of their own accord, out of her control.

'Stop! Molly Sue, stop! Please!'

Her hands wouldn't listen, they carried on towards Melody.

'No!'

Her feet, however, did obey. Sally turned and ran for the door. She swung it open and collided with Mrs Vine.

'Is everything OK?'

'Yeah. Yeah, fine. I just have to go . . .'

'Oh, OK. Thank you for coming.'

Sally was already pelting down the corridor, far, far away from where she could do Melody more harm.

That evening, Sally lay on her bed and cried. There was nothing left to do. She couldn't talk to Todd, couldn't talk to Stan, couldn't talk to Jennie. She was repulsed by the thing on her body and however far or fast she ran, she couldn't get away from her. She thought of that episode of *Satanville*, the one where the guy had the parasitic demon on his back. How was this any different?

She wished *she* could float up out of her body, and go to live inside someone else's skin. Everyone else made it look so easy. What would it be like to be certain like Annabel Sumpter, or vibrant like Keira Stevens or respected like Duncan Curtis? An awful thought occurred to her – what if wherever she went, whoever she was, she felt this loathsome? *I was miserable before Molly Sue, I'm miserable now.* Sure, the outside shell was looking prettier than ever, but below the surface she was festering. A peach with maggots at the core.

As dusk fell, she could no longer abide the noise in her head. She shoved some shoes on and told her mother she was going to Stan's. She didn't, though, and carried on walking past that traitor's house. When it started to rain – dots on the pavement quickly turning to puddles – she still didn't stop walking, even though she didn't have a coat. It was good. The rain hid her tears.

By the time she reached the rough part of town, she was soaked. Her stripy T-shirt clung to her body and her hair swung around her face in dripping rat's tails. Her socks squelched in her trainers, but she didn't care. *I deserve worse*.

When she saw there were still lights on in St Francis De Sales church she almost cried anew. A tiny ember of hope glowed in her heart. She ran up the slick stone stairs and threw herself at the doors.

Inside, votive candles flickered in their waxy jars and it smelled thickly of incense. Sally wondered if a service had just finished. She scanned the chapel for Sister Bernadette. There was no one else she could talk to. It was time to tell the whole truth, whether the nun thought she was insane or not.

She couldn't see anyone around. 'Hello?' Sally walked down the central aisle towards the altar, checking the pews. 'Is there anyone here?' There had to be someone around, surely.

Out of the corner of her eye, she saw the font standing to one side of the altar and approached it. It was a grand marble basin, intricately carved with leaves and cherubs. Sally saw it was full. 'Worth a try,' she murmured. She scooped her hand into the font and brought the water to her lips. She swallowed a mouthful and waited. She wasn't sure what she'd been expecting – to burst into flames? Foam at the mouth? Dissolve into a heap like the Wicked Witch of the West?

None of those things happened.

'Thirsty?'

At the voice, she whirled around, almost tripping over her feet. She turned to see an old priest with leathery olive skin. In his day he must have been devastatingly handsome, in a George Clooney way. 'Oh, I'm sorry!'

'That's OK. I'm Father Gonzales. Are you lost?' He spoke with a light Spanish accent.

Sally realised she must look like something that had crawled up out of a drain. 'No. I . . . I was looking for Sister Bernadette. She, she knows me. I need her help.'

Father Gonzales frowned. 'Sister Bernadette?'

'Yes. Is she here?'

He could only shake his head. 'I'm sorry, dear, you must be mistaken. There is no Sister Bernadette at this diocese. There never has been.'

Chapter Twenty-Five

Sally's harsh laughter echoed around cavernous church as Father Gonzales's eyes bulged in shock. 'Well, of course!' Sally giggled, fully gripped by hysteria. 'Why would she be real? What was I thinking?'

Judging from his face, Father Gonzales must have thought she was an escaped mental patient. To be honest, she didn't feel far off it. She couldn't stop laughing, although she wanted to cry. 'Are you all right, my child?'

Sally pulled herself together, although her skin still tingled. Sister Bernadette was as impossible as Molly Sue. She should have seen it coming. 'I'm so sorry,' Sally said. 'I should have never come here.'

'I could check at the convent . . . it's possible they have a new member.'

'No. No, it's fine. I'm sorry I bothered you.'

'Would you like me to call someone? Is there someone who's taking care of you?'

Sally was already backing towards the door. 'It's fine. But thank you.' She turned and ran out of the church.

It was still raining, but not as ferociously as before. Sally clung to herself for both warmth and sanity. One of two things was true – and she was more certain of this than she had been of anything in weeks. Either she was entirely insane – seeing and hearing *multiple* people – or there was something *incredible* going on. Not incredible like good incredible, but like . . . unfathomable, uncanny.

As she walked through the rundown streets of Old Town, Sally felt tiny. She was the smallest thing in the world. Molly Sue and Sister Bernadette, Rosita and Boris . . . somehow Sally knew they were older, bigger, greater than she was.

I am a pawn, Sally thought. *I'm being used.* She was nothing more than a host body for something far more powerful.

Good and Evil. Capital G and capital E. They were too abstract to picture, but Sally was starting to get a *sense* of each. The warmth she'd felt around Sister Bernadette, the trust, the kindness. Compare that to the icy shard in her mind that was Molly Sue. Maybe they weren't just concepts from an RE textbook.

She thought of the homeless man who'd been killed outside the school. She was determined she wouldn't end up like him, as easy as it would be to scream and shout and wail. Sally didn't feel like an insane person, she felt like a stupid person, a gullible person. Cold, hard fact time: killing herself would be the best option, she knew it would, but she didn't *yet* have the strength. But she wouldn't rule it out. If it meant ridding the world of Molly Sue . . .

But not yet. There had to be a way. She had to think of something.

Sally thought about it all the way home. Molly Sue remained mercifully quiet, if she was even listening in to her thoughts.

It seemed Bernadette was right, Molly Sue couldn't always hear her. Either Molly Sue didn't have access to every last thought in her head, or Sally had instead mastered the skill of *thinking quietly*.

It was after midnight by the time she reached Mulberry Hill, and it had stopped raining, although she was still wet to her underwear when she let herself in through the kitchen door.

With no lights on, Sally didn't see her mother sitting at the breakfast table. 'You scared me!' Sally gasped.

Wearing a white terrycloth bathrobe, her mother stood and tucked the chair she'd been sitting on under the table. 'I was worried about you,' her mother said sadly. There were grey circles under her eyes. 'I didn't want to go to bed until I knew you were home.' Dragging her slipper-clad feet across the tiles, she shuffled towards the hall.

'I'm sorry,' Sally offered, but sorrys are cheap. The truth was on the very tip of her tongue. *Just tell her. Maybe she'll be able to help.* 'Mum . . .'

'Goodnight, Sally.' Her mother was already halfway up the stairs.

Sally honestly didn't know if she'd be more of a disappointment alive or dead. But one thing was clear: it was too late, and she was beyond the type of help her mum could deliver. A damp flannel and some Calpol wasn't going to make much difference this time.

Sally awoke. It was still dark behind her curtain. *Molly Sue?* The tattoo appeared to be dormant. The was a banging noise. From downstairs. Was her mother still pottering around? Interest piqued, Sally pushed back her duvet and tiptoed onto the landing.

There was a further crash from below. 'Hello?' she whispered. She took the stairs lightly, not wanting to rouse her parents if they were still asleep. 'Is anyone there?'

Cautiously looking around the banister, Sally saw the back door was open, swinging in the wind. She must have forgotten to shut it properly when she got in. There didn't look to be anyone around so she padded into the kitchen, closed it and fastened the bolt.

There were glass panels in the back door. The garden looked empty enough, but at night the shadows that swayed over the lawn looked like teeth and nails.

Only then she heard another noise – this one much closer. A dragging sound, something snapping.

The hairs on the back of her neck bristled. Slowly, somehow knowing what was behind her, she turned.

Melody Vine hauled her body down the hallway towards her, twisted legs trailing behind her uselessly. Her jaw was broken, her mouth hanging open at a sickening angle. A broken arm, wrist bent back ninety degrees, clicked out towards Sally. 'Why, Sally?' she slurred, 'why did you push me?'

Sally awoke, drenched in sweat, and turned the bedside lamp on.

Chapter Twenty-Six

'Hey, are we OK?' Stan asked her on the way to rehearsal the next day. Most people were leaving school, so they were swimming against the tide. The nightmarish vision of Melody was burned onto the inside of her eyelids so she'd barely slept – and now she was close to tipping into Crankyville.

Sally really wanted to track down Sister Bernadette, or whoever or whatever she was, but had no idea where to start. School, and especially the play, were all feeling like a waste of time but also gave her a sense of normality she much needed.

'Yeah. Why?' Sally could barely speak to Stan and had been avoiding him where she could. The bitterness of his betrayal was like acid in her stomach.

Stan had the nerve to look hurt and that only made her angrier. 'You've been miles away the last week or so.'

'Just busy.' She knew she was being short, but she couldn't bring herself to play happy families. She was still stuck to the wheels of the bus he'd thrown her under.

'You haven't been over all week.'

She mentally counted to ten. 'Between homework and

rehearsal I'm exhausted. I've been going to bed at about half eight every night,' Sally said, and noticed they were climbing the very same stairs Melody had tumbled down. She had to cling to the rail for support.

'Where were you going in the rain last night?'

She stopped and properly looked him in the eye. 'Are you stalking me now?'

He looked even more hurt and for the first time she didn't care. 'What? No! I just saw you going out.'

'Stan, I love you but you are not my warden! I don't have to report my movements to you!'

'Sal, I know! I just wanna hang out and watch *Satanville*! You know there was a new episode last night right?'

What? That shut her up. With everything going on, she'd completely forgotten. For the first time in three years, she'd missed an episode of *Satanville*. 'Oh. I totally forgot.'

'Well, clearly. Are you like ill or something? I downloaded it, but didn't want to watch it without you and Jen.'

She forgave him a little. But not all the way. 'Thank you. I'll stop being sketchy once the show's over, I promise.'

Stan held her back from going into the hall. 'Just a second. Is there something going on with you and Todd?'

And there was the angry again. Sally bit her tongue. 'No.'

'Because —'

'Stan. Stop it, OK? Just give it a rest.' She pushed past him and entered the hall.

Mrs Greene swooped on her like a vulture as soon as she stepped in. 'Oh, Sally, sweetie, could you just come and try on your costumes, please?'

Sally gave Stan a final displeased look and followed the teacher. Stan looked wounded, but she was tiring of the sad puppy thing.

Sally had (somewhat smugly) learned she was a little thinner than Melody so all the Audrey costumes needed alterations to fit her. Mrs Greene fluttered her into the poky dressing room backstage. 'OK, I've got all three for you to try on.' She pulled them off the rack. Sally waited for her to leave to let her get changed, but Mrs Greene didn't move. 'Quick, quick, dear. I've seen it all before.'

Realising she wasn't going to be left, she pulled her T-shirt over her head. She had only just unbuckled her jeans when Mrs Greene saw Molly Sue. 'Oh my! Is that real?'

Sally nodded. Suddenly the poky room was much too hot and Sally struggled to breathe.

'That's really something!' Mrs Greene gasped with admiration. 'Where did you get that done?'

Tattoo parlour of the damned. 'Oh . . . erm . . . just somewhere in the city.' Sally couldn't think of any actual parlours or make one up fast enough. It was reassuring, in a way, that someone else could see the tattoo. If other people could see it, at least she wasn't a hundred per cent psychotic. That really would have been an anti-climax.

Mrs Greene gave her the dress to pull on. 'Oh, you must tell me where. I got one when I was about your age and I want to get it covered up with something better.'

Sally breathed a sigh of relief. 'Sure. Could you . . . not tell anyone? My parents don't know.'

Mrs Greene winked. 'Your secret's safe with me!'

A few minutes later, Sally admired herself, if that was the correct word, in the mirror. *Well, I guess I've completed the transformation. I look like a hooker.* She was wearing a skin-tight leopard-print tube dress with electric blue tights and white stilettos.

'Sugar, you look smokin'.'

She hadn't spoken in so long that Molly Sue's voice made her jump. Thankfully Mrs Greene had gone to find the patent leather belt that was supposed to go around the middle of the dress. 'A little trashy, I'll give you that, but there's no harm in a little dressin' up. Guys love that! Like whore and pastor, naughty school girl and teacher, strict school ma'am —'

I beg you to stop.

'Oh, get the rod out yo ass! You look better than a popsicle in a desert.'

I can't walk. Her ankles threatened to give at any second. Sally tried to walk up and down the dressing room but looked like a drunk baby giraffe.

'Oh good God, girl, you walk like you is on crack,' Molly Sue drawled. 'Just put the weight on the balls of your feet. And walk like you just shot your cheatin' husband.'

Despite everything, Sally laughed out of her nose. There was a tap at the door. Assuming it was Mrs Greene, Sally told her to come in. 'I'm decent.' Todd stuck his head around the door. 'Oh, I thought you were Mrs Greene.'

'Wow, you look amazing.' He came in and closed the door behind him.

Sally pursed her lips. 'I look ridiculous.'

He ran his eyes up her body. In the Lycra she felt pretty

233

much naked. 'You don't. I wouldn't wear it to school if I was you, but . . .'

Sally smiled. 'Can you imagine? I think it's actually flammable. How's Melody?'

'Oh, she's better today. Didn't you hear? She's conscious and talking a bit.'

With that it felt like the floor buckled beneath her feet. Melody was awake? Talking? *What* was she saying? Sally had to grip the edge of the dressing table.

Todd went on. 'She's drugged up to the eyeballs. She doesn't remember anything – the fall, going to hospital . . . nothing.'

Sally tried hard to suppress the wave of relief that washed over her. It felt so selfish.

Todd looked awkwardly at his hands. 'Sally, can we talk?'

She looked up at him, reminding herself how inviting his eyes were. Snapshots of the kiss by the lake entered her head, but that was selfish too. 'Talk about Melody? It's OK . . . I know you have to be with her . . . she needs you more than I do.'

He moved closer, checking there was no one else in the dressing room. 'I don't want to be with Melody. I want to be with you.' The tips of his fingers found the tips of hers and they interlocked.

'What?' *Is this a joke?*

He took hold of her hand properly. 'I felt so bad about the fall, like it was karma for thinking about you or something.'

Sally shifted uncomfortably. 'It was an accident.'

'I know,' he said, 'but Melody's going to be fine and it doesn't change anything. I don't want to be with her any more.'

She needed a moment to process that. After waiting five years to hear these words, they sounded all wrong. Sally let his hand drop. 'Todd, she's going to need you. She's going to be out of action for months . . . I . . . I saw her at the hospital. She's going to need you more than ever.'

He at least had the decency to look a little ashamed. 'I can't stay with Melody because I feel sorry for her, and she's got her family to care for her. Look, I get that we'll have to be careful. It won't look good if we get together while Mels is in the hospital, but we can keep it on the DL for a while, right?'

Was this meant to be as cold as it sounded? Sally wasn't sure she was hearing him correctly. 'I . . . I don't know. It doesn't feel right, Todd.'

'It won't be for ever. Just until Mels is up and about and stuff.' He moved closer again, stroking her hair. 'I know it sucks, but it could even be kind of hot.' He leaned in and kissed her on the lips. It was slow and steady and delicious.

Sally pulled away. 'Maybe we should just wait a little while, see how Melody is. At least until she's back at school.'

'I don't know if I can, Sally. I can't stop thinking about you.' He grinned. 'And that dress . . . I'm like whoa!' He kissed her again, more hungrily this time. It was a very different type of kiss to the one he'd given her at the lake. He held her head like a clamp with one hand and grabbed at her chest with the other. It didn't feel good.

'Todd, wait,' she managed to say between kisses. He positioned her against the long dressing table that ran the length of the room. Her bottom pressed up against the counter, she couldn't back away. Kissing her more furiously, his hand moved from her chest to the hem of the dress. 'Todd, please . . .'

'It's OK . . . relax.' His hand went under her dress.

'No!' With a strength she didn't know she had, she shoved him away. He stumbled back into a clothes rail and, pulling costumes with him, slid to the floor.

'Are you deaf or somethin'? She said get off of her!' Sally's mouth cried.

Todd clambered out of the clothes as Mrs Greene burst back into the room.

'What did you just say?' Todd looked at her wide-eyed.

Sally's heart pounded; she could feel the adrenalin twitching in her veins.

'What's going on?' Mrs Greene asked.

'Nothing,' Sally said, although she had no idea why she was protecting Todd. He had scared her. Properly scared her.

'Nothing,' Todd agreed, although he continued to regard Sally with suspicion. 'I'll see you later.' He skulked out of the dressing room.

But Sally could still feel Molly Sue's rage. It burned white hot inside her.

Chapter Twenty-Seven

'Sally?' Mr Roberts asked. 'Are you OK?'

'I'm fine,' she said as she came to the stage. 'I'm just trying to get used to the shoes.' She'd decided to keep them on, but had changed back into her regular clothes. How else was she going to learn to walk in high heels? At the end of the day, while Sally Feather wouldn't be caught dead in white stilettos, Audrey would have loved them.

Her heart rate had now returned to something resembling normal. She'd tried on the other costumes and everything was fine. Actually, it wasn't fine. Her head was messy. Was Todd a grade A douche or was that how boys got when they were horny? She was angry. Angry at him and angry at herself. She shouldn't have been scared, she should have been . . . assertive. She shouldn't have needed Molly Sue to push him off.

'Hey,' her tattoo snapped. 'Ain't nobody to blame for Todd's busy hands but Todd. Don't you go beatin' youself up over what he did now.'

I can't help it, Sally admitted. *I guess he got carried away.*

'No, girl, no. You don't make excuses for him. Men get enough of those.'

At the back of the hall, out of earshot, Todd was saying something to Duncan. He didn't look happy. He threw her a final look and sloped out of the room. A part of her was glad he'd left; a part was worried she'd disappointed him.

What's wrong with me?

'Can we get started, please?' Mr Roberts said and Sally was snapped back into harsh reality. 'I want to start from "Suddenly Seymour"! Sally? Are you sure you're ready?'

Sally saw Stan and Jennie painting the Audrey II model at the back of the hall and she longed to join them, to break down and tell them what had happened, but it felt like there was a wall building up between them. She was so angry at Stan, and Jennie was still so fragile over Kyle. 'I'm fine,' she said and tottered on her heels towards Seymour.

All she could do was channel it into Audrey, another girl, albeit a fictional one, with a boyfriend with busy hands. *Oh God*, Sally thought as she sang, *is Stan Seymour?* The loveable dork who doesn't beat her up? No. Audrey *loved* Seymour. Stan was her friend, and he was pushing his luck at that.

By the end of the rehearsal, Sally was fairly certain the white stilettos were slowly filling with blood. She sat on the edge of the stage and pulled them off. Her toes were numb and she had a cushion-sized blister on her heel, but her feet were otherwise intact. *Why do girls wear these?* Sally thought, trying to massage life back into her soles.

'Sally,' Mr Roberts called. 'Can I just have a quick word, please?' She obediently trotted over, but the teacher steered her backstage. 'Sally,' he said in a hushed voice. 'Something's been on my mind.'

'Am I doing it wrong?'

'Oh hell no!' His artificially white teeth shone in the gloom behind the curtains. 'Sally, you are killing it as Audrey. I mean that. I should have cast you in the first place . . . I was just worried you didn't have the confidence for such a big part. To be brutally honest, you're far more authentic than Melody ever was and that's sort of my problem.'

Sally waited for him to go on, unsure what he meant. 'I don't understand . . .'

'There's no easy way to say this, but, Sally, did you push Melody down the stairs?'

Oh God oh God oh God. 'What?'

'Good! I just wanted an honest reaction.'

Tears clouded Sally's vision. 'Of course I didn't!' *Molly Sue did it*, she told herself, clinging to that possibility.

Mr Roberts let out a sigh of relief and his shoulders seemed to sink. 'My mind ran away with itself. I just couldn't stop thinking about how you were with her when she fell, you were behind her on the stairs, you were the understudy . . . I kept thinking, "No one wants to be Audrey *that* badly," but then the CCTV from that day got wiped when we had the break-in and I sort of thought how clever that would be, to make it look like a burglary when it was actually a cover-up.'

He viewed her with shrewd eyes. All Sally could do was shake her head. 'Sir, I swear I had nothing to do with it. I was nowhere near her when she fell.'

'I asked the cleaner and he said you left together . . .'

Sally's legs felt brittle and hollow. *Please don't faint.*

Molly Sue finally spoke. 'Just deny everything, you hear me?'

'We . . . we did, but didn't stay together long. Melody didn't even like me; she thinks I'm a loser. There's no way she'd walk home with me. I . . . I . . .'

'Sally, it's OK. If you tell me you didn't do it, I believe you. I'm sorry, don't get upset.' He rubbed her arm.

'I didn't!'

'That's all I needed to hear. I just had to ask, you know? Keep up the good work with Audrey. Dress rehearsal next week! Can you believe it?' Apparently satisfied his interrogation had worked, he swished off the stage, leaving her alone in the wings of Skid Row.

Oh. My. God. Sally let out a shaky breath. Her hands were trembling. *That was way too close.*

Her voice cut through Sally's thoughts like a blade. 'What are you talkin' 'bout, darlin'? What if he tells the police his little theory? He needs to be stopped.' Molly Sue was deadly serious.

Sally slammed her bedroom door shut and pulled her T-shirt off. She went straight to the bathroom as Molly Sue slid round to her front and looked her in the eye. 'Are you listening? We aren't doing anything! We got away with it – he believed me!'

Molly Sue arched an eyebrow. 'Girl, he got your number. He's snooping around askin' all kinds o' questions!'

'He hasn't got a shred of proof! There is none!'

The look Molly Sue gave her was sour to say the least. 'What, are you the village idiot or somethin'? What about when Melody remembers what happened? The biggest piece of proof is layin' in the hospital. We gotta tie up these loose ends!'

'No! No more! I don't want anyone else to get hurt!'

'Little late for that, don't you think? Shoulda thought 'bout that before you sent Jill tumblin' down the hill. Look, what if that negro teacher asks Melody what happened and it all comes floodin' back?'

Sally was appalled. 'I can't believe you just said that.'

'Yeah, *that's* the worst thing I done.'

'End of discussion, Molly Sue! I won't let you hurt anyone else. I won't. I —'

Where am I? This isn't my house.

Sally stood in an immaculate townhouse. A furball of a Persian cat was curled up in a ball on a chaise longue under the window – a window that had been prized open. She was in a dining room-slash-library – there was a polished wooden table with a pretty candelabra at the centre, while the walls were fully lined with books.

Her feet moved without her permission. Once more, she prowled, ghostly footsteps over the carpet. She wore the same all-black outfit she'd worn when they broke into the school.

What are you doing? Stop!

Molly Sue didn't reply.

Sally's body slipped through the open door into the hallway. Framed Playbills lined the walls – signed by Patti Lupone and Idina Menzel. That's when Sally figured out where she was – Mr Robert's house. She did know where he lived – Jennie had once pointed it out in passing – and Molly Sue had access to that knowledge.

Molly Sue, please! This is just going to make it worse!

The tattoo ignored her and she slipped into the kitchen. It was sleek, clean and modern. Mr Roberts was a house-proud

241

man. Stainless steel handles jutted out of a knife block on the counter. Sally's hand reached out for a handle and she tested each, checking what type of blade hid within the wood. Molly Sue selected the biggest carving knife, pulling it out with a deadly sounding zing. Ice blue moonlight leaked in through the blinds and reflected off the blade.

Sally caught sight of herself in the steel. Her eyes were narrow, resolute and lethal. They were hardly her eyes at all, more like a predator's stalking her prey. *Oh my God – STOP!*

Molly Sue tested the weight of the knife in her hand, sizing it up. Satisfied, she gripped it tightly. It was cool on her skin. Moving like liquid, Molly Sue slunk back through the hall towards the stairs. She took each step on tip-toes, testing each floorboard for groans and squeaks.

Molly Sue! What are you doing? Sally was caged in her own skull, looking on helplessly. She imagined pounding on the walls of the cell, wondering if she could somehow give her alter-ego such a crushing headache she'd have to give up and go home.

They reached the landing. Three doors to choose from. Two stood ajar. Behind the first, Sally saw white tiles – a bathroom. Molly Sue tried the next. It was dark inside, but the curtains stood open to cast light over a home office. There were yet more books and huge piles of marking next to a Mac. Molly Sue disregarded the room and slipped back onto the landing. 'I'll take what's behind door number three,' she whispered.

Chapter Twenty-Eight

Molly Sue pushed down on the handle and oh-so-slowly opened the bedroom door. Sally prayed it would screech, alert her teacher, but it glided across the carpet without even a hiss. She poured through the crack and closed it behind her.

Molly Sue waited a moment to let her eyes adjust to the coal black bedroom. Sally made sense of the dark shapes: a bed in the centre of the room with bedside tables on each side, and she was standing next to a built-in wardrobe that ran all the way to a door in the corner, which she guessed led to an en-suite.

Mr Roberts was a bump under a duvet that rose and fell with his chest. Air whistled through his nostrils. He slept alone. Molly Sue took another silent step towards him. Sally couldn't even breathe. *She's going to slit his throat while he sleeps*. Sally imagined a crimson cloud spreading across the pillow as Mr Roberts clutched his neck, eyes wide. She couldn't . . . she couldn't look.

Molly Sue took another step. One step closer.

Think, Sally, think! She recalled the very first time Molly Sue had taken her over at the hairdresser – the way it had felt, like a serpent slithering up into her head. Now Sally felt for it again, searching her mind for Molly Sue's presence.

Molly Sue raised the knife, held it over him, ready to plunge it into his back.

There you are. She could feel her, as slippery as an eel coiled around her brain. Sally focused everything on that single feeling; she pictured Molly Sue and just squeezed and squeezed, as if she were trying to physically push a headache out of her head.

Sally blinked and she was in the room.

The knife fell from her hand and bounced across the carpet with a metallic ping. The hump in the centre of the bed stirred. Sally's mouth fell open. *Move!* She dropped to her knees and lay flat on the floor alongside the bed. She'd once read pythons do that to size up their dinner before they attempt to swallow it.

Above her, Mr Roberts coughed and wheezed. Sally dared not move a muscle. She didn't even breathe. The knife still lay in the middle of the carpet. Quick as a flash, her hand shot out to draw it to her side. The bed springs creaked and groaned as her teacher rolled over. *He's getting up!*

All Sally could do was roll under the bed. She forced a space for herself next to a pair of suitcases. A split second later, a heel appeared an inch from her nose. Her eyes widened and a single tear ran from the corner of her eye. Her mouth was clamped so tightly shut her jaw ached.

Rubbing his head, Mr Roberts padded across the carpet towards the en-suite. He flicked on the light and the whirr of an extractor fan started up. Sally grimaced; he'd left the door wide open. Of course he had. Who pees with the door shut if they live alone? He stood with his back to her, thankfully peeing standing up.

She had to go – *now*. Shuffling out from under the bed, she awkwardly rose to her feet. He was still going – all that coffee, she guessed. In three soft strides, Sally reached the bedroom door. Biting her lip, she opened it a crack and ducked into the hallway. The toilet flushed at the same time as she clicked the door shut. She listened for a second. The bed squeaked as he clambered back into it.

Sally edged towards the stairs, wondering if maybe she should give him a few minutes to fall asleep before making her escape. She just wanted to be out in the open night where she could breathe again.

'That was a dumb thing to do, darlin',' Molly Sue hissed.

Sally wasn't sure whether she meant not killing Mr Roberts or taking back control of her limbs.

No. It's over, Molly Sue. No more.

When Sally got home, although it was almost three in the morning, she was wide awake. There was so much to do before dawn. She also didn't want to give Molly Sue a way in. She'd forced Molly Sue out of her head once, but it had taken everything she had, she wasn't so sure she'd be able to do it again in a hurry.

Sally felt steelier than she ever had. Somehow, she wasn't sure how yet, she had won the tug of war in Mr Roberts' bedroom. She'd wrestled back control. But how? And what did that mean? She mulled it over and over in that secret part of her mind that Molly Sue didn't seem privy to.

If only she had more time to dwell on it, but she didn't. If she didn't do something drastic and NOW, she truly believed someone was going to die. It was a miracle that Kyle and Melody and Mr Roberts were still breathing. Molly Sue was out for blood, and Sally had learned by now that Molly Sue always got her own way.

As the sun rose and the birds started their chorus, Sally wrote two letters. Each took her several pages of the notebook, with crossed-through first attempts being torn out, screwed up and thrown in the bin. The first was to her parents.

Dear Mum and Dad,

If you get this letter it probably means I'm dead. I'm so sorry. I hope, with time, you can forgive me. I got involved in something terrible, something that I couldn't control. No, it's not drugs.

I want you to know that you didn't do anything wrong. You tried your hardest for me and for that I'm very grateful.

I know I'm a disappointment. I did try, I really did. I'm sorry if it wasn't enough.

Goodbye, and all my love always,

Sally x

The last part was hard to write. The love was more for them than it was for her. She thought about it. She *did* love them.

246

They had given her life, they had kept her safe and fed and physically warm, if not emotionally. They weren't her friends, but they were her parents. She'd never had to live without them – she only hoped they would readjust to the life they'd had before her. She fingered the old photo of her mum laughing; once she'd been happy. They'd be happy again.

The second letter was to Stan and Jennie.

Dear Stan and Jen,

If this doesn't work, I want to say goodbye properly.

I wonder if you have any idea how much I love the two of you. When I feel weak, just picturing you makes me stronger. When I'm down, I replay the stupid stuff you say to perk myself up. I never don't look forward to hanging out with you. Does that make sense?

I know we're meant to say how awful our lives are, but I think we have fun. I don't hate being me and that's because I've got you. It feels like I'm one third of a whole.

When I'm gone, I need you two to stick together. You only have a year of school left. Go to the same university, or if you don't, write to each other – like, proper letters, not texts. Jennie, do not get back together with Kyle: he's vile and how can you defy a dead girl's dying wish? Sorry, but it's true!

Whatever you do, don't stop watching Satanville.
Record it for me in case they don't show it in the
afterlife.

You're going to be fine.

I love you.

Sally x

By the time she finished the second letter she was ugly crying. She didn't want to go . . . but she had to. It was almost six. It was time.

Chapter Twenty-Nine

Sally arrived at Jennie's house at about seven, having showered and changed. Jennie answered the door with curiosity. 'Hey there, early bird, what's going on? Do you have an early rehearsal or something?'

'Can I come in?'

'Sure!'

'Have your parents gone?'

'Yeah.' Jennie led her through into the lounge. It was as neat as her own house but much more minimalist. There were cream leather sofas, glass coffee tables and twigs in vases. It was that kind of house. 'Their flight leaves at half nine, so they had to check in at half six.'

'Cool.' Sally had dressed simply in a slouchy vest with some jeans and the leather jacket. It was still cold this early and the lawns of Mulberry Hill were covered in pearls of dew.

'What's going on? Would you like some brekkie? We've got crumpets.'

'No, I'm OK, thanks.'

Jennie headed into the kitchen to prepare her own breakfast. She was still in her Minnie Mouse pyjamas.

'Jennie . . .' The words caught in the back of her throat, but she needed to spit them out in case Molly Sue took over again. 'I need to talk to you.'

Jennie splashed the juice carton down onto the worktop. 'Oh, God. Is it true? Did you send Lucas pictures of your boobs?'

Sally snorted. 'No!' She thought on that for a second. '*But seriously*, it'd be so much easier if that was it.'

Jennie knew at once what their code meant. 'Then what is it? You're kinda freaking me out, Sal.'

Sally nodded, considering her next sentence. 'I'll tell you everything. But first . . . I need you to tie me up.'

Needless to say, Jennie took some convincing.

'Do it,' Sally instructed.

Jennie frowned, but on seeing the expression on Sally's face, secured the handcuffs around one wrist. She then fed the cuffs around the bars of the old-fashioned cast-iron radiator before clicking the second cuff into place. 'Jennie, whatever happens, I never, *ever* want to know why you own these handcuffs. Is that clear?'

Jennie allowed her a brief smile, although she mostly looked concerned. The cuffs felt sturdy enough. At the end of the day, Molly Sue only had Sally's muscles to work with and while skilfully rowing a boat is one thing, tearing a radiator off the wall is quite another. 'Do you know where the key is?'

'Yeah . . .'

'Good! Don't tell me. Whatever you do, don't tell me.'

'OK . . .' She was looking more baffled by the minute. 'Are you comfortable like that?'

Sally was now sat with her legs straight out in front of her, her back up against the cold radiator in Jennie's bedroom. 'I'll be fine,' she said, although suspected she wouldn't remain comfortable for long in that position.

'Let me get you a cushion.' Jennie hopped up and grabbed a fluffy throw pillow off her bed. She tucked it between Sally and the radiator before pulling the blinds down, although how the neighbours would be able to see her was anyone's guess.

'Thanks.'

'Sally, what is going on? This is insane.'

Sally had already told Jennie to call Stan to tell him they were both sick and wouldn't meet him at the corner today. There was an absence hotline to call at school too. 'It's about to get a lot more insane. Sit down.'

Jennie did as she was told, leaning against her bed. Stripes of vanilla sunlight shone through the blinds across her arms, making her look like a zebra. 'Jennie, I did something so, so stupid.'

'What?'

'What I'm going to say is going to sound fully crazy, OK? I really need you not to laugh . . . just listen to what I've got to say . . .'

'I promise.' Jennie looked a little hurt. 'I'm not going to laugh. I know you and Stan think I'm Princess Sparkles or something, but I'm not. I can be serious.'

'I know.' Sally took a soothing breath and begun. 'Do you remember that homeless guy who got killed outside school? That was when it started . . .' Sally told her everything, only leaving out the Kyle episode. She felt that wouldn't be a great idea when she needed to keep Jennie on side.

Jennie took a second to process what she'd been told. 'Are you saying you pushed Melody Vine down the stairs?'

'No! Jennie, it wasn't me! It was Molly Sue. It's all Molly Sue. She wants me to believe I did it, but I didn't . . . it's all mind games. I can show you. Lift up my vest.' Tentatively, Jennie crawled forwards. 'She's on the right of my back.' Jennie lifted the rim of her shirt.

Sally heard her gasp. 'Oh my God! Sally! That's beautiful.'

'Don't be fooled. That's not what she really looks like.'

'And . . . she moves and talks? But seriously . . . ?' Her tone left little doubt she thought Sally was nuts. Even the cast of *Satanville* looked down from their posters with judgement in their eyes.

'Only I can hear her. I don't think she'll move while you're watching. She's been getting away with this for a long time.'

Jennie sat directly in front of her and crossed her legs. 'Sally, you know I love you, but do you have any idea how this all sounds? I mean, evil, vanishing tattoo parlours? Ghost nuns? It all sounds . . .'

'Let me ask you something,' Sally said, her eyes glazing with tears. 'Does it matter? Either Molly Sue is real or I'm having a total breakdown. Either way, I'm dangerous and I don't want to hurt anyone else. Jen, I need your help.'

Jennie, tiny little Jennie, reached forward and grasped Sally's knee with a surprisingly strong fingers. 'I will do anything you need. You know that.'

'Thank you. No more questions?'

'I can't promise that, but I'll do what you tell me to do. How about that?'

'Deal.' Sally felt better than she had in weeks. Jennie had taken on some of her burden. 'I need to get her removed. It's the only way I can think to stop this, but the last time I tried it she said she'd hurt me . . . or worse.'

'So what can I do?'

'I need you to get me to the clinic in the city. If I go there alone, she'll take over. I need you to be with me the whole time. You'll need to chain me to the chair. And . . . and somehow you'll need to convince them that whatever I say, however many times I tell them to stop, to carry on. She'll do anything to save herself.'

Jennie's mouth turned down at the edges. 'Will that work?'

'I don't know, but we have to try – you promised. The other alternative . . .' Sally really hoped it wouldn't come to this, '. . . is that you get some acid from school and we do it ourselves.'

'What?'

'I'm serious.'

'Oh my God, no! I can't do that! You'd be in agony!'

'So we try the first option?'

'Sally, I dunno.' She chewed a bit of skin on the side of her fingernail. 'Wouldn't Stan be better for this job? I mean, he's twice my size for one thing. He can put up more of a fight or . . . sit on you or something.'

Sally knew she was right. 'I know, but things are weird with me and Stan at the moment. I didn't know if he'd do it.'

'He would. You know he would. He'd do anything for you.' Jennie flipped her hair over her head. Maybe the pink and purple strips in her hair did sometimes betray how wise she truly was.

Sally shrugged as best as she could with her arms behind her back. 'I'm not gonna lie. This might not be safe. If I turn, I don't know what she'll do . . . she's gonna be so mad. The last thing I want to do is hurt you, but I've completely run out of ideas.'

'Do you think she'd try something in public?'

'I honestly don't know. She's capable of anything. God, that sounds like a line off the TV.'

Jennie smiled a wry smile. 'How do you want to do it?'

'In my coat pocket there's my dad's credit card. I know the PIN. If anyone asks, I'm Mrs G Feather, child bride.'

'OK, where's the clinic?'

'The address is on a piece of paper in my pocket.'

Jennie fetched her jacket. 'I'll give them a ring and make an appointment.'

'You'll do it?'

She nodded slowly. 'Yeah. If it's what you need.'

A fat tear rolled down Sally's cheek. She'd never felt so loved.

Jennie showered and dressed before giving the clinic a call as soon as they opened at nine. Sally heard her talking with them on the landing although couldn't make out every word. When she came back in the bedroom, Sally could tell it wasn't good news. 'They're totally booked up today,' she reported. 'I tried . . . I begged, I said it was an emergency. The receptionist told me there's no such thing as a tattoo emergency!'

Sally rolled her eyes. 'I beg to differ.'

'But they can see you first thing tomorrow. You know it'll take lots of sessions though, right?'

'I know.' Sally nodded. 'I'm just hoping that as she fades, so does her power.'

'What do we do now?'

'I'll need to stay here.'

'All night?'

Sally nodded. She wasn't thrilled about the situation, but there was no other way. 'Maybe we can cuff me to a bed tonight? If I'm free, she'll run – I know she will.'

Jennie kneeled next to her. 'You're really serious about this, aren't you?'

'Without wanting to sound histrionic, I'm deadly serious.'

Jennie thought about it for a second. 'Well,' she said brightly, 'we have a whole night and day to get through. We're gonna need snacks and my laptop. I'm gonna have to feed you like a baby!'

'Thank you, Jen. This means everything to me.'

'I'll go get some supplies. Any requests?'

'Just whatever you want.'

Jennie hurried away to get provisions from the kitchen. Sally shuffled on her bottom, her buttocks already going numb. If it got really bad, she'd be able to kneel or sit on her side. This wasn't too bad.

'Bet ya think you're pretty goddamn smart, donchya?'

The voice made Sally jump. It was a low, guttural growl. With Jennie out of sight, Molly Sue was back, pacing angrily across her back.

I sort of do, Sally told her.

'Just try it, darlin'.'

What are you gonna do? Pull my hands off?

255

'Why not? It'll do for a start. And just wait and see what imma gonna do to your little friend downstairs. I'll make you watch while I pull her insides out.'

What? You'll do that with no hands? You can't do anything, Molly Sue. Just give up now. It's over.

'Oh, the kitten finally got her claws. Pride, sugar . . . it comes right before a fall.'

Sally said nothing, but knew that she and the thing inside of her had reached checkmate. There was only one move left, and it was hers to take.

Chapter Thirty

The day dragged on for ever. The walls of Jennie's bedroom seemed to be shrinking in around Sally like a funhouse illusion. Sally just wanted it over. If Molly Sue had any more tricks up her sleeve, Sally wanted them where she could see them. There was some security in the fact that she'd told her parents she was coming here to help Jennie look after the house while her parents were in Seoul. She knew Molly Sue wouldn't be so stupid as to kill Jennie here when she'd be the only suspect – unless she killed her and fled.

Sally kicked that thought right out of her mind, hoping Molly Sue hadn't considered it.

Sally and Jennie passed the day watching *Satanville* and a couple of films that had the actors who played Dante and Zeke in. On a normal day that would be bliss, but each forty-five minute episode seemed to last for a month. Being fed by Jennie was somewhat humiliating, but Jennie seemed to quite enjoy playing Mummy and Baby so Sally didn't complain.

After they'd eaten dinner, the doorbell rang. It was starting to get dark behind the blinds so Sally guessed it was around seven. She frowned at Jennie. 'Who's that?'

Jennie bit her lip and looked sheepish. 'Look, don't get cross, but I told Stan to come over.'

'What? Jennie!'

Her friend stood, hands on hips. 'Oh, come on! If this Molly Sue character is real then we need all the help we can get! And Stan has been doing his press-ups or whatever and I clearly haven't!'

Sally sighed. She was right. This was bigger than her beef with Stan. 'Whatever.'

Jennie went to answer the door and returned with Stan a minute later. His square shoulders filled the doorframe of the bedroom. Initially, he looked blindsided, like he was trying to work out what he was seeing. He stared down at her, his face unreadable; was it pity? Was it confusion? Hate? All of those things? 'What the eff is going on, you guys? Seriously. If this is a joke, I don't get it . . .'

Sally couldn't say anything, she couldn't even look him in the eye.

'Come in,' Jennie said, ushering him into the room and sat him stiffly on her bed. 'We can explain everything.'

'Can we?' Sally muttered.

'Sally, what's happening? Please tell me. You're scaring me.' Stan's blue eyes looked watery. It sounded like he was only just holding his voice steady.

Sally began, 'Stan, this is going to sound like an episode of *Satanville*, but please try to believe me. You *know* me . . . you know I don't lie.' Well, she certainly never used to. She told him the same version she'd told Jennie. Stan listened without interruption, eyes on his lap, with Jennie next to him on the bed. 'So, do you think I'm insane?'

After a beat, Stan shook his head. 'No.'

'Really?' Sally half-laughed. 'I wish I were so certain.'

He came to her side. 'May I?' Sally nodded and he delicately lifted her vest, taking care not to pull it up too high. He ran a finger over her tattoo and she shivered at his touch. 'In a way it explains everything. Things have been so different these last few weeks. I thought you'd changed, but I had no idea we were talking, like, possession. . .'

Sally looked into his eyes, struggling for the right words. 'I . . . I think she called to me somehow, and I walked into her trap. She used me because I was weak.'

'You're not weak,' Stan said softly before turning to Jennie. 'Jen, could you give us a second by ourselves? There some stuff I should have said ages ago.'

Jennie concealed a knowing smile. 'Sure, I'll go put the kettle on. It's dangerously close to an hour since my last cup of tea.'

Once she'd left, an awkward, endless silence fell over the bedroom. Stan sat with his back up against the radiator next to her. 'I thought there was so much I wanted to say,' Stan started.

'Do you believe me?' Sally broke the ice that had descended on the room.

'A hundred per cent. I don't believe this is something *you'd* make up. You're the rational one.' He threw his hands wide. 'Just because I've never seen a ghost or a demon or an alien doesn't mean I'm stupid enough to think my eyes are the final word on the matter.'

If Sally hadn't been shackled to a radiator she'd have thrown her arms around him. As it was, she turned to him, eyes wide and earnest. 'But tomorrow we can stop her. Will you help?'

'Well, duh.'

'Thank you,' she said, her voice wobbling. She should have trusted Stan, but then . . . 'Stan? I have to ask . . . why did you tell Melody about me and Todd?'

He winced. 'God, Sal, I'm sorry. I was such a dick. I was just so angry. It was like this red mist fell over me or something. I couldn't believe it . . . like, *you* and *Todd* . . .'

'What's that supposed to mean? That I'm not good enough for Todd Brady?'

'No! That he's not good enough for you.' Another dense silence followed. The air between them felt stodgy. 'Honestly . . . I just wanted to hurt you because it hurt me. I know, it's mean and petty and stupid. It was a . . . low blow. I knew Melody would finish it one way or another so I told her and kept my hands clean. I was a coward. I was jealous.'

All those rumours at school about her and Stan, all the whispers in the common room that she'd brushed off for so long. Everything that Molly Sue had said. She'd been so blind. Perhaps wilfully so. Now she had to face it head on. 'You were jealous? But, Stan, why?'

'Because when I think about us growing up, everything is this shape-shifting shit of a confused mess. The only thing I see for definite in my future is you.'

Perhaps she'd always known, but hadn't believed anyone could want her in that way. This certainly complicated things and she didn't have a clue what to say. 'Stan . . .'

'It's true. You know how everyone always thinks we're together? Well, I let them. I just assumed that we'd end up together. That one day we'd stop being friends and become something . . . more. Like, who doesn't want to fall in love with their best friend, right? I thought you felt the same . . . and then I saw you with Todd.' He spat the last word as if it had a bad taste.

Sally couldn't untangle words from the spaghetti in her head. She'd never heard Stan speak for this long without making a lame joke or pulling a goofy face. This version of Stan was something new. He was older somehow, wiser . . . This wasn't the little boy who used to catch frogs with her down at the pond, and yet there was still that Stannish Stanness that was, well, Stan. 'I . . . I thought I liked Todd, but . . .'

'Now you don't?'

'I think I liked the idea of Todd more than Todd,' Sally admitted. Stan's bare arm was pressed against her bare arm. His skin on her skin. It was electric. 'I wonder if I got hung up on him because it was safe. It was like fancying Dante or something, you know – nothing was ever gonna happen. As soon as it became real, I didn't like it so much.'

His relief was almost tangible. 'It was so scary,' Stan went on. 'I never realised how much I took you for granted. I thought we'd always be together and then you started to change . . . your hair, your clothes. I thought we were losing you.'

Sally sighed. 'Everyone changes. You've changed too, Stan.'

'I haven't!'

'You have.' Sally smiled. 'Look at you.' Oh, she looked. There was a long, stodgy silence. And then it happened. She wasn't sure if it was how close he was to her, or his scent, or how good he looked but she was suddenly kissing him.

If he was surprised, he adapted quickly. He moved in closer, so close she could feel his heart thundering in his chest. He cupped her face with a bear paw hand, taking charge of the kiss. If this was his first kiss, and she thought it probably was, he had a knack for it. His lips were confident. There was a strength to him, but no eagerness. It was ... well, good. She'd been nervous as hell with Todd, but with Stan, although it was weird because she was KISSING STAN, she could just relax. No need to think, only to do. She wasn't worried about how good she was or what he thought of her, it was just Stan. And Stan was highly skilled at kissing.

He pulled away, a broad smile on his face. 'God, I have spent so long wondering what that would be like.'

Sally smiled back. 'And how was the real thing?'

The smile grew even wider. 'Better than I ever imagined.'

Sally couldn't stifle a smile. 'Smooth! Who knew you could be romantic?'

'Are you kidding? I've spent four years watching Dante and Zeke brood at Taryn.'

She laughed for what felt like the first time in months. 'Of course! I should have known!'

There was a tap at the door and Jennie poked her head through. 'I heard laughing so I thought it might be safe to come back in?'

Stan sprung up like he'd be caught behind the bike shed, not that their school really had one. 'Yeah, sure, come in.'

'Did you guys talk it out? Are we all good?'

Not really. God, that kiss had been *something else* but if anything, Stan was one more task in her inbox and she had no idea how she felt about it. Sally wasn't sure what *anything* meant any more, and she was nowhere near good. 'We're fine,' she lied. She and Stan could deal with the fallout from that kiss once the tattoo was lasered off her back.

Stan Randall was still beaming. Apparently dealing with excess adrenalin, he paced the floor, wiping his palms on his thighs. 'Have you eaten? I'm starving? I might get something to eat? Is that OK?'

Jennie wore a sly smile. Sally suspected she'd been listening to every word through the door. 'Work up an appetite?' She grinned. 'We already ate but there's loads of provisions in the fridge. Go nuts.'

Stan thanked her and trotted downstairs.

'Did you hear everything?' Sally asked once he was out of earshot.

Jennie sat down next to her and folded her legs like a Buddha. 'Pretty much. How gross does kissing sound on audio only? Slurpy!' she giggled.

'Oh, don't! I don't know what came over me!'

'You started it? Wow. Was it good?'

Sally couldn't lie. 'I never thought I'd say this, but it really was . . .'

'Sally Feather, you have a look of faraway longing in your eyes!'

'I do not!' she said, although wondered if she might. She was probably in shock.

There was a sudden crash from below, something smashing in the kitchen. Sally jumped, banging the back of her head on the radiator. 'Ow! What was that?'

Jennie scurried to the door and shouted down the stairs. 'Stan, whatever you just dropped, clean it up!' There was no reply. Jennie leaned over the rail on the landing. 'Stan? What did you do?' She turned back to Sally. 'God, he better not have broken anything expensive. I'll be right back.' Jennie followed Stan downstairs.

All Sally could do was wait, straining her ears to hear conversation, but there didn't seem to be any. What was going on? Eventually she heard light footfalls climbing the stairs. She craned her neck around to see Jennie emerge back onto the landing. Her face was hovering somewhere between confusion and concern.

'What is it?' asked Sally.

Jennie shrugged. 'Stan's gone.'

Chapter Thirty-One

Sally was equally baffled. 'What? Where?'

'I don't know.' Jennie crossed to her window and looked out at the street, trying to locate him. 'The back door was wide open and there was a plate of chicken wings smashed all over the floor.'

'Can you see him?'

'No.'

'OK, that's weird.'

'I don't get it. Why would he just wander off?'

Why indeed, Sally thought. *Molly Sue, what are you up to?* She waited for a response. Nothing came. Maybe it was because Jennie was in the room. 'Jen, will you give me a second alone with Molly Sue?'

'Oh. Yeah. OK.' Jennie, still looking a little sceptical, shuffled out of the room and closed the door behind her.

'Molly Sue, have you done something to Stan?' Again there was no response. 'Cut it out, I know you can hear me, so tell me.' Still nothing. With her mind, Sally reached out around her body and head, searching for the greasy black tendrils that were the real Molly Sue.

And then she started to panic.

She started at her feet and scanned the length of her body. She'd become accustomed to the strange sensation of Molly Sue's *presence* but now it was nowhere to be found. *No way . . . she couldn't have . . .*

Oh, but she could. It had only taken fleeting eye contact between her and the old homeless man outside school . . .

The kiss. Now that she replayed the moment in her head, she hadn't initiated it. There had been a split second of darkness and that was all it had taken to spur her on. Molly Sue had lit the match and it had been enough to start a blaze between her and Stan.

Molly Sue, are you in here? She tried again as a desperate last bid, but knew there would be no reply.

Because Molly Sue was in Stan now.

'No!' she cried aloud. 'No, no, no!' She rocked against the radiator, the handcuffs digging into her wrists.

Jennie barged back into the room at once. 'Sally? What's up?'

She grit her teeth so hard her jaw hurt. 'She's in Stan! She went into Stan!'

'What?' Jennie's eyes widened.

'Molly Sue! When we kissed, she travelled into Stan. She's taken him.' Jennie rubbed her forehead, processing this information. 'I know it sounds insane, but it's true. I can't feel her inside me any more.'

'What is she going to do?'

'I don't know.' Sally forced back tears. Crying time was over. 'Jennie, you have to release me. Quickly, I need to catch up with him.' She tugged against the handcuffs.

Jennie spun in a confused circle in the middle of her rug like a dog chasing its tail. She snapped out of it and climbed over her bed to the bedside table from which she took the key. She returned and crouched down next to her. 'Wait.'

'What? Quick! He's getting away.'

Jennie eyed her with suspicion. 'Wait a second.' She backed up. 'You told me that I wasn't to let you out under *any* circumstances.'

'Jennie! That was before this happened. Hurry up! Stan is in deep trouble!'

'But isn't that exactly what this Molly Sue would say to get me to untie her?'

'I'm not Molly Sue! I'm me!'

'Well, of course she'd say that!'

'Jennie, please. We're wasting time.'

'Tell me something that only Sally would know.'

Molly Sue had access to all her memories anyway, but she didn't let on. Sally searched for the most intimate secret she knew. 'OK, what about the time in Year Five when you farted and a bit of poo came out and you had to borrow my gym shorts?'

Jennie considered that for a moment.

'Or what about the fact that the first person you ever kissed was your cousin in Seoul?'

Jennie's mouth fell open. 'OK! I believe you! I told you to never say those words aloud!' She kneeled down and released her wrists.

Only when Sally struggled to her feet did she truly feel the extent of how achy and stiff she was. 'Ow, I'm numb.' Nonetheless, she hobbled over to the bed and pulled her leather jacket on.

'Where are we going to look?'

Sally was already on the landing. 'We aren't going anywhere. I need you to stay here.'

'What? No way.'

She took the stairs two at a time. 'Jennie, this is serious. I can't put you and Stan in danger. I'd feel awful if something happened to you both. I need you to be OK.'

'But I want to help.'

'And you are. If something happens to me, and it probably will, I need you to give a letter to my parents. I left them in my bag. There's one for you too.'

They reached the kitchen, but Jennie grabbed her arm and pulled her back. 'Stop. What do you mean *if something happens to you?*'

Sally wished she had an answer. 'I don't know. I don't know what she's capable of, but I think I know where she's heading.'

'I can't just sit here waiting to hear if you're dead!' Tears filled Jennie's eyes.

'Please! I know it's a big ask, but worrying about you *and* Stan is only going to throw me off my game.'

Jennie caved. 'OK, go. But you better get back here in one piece with Stan.'

'I promise I'll do everything I can. I have to go.' Sally stepped over the chicken wings and to where the back door was flapping in the wind.

'Be careful,' Jennie said, but Sally had already gone into the night.

* * *

Stan didn't have that much of a head start and he had to be either on foot or on the bus, which was almost as slow. Sally ran until her thighs and calves burned. She had to stop every few minutes to rake in breath and at one point her stomach heaved painfully. Following the river was probably the quickest way down into the valley and she guessed that was the way Stan must have gone. Below her the swollen river roared through the ravine and the tops of the trees strained and bowed against the wind. Tonight the forest was alive.

Sally took the fastest possible route towards the House of Skin. She *had* to be taking him there. Molly Sue had been able to manipulate her from that first meeting, but her possession hadn't truly started until she'd got the tattoo. That *must* be where she was steering Stan. In a way, Sally had won; she had Molly Sue on the ropes. The tattoo apparently believed her resolve and had gone to plan B – a new host.

But Sally would die before she let Molly Sue have Stan.

The thought powered her on. She had to get there before they tattooed him. Would it be the same tattoo or could she manifest in different ways? What would Stan's Molly Sue be? A dragon? A mermaid? A skull? How would it speak to him? Sally had been thinking for a long time now that Molly Sue, or whatever her true name was, must be someone different to each host she inhabits – Molly Sue was tailor-made to exploit *her* weaknesses. *I'll be your best friend, just do everything I say or I'll kill you.* The Molly Sue character felt old, but Sally suspected her true entity was older still. Who knew what the voice in Stan's head would sound like.

Whatever she really was, Molly Sue hungered for pain, suffering and death and took joy in them. *If that's not evil, I don't know what is. I have to get to Stan.* She ran faster.

Sally left the woodland footpath and leaned against the turnstile, catching her breath again. She might yet vomit. She coughed and spluttered but nothing came up.

Not Stan, please not Stan. It was strange. How much *she'd* taken *him* for granted. It was so clear now. She'd been vile to Stan. This whole time she'd suspected – no, more than suspected, *known* – how Stan felt. He'd been an insurance policy. If no one else wanted her, there'd always be The Boy Next Door. He'd always be patiently waiting, some faithful Labrador trotting at her heel.

And I knew, she told herself, choking on a sob, *I knew*.

Well, Molly Sue wasn't gonna win this one. *I owe him that much. You're not having him, Molly Sue. He deserves better than either of us.*

Move. She took flight again, this time over the tin bridge and onto the damp pavements leading into Old Town. Out in the open, a fierce wind whipped through the streets. Dirt and litter swirled in circles around her feet but she fought through the gusts. Sally ran past the school, past the diner, past the rec ground. *You're close now.*

Something felt wrong. Her skin prickled. She stopped. From nowhere, a furious gust bellowed down and she was almost swept off her feet. The opening to the chain-link fence around the warehouse flew open, clanking and banging against the wall. Sally froze. She remembered what was behind that fence . . .

Sure enough, the rabid hound barrelled out of the yard, almost tumbling over its own feet. Sally couldn't believe how fast it was; it moved like a bullet.

Fight or flight? She couldn't run away. She couldn't go in the opposite direction. Stan needed her. Sally stood her ground.

Spittle flying from its jaws, the dog reared up at her, gnashing its teeth. All Sally could do was cover her face with her arms. She felt needle-like claws rip at her sleeves and she stumbled back.

The Doberman fell to the floor, snapping at her heels, driving her back. 'Get off me!' she cried, kicking out with her foot. The hound backed up, baring blood red gums. Its eyes were wild. Saliva foamed around its mouth.

And then another Doberman, identical to the first emerged from the kennel. And then another. The dogs seemed to be carbon copies of each other. How was that even possible?

'What the . . . ?' Sally's mouth fell open.

The twin dogs joined their brother. Three grinning, growling, hungry dogs circled around her.

Sally was trapped.

Chapter Thirty-Two

Sally had no weapons, nothing she could even use as a weapon. Backing away, she scanned the empty road. The windows – the ones that weren't boarded up – were black and even the streetlights flickered and swayed in the wind.

The first dog – she thought, but they were impossible to tell apart – lunged for her. Vice-like jaws clamped around her arm and she yelped, shaking it off. The leather of her jacket prevented it from getting too firm a grip and she flung it loose, but a second was already gnawing at her boot. She staggered, trying to remain upright. If she went down, they'd tear her to ribbons.

She kicked and kicked, trying to shake the dog off. The third dog bounced up and down on its hind legs, teeth snapping in her face. Claws scraped her cheek and she felt the warmth of blood flowing from the wound. Sally swung her arms like a windmill, trying to confuse and deter the animals, but they were tireless. The constant barking rattled her skull.

I have to get to Stan! Her inner voice screamed as loud as the dogs were barking.

And then – they stopped. Breathing heavily, Sally cautiously lowered her arms from over her eyes. The wind was stronger still, whipping her hair around her face. Veins of lightning lit the sticky sky, each followed by an angry growl of thunder. *What is going on?* The dogs had backed off, whimpering. They looked downright sheepish. Bad doggies. But why?

'Don't you have somewhere to be, Sally?'

Over the wind, Sally could hardly hear her. She turned, pulled the hair out of her eyes and saw Sister Bernadette, all in white, standing in the very middle of the street. She wore a thin cotton dress, almost translucent as lightning flickered, and her wimple was gone. Her raven hair was down, blowing around her face. She looked completely different – wild, beautiful and powerful. 'Sister Bernadette . . . how did you know?'

The dogs slinked over to the sister, heads bowed. They came to a rest at her feet. 'Sit!' she told them and they obeyed at once. All three sat attentively awaiting instruction.

Between the moonlight and streetlights, Bernadette's alabaster skin was almost luminous. She fixed Sally in a kindly gaze. 'Sally, my child, now is the time . . . and you need to run.'

She didn't need telling twice. Sally's eyes prickled with gratitude. 'Thank you,' she said. She turned and ran, leaving Bernadette to deal with the hounds. Sally sensed she would never see her again.

This time it took her no time at all to find the House of Skin; the neon lights blazed hot pink down the alleyway. The tattoo parlour was open for business once more. Sally hurtled down the backstreet and swung around the railings to go straight down the stairs.

Sally paused for a moment on the threshold. Her plan had only got her this far; now that she was here she had no idea what she was supposed to do. *Just stop them . . . any way you can.* With an unsteady hand, Sally pushed the door.

It creaked open with no hesitation. It was almost like the door wanted to be walked through. *Come into my tattoo parlour, said the spider to the fly.* She was probably walking into a trap. They either wanted her or Stan . . . they didn't need both. The space beyond the door was blacker than black, like stepping into ink. Arms out in front of her, Sally plunged into the dark.

The House of Skin had changed. After the World's Scariest Clone Dogs, Sally didn't bat an eyelid. Strange how quickly you can habituate to impossible things. Nothing was impossible any more. The reception had shifted and grown; no longer a cosy holding area, it was more like a hotel lobby.

Sally emerged from the marble alcove around the door and took in the faded splendour. Once upon a time this would have been a Gatsby delight, but now it was a ruin: a cobweb-strewn chandelier clung lopsidedly to the ceiling by a thread; a layer of dust as thick as snow covered the mosaic floor and the upturned chairs and sofas. Ash swirled through the dim light, which punched its way into the room through cracks in the walls.

Wait a minute. I know this . . .

It was the art deco hotel from Stan's zombie game, recreated in minute detail. Or certainly as Stan would remember it. This whole place had been created from his mind. Molly Sue had read his mind. One key difference: the once glorious pictures of the tattoos were now either flat on the floor or hanging at broken angles in broken frames.

What is this place?

When Sally was here before, she felt out of time somehow, as if the entire structure existed independent of the world. A spider's web Molly Sue could hide in, waiting for unsuspecting flies. Like a web, perhaps it could bend and flex. She remembered the room as warm, but now it was glacial. Her breath frosted in the air. Sally wrapped her arms around herself.

I'm in Stan's nightmare. Molly Sue was trying to scare him, show him how powerful she was

She took a few more steps into the mouldering space. Sally yelped. Her hand flew to cover her mouth. There was a corpse splayed out on a chaise longue.

Stan?

She rushed to the sofa. Although it was hardly recognisable as human, she was pretty certain the body was female. Leathery skin was taut around her skeleton, eyes sunken back into her skull. Her lips were stretched over teeth that now seemed too big for her decaying head.

The eyes snapped open and Sally shrieked. The woman groaned and raised a hand to her, pleading. Sally saw the hand was tattooed.

Backing away in horror, Sally's heel made contact with another body. She whirled around and saw another almost-corpse resting against a pillar, just as emaciated as the first. Just as tattooed. This one she recognised – not by his face, but by his amputated arms. *The man from outside school.* How was

275

that even possible? She'd seen him die. Something crawled across his skin – a faded ink scorpion. His eyes opened into slits. As he saw her he gave a pitiful groan. 'Please . . . please make it stop . . .'

'Oh God . . .' Sally looked around the room. Either her head or the room was spinning. Perhaps both. Half buried by the dust were the bodies of many men and women. The ones that still had skin were tattooed. Their eyes blinked, but they were immobile, more husk than human. They were like the skins snakes cast off – kept alive by the tattoos, she guessed. No alive, wasn't right. This was not living but they were not truly dead.

A tapping noise drew Sally's attention, and she realised a low mewling noise was coming from her own mouth. Something was moving in the room – light, scuttling footfalls. Little feet tapping on the tiles. Something like a rat . . . something like a spider.

Shaking off her disgust, Sally stood in the centre of the lobby, taking slow, cautious steps. She scanned every dark corner, but all she saw were the desiccated bodies and they weren't capable of such swift movement. 'Where are you?'

More spry footsteps. Something scuttling low to the ground. Sally shuddered. Was it the dogs? Perhaps Sister Bernadette couldn't hold them back any longer. Sally crouched to look under a sofa, but saw only dust and some items she remembered from the shop. The Day of the Dead skulls and the religious icons were scattered across the floor.

The footsteps grew louder. It was close. Sally shot to standing and whirled around.

Too late did she think to look *up*.

A black shape crawled across the ceiling. Sally screamed, a reflex. Its face twisted to look at her and Sally screamed again. It was Rosita.

Chapter Thirty-Three

With a hiss, Rosita let go of the ceiling and plummeted towards Sally. There was nothing she could do. She tried to dive out of the way, but Rosita was on her in less than a second.

Sally hit the tiled floor awkwardly, her hip bearing the brunt of the fall. Rolling onto her front, ignoring the pain, she tried to crawl away, but Rosita's nails dug into her flesh, pinning her down. The spider-woman straddled her, her hands closing in around Sally's neck.

Now that she was close, Sally saw Rosita's irises were jet black and inhumanly swollen. When she smiled her deadly smile, her teeth seemed sharper than before. 'Back so soon, Sally Feather?' Her grip tightened. 'Was Mother not everything you desired?'

Sally gasped and choked, trying to prize the fingers off her throat. *Mother?* Rosita was Molly Sue's daughter? No . . . not Rosita – whatever was *inside* her. 'You . . . tricked me! She's evil!'

Removing one hand, Rosita slapped her hard across the face. 'You ungrateful little bitch! Did Mother not give you everything? Popularity, beauty, love . . . you could have had

278

it all.' A tiny black spider tattoo elegantly lowered itself down her slender neck on a silk strand. Rosita was more than just Molly Sue's slave. The darkness, the power inside her came *from* Molly Sue.

Sally could no longer speak as thumbs dug into her windpipe. Tears ran down her face and glittery silver shapes swam in the periphery of her vision. *It's not worth it. It's not worth it if I have to become like her.*

Maybe Rosita heard what she was thinking, maybe she didn't, but she went on, pressing harder and harder on her neck. 'You were *weak*. You couldn't handle her power. You were an unworthy host. Not like Boris and I . . . we are her special children. We take good care of Mother and so she gives us gifts.' Gifts, Sally guessed, like being able to walk on ceilings.

Rosita squeezed harder. Like curtains closing at the theatre, darkness swooped in over Sally's vision. This was it.

'But fear not, little one. Now you'll stay with us in the House of Skin,' Rosita cooed. 'Join the family . . . for ever and ever and ever . . .'

Stan. The image of his face gave her the jolt she needed. She let go of Rosita's wrist and let her hand feel its way over the tiles. Her fingers found a smooth, cool object. Porcelain. One of the Day of the Dead skulls. Sally gripped it by its eye sockets and drove it into Rosita's tattooed face with everything she had left.

There was a crunch as it made contact with her nose. Rosita screamed and fell off her. Not letting go of the skull, Sally bashed it onto the side of her head. This time, the woman crumpled to the ground. Exhausted, Sally flopped onto her back, gasping for breath. Her body lulled her to sleep, but she knew if she closed her eyes, she'd be done. Covered in dirt and grime, Sally woozily stumbled to her feet.

Get Stan.

Rosita groaned, clutching her temple. She wasn't dead, but only just conscious. Sally moved. There was only one door that she could see, partially hidden behind a torn curtain at the back of the lobby. The floor and the door seemed to slope as Sally ran for it. Everything here was topsy-turvy and Sally was still light-headed. She steadied herself against the doorframe for a second before pushing her way in.

It was the same workroom, but much, much larger. This time, the room seemed to go on for infinity, the chessboard floor stretching into the shadows with no walls in sight.

There were many chairs and tables this time, all with clients stretched out on them. They weren't in the same state as the corpses in the lobby, but not far off. They writhed in pain, backs arched, mouths open in silent screams. Their pale, naked flesh was infested, swarming in tattoos of all different shapes, colours and sizes. Each tattoo crawled over their bodies. How many entities here needed new hosts? How many demons were housed here? Or was each a fragment of one larger being? Were they all controlled by Molly Sue, like the being inside Rosita? Like the being that had been inside *her*?

It all made sense – well as much as something so insane can ever hope to. They, whatever they were, must move from host to host until they were spent like the husks outside. The host only died when the parasite allowed it. Oh, with the exception of Boris and Rosita – Molly Sue must preserve and enhance them to do her dirty work. *How many years*, Sally wondered, *until she'd have used me up and bled me dry?*

All excellent questions, but questions Sally didn't have time to deal with, and, by the looks of it, it was way too late to save these poor souls. One of the human cages – a girl not much older than her – peered at her with sunken, glassy eyes. Despair contorted her face into something inhuman and Sally had to look away.

Where is he? She followed the buzz of the needle. In the centre of the hall, under a single feeble lamp was Boris. He held his needle just centimetres above a clear expanse of skin: Stan, hunched over a chair, his shirt off.

'NO!' Sally screamed, her voice echoing through the chamber. Boris's amber eyes gleamed above his mouth mask and she tore across the room, pushing past trolleys and tables. Ignoring the artist's height and weight, she threw herself at him, grabbing for the needle. He wasn't expecting the attack and, to even Sally's surprise, she knocked him back. He collided with his trolley – inks and jars toppled over with a smash. An overwhelming blast of alcohol filled her nostrils. Antiseptic.

Boris batted her away like a fly, knocking her into a cold puddle, and turned back to Stan. *No.* Sally pounced onto his back, tugging him away. 'Let him go!' she cried before biting his ear. She bit so hard she tasted blood. This time, Boris howled in pain. He threw his shoulders left and right, trying to loosen her but she only clung on tighter, wrapping her legs around his waist. 'Stan! Run!' she yelled, but he didn't move, draped where he was.

With her left hand she grabbed at Boris's jaw and the surgical mask came away. Sally screamed and crashed to the floor, and saw his face for the first time. She couldn't look away. It was *hideous*. Where there should have been a jaw was just a *hole*. A long, thick, pink tongue thrashed around like a fish out of water. His top teeth were normal enough but the tongue was loose, flopping around his neck with no chin or lower teeth to support it.

All Sally could think was that Boris, the man, not the creature inside him, had tried to tell someone the truth. Only Molly Sue could have done this. Sally pressed her hand to her own mouth, knowing Boris had most likely ripped his own jaw off under the influence of his tattoos.

Furious, his eyes burned like fire. He made a horrid, slurping moan and came for her. He would surely crush her.

'Stop!' Stan's voice rang around the room. 'Sally, just stop.'

Both she and Boris turned to him. 'Stan . . . you're OK!'

'I'm fine.' He rose from the chair, a little woozy, but otherwise unharmed.

Sally ran to him and examined his skin. It hadn't been marked. 'Oh, thank God. I got here in time.' She reached out for his hand. 'Let's get out of here!' In this place, he was the only thing that seemed real. A lifeboat in a sea of nightmares. She clung to him.

He pushed her away. 'Sally, I have to do this.'

'What?' She looked at him like he was insane. 'No! No way!'

'Rosita told me everything. If I take Molly Sue, you'll be free and things can just go back to how they were.'

Sally shook her head, hardly able to believe what she was hearing. 'No. Stan, you don't know what she's like.' The door creaked and Rosita prowled in, sticking to the outskirts of the light. Sally ignored her. 'She'll make you do the most terrible things. You don't get a say in them. She'll steal your body.'

Stan seemed resigned to this; his eyes were dim. 'I can *feel* her . . . it . . . in me. It just wants to exist.'

'For ever,' Sally spat. 'She wants to live for ever. She'll go on and on. When you die she'll just keep going.'

'I . . . I don't mind. She says she just wants a home. I'll do that if it means you can be free.'

Rosita edged ever nearer. Sally grabbed another jar of antiseptic solution from a different trolley and hurled it at her. She side-stepped it, and it smashed into the wall behind her. 'Stay where you are!' Sally growled at Rosita, who cowered behind a table. She turned back to Stan. This was a trick. 'You're not Stan. It's Molly Sue. You're making him do this.'

'She isn't,' Stan insisted. 'She says her hosts must willingly submit.'

'I don't believe you.' *Although I did.*

'It's true! Sally, please, just let me do this for you.'

Her hands curled into fists. 'Stan . . . I don't need you to *save* me. I need you . . . to go. I just need you to be OK. You want to free me? I can't ever, ever be free knowing I did this to you. I would rather die.' She took at deep breath. 'Molly Sue, if you're not making Stan do this, prove it! Come back into me . . . now.' She grabbed Stan's face and planted another kiss hard on his lips. She pulled back and Stan blinked, stunned.

A pause and then it hit her. Once more she felt the shadow tendrils unfurling in her mind. Like tangleweed, Molly Sue wrapped herself around Sally's thoughts. As much as she hated to admit it, she hadn't quite felt . . . complete . . . without her.

'Did ya miss me, darlin'?'

'Let Stan go,' she said aloud. Stan now slumped into the tattooist's chair, the possession or transfer apparently draining him.

'But he seems so willin', dontchya think? And I could have a real good time with all that body. No offence, darlin', you ain't exactly the life and soul of the party . . .'

Sally ignored her. 'You have me. You don't need him. What is it they say? *Better the devil you know?*'

Molly Sue hesitated but seemed to agree. 'They also say, *there's no place like home.*'

The ball was in Sally's court.

Well, this really, really sucked. This is what tomorrow was like now. Every tomorrow. Ever. Sally Feather and Molly Sue: BFFs 4eva. She felt that last dribble of hope gurgle down the plughole. 'I guess we're stuck with each other. I made my bed . . .'

'And now we'll get real cosy in it together. I'm not so bad, am I, sugar?'

Sally felt her blood turning black; revulsion crawled under her flesh all the way to the bone. 'You're . . . a disease, Molly Sue. A plague.'

Stan, his torso slick with sweat, examined her, no doubt looking for signs she was possessed. 'Is she back in you? Sally, no!'

Sally slipped her hands in his. Time to say goodbye. 'Stan, this . . . is right. It's how it has to be. I can't stand the thought of anything happening to you.' She looked him in the eye and saw how blue they really were for the first time. They were the colour of the sky in summer, a blue you could swim in. 'Stan, I love you. Not love like in a cheesy Valentine's Day card or boy-band song . . . something bigger and better than that. You are like the scaffolding around my heart and you always have been. I *need* to know that you are OK.'

'Mary, Jesus and Joseph, I'm a gonna hurl,' Molly Sue muttered.

'Stan, please just go.'

The muscles in his neck tensed. 'Are you coming with me?'

Tell the truth or lie? Lie. 'Yes, but I need to get some things straight first. I can't go on like this for ever. I'll be out in two minutes. I just want you out of here . . . I don't trust them.'

'I'll wait.'

'Stan, please.' At that moment she needed Stan to understand without her even thinking about it. She looked deep, deep into his eyes, willing him to go and telling him to trust her.

He caved, although he seemed far from pleased. 'I will be right outside. I'm not going home without you.' He scowled at Boris, trying to give the Stan Randall interpretation of a menacing glare. It didn't really come off but Sally appreciated the gesture. Reluctantly, he backed towards the door to the lobby.

Sally waited until he had left. Rosita sidled up alongside Boris. 'We cannot let you leave the House of Skin,' she said. 'You'll just go back to your friends and have the tattoo removed. We live to protect Mother.'

Sally wondered what kind of deal with the devil Rosita and Boris had signed. Immortality in exchange for bringing in willing victims? There was every possibility they weren't even human at all any more. Sally half smiled. 'I wish it were that easy. It didn't work last time. I'll give it to Molly Sue, she's resourceful.'

The tattoo spoke to her children – apparently they could hear the tattoo too. 'Stop her. She's plannin' somethin'. I can feel it and she's blockin' me out!'

Boris stepped forward, but Sally was quicker. Her hand ducked into the pocket of the leather jacket and pulled out Kyle's lighter. With her thumb she flicked the lid open and found the spark wheel. She pressed it hard and a healthy flame leaped from it. 'Stay back.'

The flame danced in their inhuman eyes. Sally looked to her feet and saw she was still standing in a thin puddle. 'The floor is covered in alcohol. You know what'll happen . . .' For good measure she tipped over another trolley. More antiseptic spilled over the floor, the alcohol stench burning in the back of her throat.

'How do you even know it would work?' Rosita said. 'Down here the rules are meaningless.'

It was a bluff worth calling. 'Because I can see how scared you are.' The flame burned her fingers. 'This has to stop. I don't know exactly who or what you are, but it's evil. Old-school evil.' Sally knew Molly Sue now and she was unquestionably evil. There wasn't a more appropriate word. Selfish, immoral, wicked, yes, but something worse than just those things. Sally could understand it now; this was how people did unspeakable things . . . they had *this*, even an essence of this, within them.

'There is no such thing as evil, darlin',' said Molly Sue.

'There is,' Sally said, remembering Sister Bernadette's sermon. 'And it lives in the hearts of men. But so does good. If I can do a good thing, I probably should. I can end all this. I can stop you from doing this to more people, and set these ones free. Even if it means . . .' She smiled wryly. 'Standing back and letting evil happen is its own kind of evil.'

'You don't want to die, Sally Feather,' Rosita purred, reaching out for the lighter.

'I don't. But it's the right thing to do . . .'

Molly Sue hollered over her. 'Quit wastin' time, Feather! We both know you don't got the balls!'

Sally closed her eyes. 'Who needs them?'

She let the lighter fall to the ground.

Chapter Thirty-Four

Having never played with candles and matches, I never thought of fire as a physical thing, but I'm wrong. The heat's like an eighteen-wheeler truck hitting me front on. I'm thrown clean across the room, colliding with one of the tables.

The heat . . . the heat is unbearable. As stupid as this sounds, I'm not ready for how HOT it is. You feel it, you know, you feel it on your skin. Oh, and the smell, the smell of your own flesh burning. I don't know what's worse, that or Rosita's screams. Through the flames I see their flailing bodies alight. They thrash and crash with nowhere to go.

'You stupid little bitch! What have you done?' Molly Sue is screaming.

I've never heard her like this. No funny quips now, eh?

'Get on your feet and run! What are you doing? Run!'

My urge to run is strong; every cell begs me to get away from the flames. After a second, I realise I've been thrown clear of the inferno but the flames are spreading, chasing across the floor. Can you remember those old cartoons with the cute dancing flames? It's like that – just not cute. Tongues lick at me.

'Nowhere to go, Molly Sue,' I tell her. 'We're going together.' This time there's no one for her to jump into either.

The smoke's as oppressive as the fire itself. Thick, black clouds billow and ripple, rolling over the ceiling and then back down like a tide. Yes, that's precisely what it's like – a sea of fire and smoke and I'm drowning.

I have to stay. If I run it would be for nothing. I can't get up, anyway. My clothes are on fire. I was covered in the alcohol so my jeans have gone up. I feel the denim fuse to my skin. My face is taut as the flames bluster towards me. I cover my eyes with blistered hands.

I can feel it, I can feel it in the room. Something thick and heavy and malign. She circles the flames. I hear her ghastly, feral screams. The real Molly Sue.

This is what all those stories warned us about. This is the dark at the heart of the forest; this is the Big Bad Wolf; this is both serpent and apple. There were warnings everywhere – in the Bible, on TV, in nursery rhymes. I always thought they were metaphors or allegories to get me to go to bed, to make me eat my vegetables. I ignored them. I think we all do.

And now it's too late. I was weak and now I am dead.

Oh, it's for the best. I hurt people every way people can be hurt. And I'd do it again.

This is not just badness.

This is not just wrong.

This is evil.

This won't last much longer. We are devoured. I am cleansed.

I have hope – a kind of hope I haven't felt in a while. Now that I know all about evil, I have to give a little consideration to Good. Capital G. I'm not sure you can have one without the other, so maybe, just maybe, there's something for me to look forward to in a couple of minutes. I cling to that and my heart lifts. There's something, even if it's nothing, just around the corner.

Chapter Thirty-Five

Let there be light.

Sally first became aware of light.

White splodges, nothing more, but there was indeed *something*.

She was tired. She slept.

Gradually, there was more light. Darker shapes moved within the light like clouds. People . . . there were people moving over her. She was still very tired, though. This sleep squashed her down, like she was caught in a riptide, being sucked under time after time. She couldn't break the surface. She slept.

The light grew brighter and clearer. It was a ceiling. She could see a ceiling with a strip light and those polystyrene tiles. But she was still so tired. This time she could feel her hands – they were where they had always been, but she couldn't really move them. They felt wrong.

She was more lucid this time. *I am not dead. I survived. How? If I survived . . .* Sally looked for Molly Sue inside, but was just too weak. Her head . . . it felt . . . quiet.

That's good enough.

She slept.

Sally heard a voice. At first she panicked, thinking that Molly Sue was back in her head, but after a moment, she recognised it as her mother's. She felt warm breath on her ear. 'Heavenly Father,' her mother whispered. 'I've only ever asked you for one thing. I asked to be blessed with a child and you sent this gift to me. You wouldn't be so cruel as to take her away. It's too soon. It's too soon for my little girl to go. Please, God, I'll do anything, I'll do anything you ask, just please return her to us. Whatever I've done, punish me, not her.'

I'm here, Mum! Sally tried to speak but she could not; there was something in her mouth, something plastic. Instead, she did all she could: with what little strength she had left in her hand, she squeezed her mother's. She was wearing some sort of glove.

'Sally?' She heard her mother's chair screech across linoleum. 'Sally, can you hear me?'

Sally again tried to speak, managing to gurgle.

'Nurse! Nurse! I think she's coming around! Nurse! Please!'

Sally heard footsteps scurrying around her bed and fell back to sleep.

'Sally? Can you hear me? My name is Dr McCulloch. No . . . no, don't try to move or talk, just lie still. You're in the hospital, my dear. Can you look into this light for me? Just follow my little light. Good girl. You're on a lot of pain medication, that's what's making you so sleepy, but you're going to be fine. You're going to be just fine . . .'

She had to live. She had to get better. She started to feel the pain and, oh man, did it hurt. All of her back, her arms, her legs. As soon as she was able to sit up independently, Dr McCulloch explained she'd sustained fifty-two per cent burns. Sally hadn't seen herself yet, but she wasn't so drugged up that she couldn't understand that more of her body was burned than not.

Her movement was limited, her skin felt impossibly tight, like latex around her bones. Even the slightest change in position was agony and her legs had to be suspended from the bed. While she'd been sleeping – for almost a week she'd been sinking in that quicksand sleep, according to the doctor – they'd already performed skin grafts on her back and legs, tackling the worst of her burns.

Dr McCulloch sombrely explained that, even with plastic surgery it was likely she would be scarred for life. Sally could learn to live with that. 'Doctor, can I ask one thing?'

'Of course.'

'What happened to my tattoo?' Sally whispered. Her mother and father were out getting a sandwich and would return at any moment.

Dr McCulloch smiled sadly, tucking a stray black lock behind her ear. 'Sally, dear, your skin was very badly burned. They were third-degree burns. I didn't even realise you'd had a tattoo.' She gave her unburned right shoulder a gentle punch. 'Years from now, you'll still be able to get tattoos, I promise. It's not the end of the world!'

293

Sally only just held back a tear of relief. 'Oh, no. I won't be getting another. Believe me.'

OK, so Sally was alive, but it wasn't going to be a walk in the park. That was fine. She'd known for a long time that she wasn't getting out of this unscathed. The only worry now was how long she was going to be stuck in the hospital. Boredom had fully set in, alongside the pain, and she'd only been conscious for five days.

Her father stayed at her bedside, not even mentioning his job or the bank. Not once did he or her mother ask what she'd been doing in the derelict building. Instead, he read to her – the *Satanville* companion novels – and he even attempted different voices for the characters.

On the sixth day, her parents and Dr McCulloch agreed she was well enough to receive visitors and Stan and Jennie barrelled in. She'd been warned that Stan had been burned while pulling her out of the 'squat', but aside from some bandages around his hands, he didn't look too bad.

'Hey, how are you feeling?' Jennie held it together for about three seconds before bursting into full-on ugly crying.

'Oh, don't cry! I'm not too bad.' That was a lie. She was so, so sore. Sore everywhere. With smoke inhalation, her voice sounded like she'd had a fifty-a-day smoking habit for ten years.

'You liar! You almost died!' she sniffed. 'I've never been so worried in my life.'

'I'm sorry. I thought it was the only way.'

Stan looked over his shoulder to check no one was listening. She was in a private room on the intensive care ward so he pushed the door closed. 'And? Did it work?'

'It worked,' Sally said as triumphantly as she could. 'She's gone.'

'Thank God,' said Stan, letting out a dramatic breath. Jennie also visibly relaxed. 'It wasn't for nothing.'

'And the House of Skin is gone. I hope. I saw Rosita and Boris burn . . . they couldn't have survived. None of them could,' she added, thinking of their many victims. Hopefully now they were free to go wherever it is dead things went. She looked at Stan's wounds. 'How are you?'

'Oh, that? It's nothing. Less than nothing. What's a little second-degree agonising burn between friends?' He smiled, wearing casual heroism well.

Sally considered him. He wasn't the same Stan any more. The whole encounter had aged all of them. This new version was . . . intriguing. She wasn't the same Sally and he wasn't necessarily the mayor of the Friend Zone any more. 'Well, thank you. I can't believe you went back into a burning building to get me . . . I told you to go!'

'You're not the boss of me,' he grinned. 'I wasn't going home without you.'

'Do you guys wanna be alone?' Jennie asked, backing towards the door.

'No.' Sally gave Stan a meaningful glance. 'I want both of you. Stan and I will talk later.'

He wrapped his bandaged hand in her gloved one. 'Sure. We have all the time in the world. I'm not going anywhere.'

Sally gestured at her bandaged body. 'Neither am I, clearly.' For the first time in a long time, everything felt right. She was with Jennie and Stan and her heart was light with love. As long as they were all together, everything would be OK. Instead of fretting about what might happen with Stan, she was excited. There was so much to explore, but that was something to cling to as time passed in this place. 'Hey, I have a question. Stan . . . what tattoo were you going to get?'

Stan blushed. 'I couldn't really think of anything so . . . '

'Oh God!' Jennie gasped. 'Don't say you were going to get Sally's name on a heart or something?'

'No! Sorry, Feather! OK, don't laugh, but I was going to get Dante's tattoo – The Order of the First numeral with the wreath of ivy.'

Sally felt toasty inside and it felt nice. 'Speaking of, did you record *Satanville*? Don't you dare watch it without me . . . '

'Jennie Gong . . . do you want to tell her or shall I?'

Jennie grimaced. 'Sorry, I already watched it. I couldn't wait!'

'Oh my God, you are so dead to me!' Sally gasped. 'Ex-friend!' They talked and laughed and teased and laughed until Sally could keep her eyes open no longer.

Later that night, Sally woke. She heard voices. 'Mum?' Some nights her mum fell asleep in the chair next to her bed. But tonight, the voice was a solemn whisper, someone murmuring. With a pained groan, Sally sat up and saw the guest chair was empty.

It was dark outside the open blinds. Rivulets of rain careered down the windowpane. Her parents must have left ages ago. It felt late – really late. Instead, Sally looked out of the open door onto the corridor. That was dark too and she couldn't see any of the nurses going about their rounds.

It was nothing so very unusual, though. It was a busy hospital and someone on the ward outside her room always needed something – her sleep had been disturbed every night. With a great effort, Sally swung her legs off the bed and got to her feet. With all her dressings she felt like a mummy of ancient Egypt, but her feet were fine to walk on and so she shuffled over to the door and closed it.

But the whispers continued. They were getting louder. Whispers became words in her head.

'No . . .' Sally said to herself, feeling that lift-going-down-too-quickly sensation. Sally limped to her poky shower room and switched the light on. The bulb was pretty feeble and only ever gave a thin, blueish, flickering light.

She had to know.

Her mother had covered the mirror in her bathroom, not wanting her to get upset by her burns. Sally had let her, not wanting to cause an argument, but now she needed to see. She pulled the cheap hospital towel out from around the edges and let it drop into the sink.

Sally cried out in shock. A monster lurched at her. It took her a whole second to realise that the deformed creature was her reflection. Her hair was gone. They'd cut most of it off, but there were bald pink patches of burned flesh on her scalp. There was a nasty burn on her cheek too. Around the edges of her hospital gown and dressings she could see bright red scar tissue creeping up her neck. It was bad.

But while Sally whimpered, her reflection just stared back at her, a stone-cold look of pure hatred on her face. And then her lips moved.

'Now don't tell me you thought it was going to be that easy,' said Molly Sue's voice.

She didn't sound happy.

Chapter Thirty-Six

'Not for a single second,' Sally admitted, gripping the sink so hard that what was left of her fingers *blazed*. The burn is a lingering reminder of the fire.

'Don't you get it?' Molly Sue went on, again using her mouth and tongue. 'I am not a *drawing* of a woman. I am something bigger and older than your limited little brain can understand and I owned you long before Boris got his hands on.'

Sally stared her reflection down. 'I know what you are.'

Molly Sue's voice changed. It became older, sonorous. Not just old, *ancient*. 'You know *nothing*. I am older than man and word. Wherever there is death and pain and hate and suffering, I am there to sip it up like red wine. I have taken countless names in a million languages, and as many forms and faces.' And then she was Molly Sue again. 'Doll, it's gonna take more than a cookout to stop me. Did ya really think yo boy toy saved yo life? *I* kept you alive. By rights, you should be deep fried chicken right now. Extra crispy.'

It was hard to admit, but she couldn't pretend. 'I knew,' Sally said. 'I knew if I was alive then you would be too. I knew.'

'I am eternal. I ain't goin' nowhere.'

Sally looked herself dead in the eye. She was done with Molly Sue's doom-filled warnings. No more playing. 'I know. And I don't care.'

Molly Sue paused. 'What?'

I'm not scared any more. OK, that was a lie. Sally *was* scared and might always be, but admitting it felt freeing, like letting a balloon filled with toxic gas float away into the clouds. She'd let go of the shame if not the fear. 'It looks like you and I are stuck with each other, so we need to get some things straight; establish some ground rules.'

Molly Sue laughed bitterly. 'I don't think you're gettin' how this deal works, darlin' . . .'

'Oh, I get it,' Sally said, pouring everything she had into remaining cool and calm. 'And I want to thank you.'

Another pause. 'Ya wanna what?'

A tear ran down Sally's face – she was allowed one tear of mourning for her former self. But just one. 'You have changed me so much and, here's the thing: I needed to change. Before you I thought I was weak and scared and uncertain.'

'You got that right.'

'No. I only *thought* I was. You made me see I was wrong. You made me realise I could do things I never thought I'd do. I found my voice, I let people see me, I *sang* . . . so thank you. I needed you.' Sally smiled at herself in the mirror. 'Just one problem, Molly Sue. You created a monster. I'm stronger than you now.'

Molly Sue laughed again. 'Is that what you think?'

Sally nodded. 'It's what I know. I can feel you inside me and, sure, you're noisy, but you're so *small*. You are just a *voice in my*

300

head. You're a parasite. You're a backseat driver. I think I get it now. I *made* you. At the tattoo parlour, I wanted something bad, maybe I wanted to be bad.' Her reflection flinched and Sally knew at once she was right. She had shaped these beings, whatever they were. 'You were something bad and Bernadette was my something good. I created you both. But I'm neither virgin or vamp. I'm . . . just *me*. And you . . . you are *nothing*.'

'Nice try, darlin', but —'

Sally silenced her. She simply made her stop. In her mind, Sally pictured grasping that blackness, which now seemed little more than ink. Perhaps Molly Sue was something vast and ancient, or maybe, just maybe, she was something that wanted her to believe she was. Before, the presence had seemed so enormous, but only because she'd been so near. Up close, even the most insignificant things look huge. Now, taking a step back, Sally felt how *tiny* Molly Sue was, hardly bigger than her little fingernail. She was dark and frightening and loud, but she was so *small*. So easy to shut away. 'You don't own me . . . and you can't control me.'

There was a dark corner in her mind that Sally thought would suit Molly Sue quite nicely. Gritting her teeth, she pushed the darkness far, far behind the things and people she loved. Mum, Dad, Stan and Jennie. *Taryn, Zeke and Dante*. She pushed her behind everything she was excited about and everything she had to look forward to, all the things she might be. There were so many tomorrows ahead.

She'd be there if Sally needed her. Maybe she'd come in handy one day . . . Molly Sue did, after all, have her uses. Sally didn't doubt there'd be moments of weakness, days where she wasn't so strong, and those were the days when she'd really have to be vigilant or Molly Sue could so easily slip back into control. But she'd be ready. She knew the signs now.

'You can't do this to me!' Molly Sue screamed like a bratty child. Sally felt her trying to cling on, trying to remain in control. But Sally was stronger. She kept pushing and pushing, filling her head with frogs at the pond; dying Jennie's hair over the bathtub; gummy bears in Stan's room. She thought about the kiss. One day soon, she *would* sing on stage.

As Molly Sue's voice faded to nothing, Sally looked deep into her own steely eyes to issue a final warning. 'Listen up, Molly Sue. I'm only going to say this once.' Her lips curled into a slight smile. 'Shut the fuck up.'

The End

Acknowledgments

Working with Hot Key Books is always so effortless, although I'm sure that like a beautiful swan, as I glide along, the team are kicking their little legs really fast. So a massive thank you to everyone who worked on *Under My Skin*, especially the editorial team of Emma Matthewson, Naomi Colthurst and Melissa Hyder. Huge thanks to Jet Purdie for the gorgeous cover and humouring my cover suggestions; Sarah Odedina; Sara O'Connor; Kate Manning; Sanne Vliegenthart; Cait Davies and Jennifer Green. Like any author, you spend a lot of time with your publicist on trains and it's always a pleasure to take a trip with Rosi Crawley and Livs Mead.

Thank you, as ever, to my agent Jo Williamson and everyone at Antony Harwood Ltd. Continued love and thanks to all the booksellers, librarians, teachers and bloggers who've supported me for the past four years.

Keen-eyed readers will have by now spotted Kerry Turner and Sam Powick are my regular beta readers and their opinion is still so important. Extra special thanks to Ana Grilo. Thanks to Erik Tomlin for trying to clear *Little Shop* lyrics. Finally thanks to Eleanor Ford (the real one) whose generous contribution to *Authors For Philippines* earned her name a spot in this novel.

To the readers, thank you so much for sticking with me. Your letters, emails and tweets help plug the hole in my heart that love leaks from.

PS – Prince says hi, too.

James Dawson

For eight years, James Dawson was a teacher specialising in Personal, Social, Health and Citizenship Education (PSHCE). As well as being a sexpert, his teen horror fiction and non-fiction writing led to him being nominated for and winning the Queen of Teen award in the summer of 2014, making James the first 'Boy Queen'. His debut, best-selling YA novel *Hollow Pike* was followed by YA thriller *Cruel Summer*. James's first non-fiction title, *Being a Boy*, the ultimate guide to puberty, sex and relationships for young men, was published in Autumn 2013.

James is also a Stonewall Schools Role Model, and his guide to being LGBT* – entitled *This Book is Gay* – was released in summer 2014, alongside his first fiction title for Hot Key Books, *Say Her Name*. When he's not writing books to scare teenagers in a variety of ways, James can usually be found listening to pop music and watching *Doctor Who* and horror movies. He lives and writes in London. Follow James at either www.askjamesdawson.com or at www.jamesdawsonbooks.com or on Twitter: @_jamesdawson

IN FIVE DAYS SHE WILL COME

SAY HER NAME

JAMES DAWSON

OUT NOW

Roberta 'Bobbie' Rowe is not the kind of person who believes in ghosts. A Halloween dare is no big deal, and when she is ordered to summon the legendary ghost of Bloody Mary, she's not surprised when nothing happens.

Or does it?

Next morning, Bobbie finds a message on her bathroom mirror - five days - but what does it mean? And who left it there? It seems that Bloody Mary was called from the afterlife that night, and she is definitely not a friendly ghost...

Thank you for choosing a Hot Key book.

If you want to know more about our authors and what we publish, you can find us online.

You can start at our website

www.hotkeybooks.com

And you can also find us on:

We hope to see you soon!